CHICAGO

W9-BSP-346

R02007 51536

Taking both her hands in his, Matt looked into her eyes.

"Jane, nothing that you discover about the person you were in the past will change the person you've created. The person I've come to—"

Matt stopped speaking. Had he been about to tell Jane that he loved her?

He was aware of Jane's slender hands in his, her eyes gazing up at him, still glistening with unshed tears. His arms ached with the urge to pull her to him, to cradle her against his chest; his lips longed to feel hers beneath them. But that wasn't love. It was desire. It was a need to connect that went so deep, it burned the pit of his stomach. Love existed for other people....

But not for him.

NORTH AUSTIN BRANCH
5724 W. NORTH AVE.
CHICAGO, IL 60639

Dear Reader,

While taking a breather from decorating and gift-wrapping, check out this month's exciting treats from Silhouette Special Edition. *The Summer House* (#1510) contains two fabulous stories in one neat package. "Marrying Mandy" by veteran author Susan Mallery features the reunion of two sweethearts who fall in love all over again. Joining Susan is fellow romance writer Teresa Southwick whose story "Courting Cassandra" shows how an old crush blossoms into full-blown love.

In Joan Elliott Pickart's *Tall, Dark and Irresistible* (#1507), a hero comes to terms with his heritage and meets a special woman who opens his heart to the possibilities. Award-winning author Anne McAllister gets us in the holiday spirit with *The Cowboy's Christmas Miracle* (#1508) in which a lone-wolf cowboy finds out he's a dad to an adorable little boy, then realizes the woman who'd always been his "best buddy" now makes his heart race at top speed! And count on Christine Rimmer for another page-turner in *Scrooge and the Single Girl* (#1509). This heart-thumping romance features an anti-Santa hero and an independent heroine, both resigned to singlehood and stranded in a tiny little mountain cabin where they'll have a holiday they'll never forget!

Judy Duarte returns to the line-up with *Family Practice* (#1511), a darling tale of a handsome doctor who picks up the pieces after a bitter divorce and during a much-needed vacation falls in love with a hardworking heroine and her two kids. In Elane Osborn's *A Season To Believe* (#1512), a woman survives a car crash but wakes up with amnesia. When a handsome private detective takes her plight to heart, she finds more than one reason to be thankful.

As you can see, we have an abundance of rich and emotionally complex love stories to share with you. I wish you happiness, fun and a little romance this holiday season!

Karen Taylor Richman
Senior Editor

Please address questions and book requests to:
Silhouette Reader Service
U.S.: 3010 Walden Ave., P.O. Box 1325, Buffalo, NY 14269
Canadian: P.O. Box 609, Fort Erie, Ont. L2A 5X3

A Season To Believe

ELANE OSBORN

NORTH AUSTIN BRANCH
5724 W. NORTH AVE.
CHICAGO, IL 60639

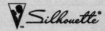

SPECIAL EDITION™

Published by Silhouette Books
America's Publisher of Contemporary Romance

If you purchased this book without a cover you should be aware that this book is stolen property. It was reported as "unsold and destroyed" to the publisher, and neither the author nor the publisher has received any payment for this "stripped book."

To Dar: For housing me and for your company on so many of my research trips, but most of all for your support and friendship on this trip called Life.
And to Dad: For everything you shared with me, from creating a window display to potato stamping, but especially for your encouragement and for teaching me that the worst four-letter *S*-word is, "can't." I miss you.

SILHOUETTE BOOKS

ISBN 0-373-24512-2

A SEASON TO BELIEVE

Copyright © 2002 by Elane Osborn

All rights reserved. Except for use in any review, the reproduction or utilization of this work in whole or in part in any form by any electronic, mechanical or other means, now known or hereafter invented, including xerography, photocopying and recording, or in any information storage or retrieval system, is forbidden without the written permission of the editorial office, Silhouette Books, 300 East 42nd Street, New York, NY 10017 U.S.A.

All characters in this book have no existence outside the imagination of the author and have no relation whatsoever to anyone bearing the same name or names. They are not even distantly inspired by any individual known or unknown to the author, and all incidents are pure invention.

This edition published by arrangement with Harlequin Books S.A.

® and TM are trademarks of Harlequin Books S.A., used under license. Trademarks indicated with ® are registered in the United States Patent and Trademark Office, the Canadian Trade Marks Office and in other countries.

Visit Silhouette at www.eHarlequin.com

Printed in U.S.A.

ELANE OSBORN

is a daydream believer whose active imagination tends to intrude on her life at the most inopportune moments. Her penchant for slipping into "alternative reality" severely hampered her work life, leading to a gamut of jobs that includes, but is not limited to: airline reservation agent, waitress, salesgirl and seamstress in the wardrobe department of a casino showroom. In writing, she has discovered a career that not only does not punish flights of fancy, it demands them. Drawing on her daydreams, she has published three historical romance novels and is now using the experiences she has collected in her many varied jobs in the "real world" to fuel contemporary stories that blend romance and suspense.

SAN FRANCISCO, CA
AREA

Marin City
Belvedere
Berkeley
Sausalito

Golden Gate
Bridge

Oakland

San Francisco

San Leandro

N

San Francisco
Bay

PACIFIC
OCEAN

San Mateo

Chapter One

"Silver bells..."

The first strains of the Christmas song brought an instant frown to the woman standing at the glass counter. She stared blankly at the burgundy-and-tan scarf draped across the palm of her hand as she heard *"It's Christmas time..."*

Hot, unreasoning anger sent blood pounding through her ears, drowning out the rest of the tune. Her fingers crushed the silk scarf as she turned toward the figure on the other side of the counter.

"Don't you think this is just a little ridiculous?"

The salesperson, a girl in her late teens with short, tousled red hair, jumped and turned from the display of necklaces she was straightening.

"I'm sorry." She blinked. "Are you, um, having a problem finding what you want?"

"What I want is to shop in peace, without being assaulted by shamelessly blatant attempts to whip the public into a seasonal buying frenzy at such an absurdly early date.''

The girl responded with a blank stare.

The woman's fingers tightened. ''I don't suppose that you could do anything about changing the piped-in music?''

A tiny frown appeared over the girl's blue eyes. ''Um, I'm sorry, no. But...'' She paused, then flashed an overly bright smile as she went on. ''You know, sometimes all the crowds and the music and the hustle-bustle of shopping can really be wearing. Have you thought about taking a break in our food court? A cup of eggnog-flavored coffee and a peppermint cookie might put you right back into the spirit.''

Back in the *spirit?* Was this young woman nuts?

''I doubt that would work. I detest eggnog, for one thing.'' An involuntary shudder ripped through the woman. ''And even if I did like the vile stuff, I certainly wouldn't consider drinking it in May.''

''M-May?'' The salesclerk took a deep breath and raised her chin. ''Um, ma'am? It's *November.* November twenty-ninth. The day after Thanksgiving.'' The girl frowned again, then went on. ''Um, you know, I could call someone from Security and...''

The woman willed the girl's next words to dull to an unintelligible hum. Obviously the young lady was unbalanced. There was no way it could be November. Only yesterday, the woman thought, she had been watching waves crash onto the shore and thinking how unusually warm it was for May.

''Silver bells...''

The refrain intruded. The woman glanced toward a wide bank of glass to her right. Sunlight streamed in. The bit of sky she could see was clear blue. However, she did notice that the hats hanging from the chrome pole at the end of the aisle were all dark—black, brown, forest-green and red circles of felt, along with a few knitted caps. Not one summery straw hat in the bunch.

Fighting off a shiver, the woman let her gaze fall on the round table several feet away. Pieces of silver and gold jewelry were nestled within open boxes decorated in a burgundy-and-green plaid.

She looked up, searching for the speaker responsible for the offending music, only to see a collection of glittery snowflakes dangling from the ceiling. As she stared at them, she heard a man behind her say, "This is Santa's first day in the store, honey, so you're going to have to be a good little girl if..."

As the voice faded in the distance, a blush heated the woman's cheeks. The salesclerk must be right. It must be November, after all. And she must be—another shudder shook her shoulders—Christmas shopping. In some store in downtown...

Downtown where? The woman froze as she asked herself, *What city am I in?* When her mind came up blank, her heart thudded to a stop. The snowflakes began to spin, quickly forming a shimmering blizzard above her. The music grew louder, while she frantically asked herself, *Where am I?*

Then, *Who am I?*

Again there was no answer. Her heart began to race. Her fingers could no longer feel the glass counter she gripped so tightly. Her breath felt as if it was jammed in her chest, unable to escape. Blood pounded in her ears.

"Ma'am? *Ma'am?*"

The second sharp-edged address penetrated the dizzying vortex. She pulled her attention to the clerk, just as the girl said, "The security guard will be here in a moment. He'll take you to our quiet lounge, where you can—"

"No. That won't be necessary." The woman added more firmly, "Really."

With that she turned and began walking quickly away, ignoring the clerk's cries of protest as she moved toward the wall of windows that she assumed, *prayed,* held the store entrance—and more importantly, its exit.

I just need some fresh air, she told herself. I just need to get my bearings, she thought as she wove past a series of clear plastic shoe displays. Once I figure out where I am, I'll know who I am, and then I'll be fine.

Desperate to escape the crowds, the decorations and the far-too-jolly notes now jangling in her ears, she practically ran up the shallow, wide staircase leading to the glass door and pushed it open. Moist, cool air hit her face as she exited, then moved to one side, away from the stream of people entering and departing the store.

She'd made it outside. Now, certainly, she would know where she was, she assured herself as she glanced around. Nothing looked the least bit familiar. Oh lord. Panic widened her eyes, sent her heart racing again. She had no idea where in the world she might be. *Yes, you do,* a voice in her mind insisted impatiently. *You* have *to know where you are. Look around again. What do you see? Think. Breathe.*

Obeying this last command first, she then slowly took in her surroundings. On the opposite side of the street, a series of brick planters stair-stepped up to an area bordered by a row of benches. Beyond these, perhaps a block away, she saw a tall ivory building emblazoned with the words Saks Fifth Avenue.

All right. There was a Saks Fifth Avenue in New York. She didn't know how she knew this or, for that matter, why she felt so certain this was not New York. But it was somewhat comforting to feel certain about *something.*

The surrounding structures weren't tall enough for New York. And—

Her thoughts stilled as she spied a car with a California license plate.

In a flash she knew this was San Francisco. The park in front of her was Union Square. The store she'd just stepped out of was Maxwell's Department Store.

She turned to the wall of windows behind her. To one side, a calendar had been posted bearing the longer holiday hours, topped by a banner warning that there were only twenty-six more shopping days to Christmas.

So, it was indeed November. Not May.

She wondered how she could have made that mistake, then brushed the thought away. It didn't matter how or why she'd fallen into this pit of amnesia. All that mattered was that she *knew* again. She was in San Francisco, at Maxwell's, and her name was Jane. Jane Ashbury.

At least, that's who she was now.

Reflected in the window, Jane saw a slender woman dressed in a red suit jacket over an ankle-length black skirt. She appeared to be in her late twenties or early thirties, and was of medium height with light brown hair. This was layered into thick bangs to cover the scar on her forehead, and the sides fell just past her narrow jaw.

In the past year and a half, Jane had come to accept that the large, gray-brown eyes, the tiny scar at the right corner of her mouth and the not-quite-symmetrical features belonged to her, just as she'd learned to answer to the name Jane. What she had looked like before, or what her name had once been, were lost in a darkness far deeper than the one she'd experienced inside the store—a darkness she'd long since given up trying to penetrate.

Jane became aware of the jangling sound of a ringing bell just as a man jostled past behind her. She fought off a shiver.

She hated crowds. They made her want to escape to some open place where she could breathe. She turned to do just that. Before she could take a step, a hand closed over her arm, then tightened, and she gasped as a deep voice said, "Forget it, honey. You and that scarf you took are coming with me."

In a small, gray room, Jane slumped in a hard chair, a slit of a window in the wall on her right, a closed door on her left. Too weary to do more than stare at the burgundy-

and-tan pile of silk in the middle of the desk in front of her, she listened to the two men sitting on the other side.

"Thanks for calling me."

Jane glanced at the speaker. With his short blond hair and linebacker's body straining the shoulders of his blue sport coat, Detective Bruce Wilcox was an imposing figure, even sitting down. She didn't feel any more comfortable with him today than she had the only other time they'd met, well over a year ago.

"Actually, it was her idea."

The thin faced security guard, in his brown uniform and billed cap, was the person who had grabbed her arm and brought her up here, then refused to listen to her explanations. Mr. Jessup continued to speak to the detective.

"She gave me this cockamamy story about forgetting who she was, then told me to call the police and ask for the detectives who had been in charge of her case. When the officer I spoke with said that neither of those men were on the force now, she came up with your name. Until you showed up, I was sure she was lying."

"Nope. She was telling you the truth. At least, the part about her being Jane Doe Number Thirteen. The scarf story we'll have to check out."

Jane barely heard the last words. Her mind was stuck on *Jane Doe Number Thirteen.* She hated that name, hated the memories it conjured up—waking to find she didn't know where she was, who she was, why her jaw was frozen shut, why her face was bandaged, what was causing the deep ache in her pelvis. Even worse had been the cheery nurses smiling at her when she shook her head in response to their questions, doctors asking if this hurt, if that hurt.

Then the detectives had arrived, with more questions. But Manuel Mendosa and Matthew Sullivan hadn't been anything like Wilcox. Patient and kind, they had never treated her like a suspect. Jane's stomach twisted as she realized she'd somehow managed to forget that, of the two detectives who had worked on her case, one was now dead and the other—

The click of a key in the lock broke into Jane's thoughts. She turned as the door swung open, then started. The man standing there was that second detective—Matthew Sullivan.

The man looked just as she remembered—black hair and dark green eyes; tall and athletically trim in his faded jeans and tan, open-neck shirt. But as he stepped into the room, Jane noticed that his face was more deeply lined, making him look older than his mid-thirties. And the expression in his eyes was almost grim.

He stopped just inside the doorway and his glance skimmed the two men on the other side of the desk. When his eyes met hers, they widened momentarily, then he smiled. That deep dimple she recalled so well creased his left cheek, but his eyes still lacked the devil-may-care expression she remembered so well.

"Hello there, Jane," he said.

She'd always found his deep voice soothing, but today there seemed to be a harsh edge to it. Conscious of the way he continued to study her, she slowly got to her feet. His gaze swept down, then back up. His smile widened, and all the carefully chosen words Jane had been about to utter tumbled out in random order.

"Matt. I'm surprised to see you. I was just thinking about you." Realizing that her voice sounded more raspy than usual, she cleared her throat. "Worrying, actually. Well, worrying isn't exactly the right word. Though I did do that when I heard you were shot, of course."

Jane knew she was rambling. She forced herself to speak more slowly. "What I was doing before you came in was berating myself for forgetting that you'd left the police force and—"

"*Forgetting,*" Wilcox broke in, "seems to be a habit with you, doesn't it?"

Jane turned toward the detective, but not before she saw Matt's dark eyebrows move together in a quick frown.

"Just what is going on here?" Matt asked.

Wilcox leaned back in his chair. "I'm here to investigate a report of shoplifting. What are *you* doing here?"

"I was at the station, trying to get some information on a case Jack and I are working on. I happened to hear Baker call you on your cell phone about a matter involving Jane Ashbury and Maxwell's. I decided to find out what was going on. I know it's not my case anymore, but call it for old times' sake. Care to fill me in?"

In the silence that followed, Jane glanced from one man to the other. Matt, with his narrowed eyes and firmly set lips, didn't look at all like a man who was asking a favor. And Wilcox, with his hard blue eyes and head cocked to one side, didn't look like one who was predisposed to grant one. But slowly the man's lips curved slightly.

"Sure. Why not? So far, we have established the fact that Miss *Ashbury* here ran out of the store carrying this scarf, valued at one hundred and thirty-four dollars. She claims that she became confused, didn't know where she was, what month it was, or even who she was. That, however, has yet to be proven."

Matt looked at Jane. Before he could say a word, however, Mr. Jessup spoke up.

"Well, actually, when the salesgirl called me, she did say she had a customer who seemed to think it was May, and was acting rather strangely."

Matt's gaze seemed to sharpen. "May?" he asked Jane.

She barely managed to nod before Wilcox spoke.

"All right. So she was confused. Familiar story, right? That doesn't explain why she took the scarf with her."

Matt turned to Wilcox and took a step toward the man as he asked, "What's wrong with you? My guess is, she forgot she was holding it." He turned his attention to the security guard. "Where did you apprehend Miss Ashbury?"

"She was standing in front of the store, staring into the window."

"I see. Where was the scarf?"

"In her hand."

"Had the tag been removed?"

The man shook his head.

"Would you mind telling me just how many shoplifters you've known to stop right outside, with the stolen merchandise in clear view?"

Jessup sighed. "None. But she was moving away when I grabbed her. And her story—"

"Needs to be confirmed," Wilcox finished as he stood up. "Mr. Jessup, let's go speak to that salesclerk. I think we can safely leave her in Mr. Sullivan's custody. He used to be a cop."

A minute later, Jessup closed the door, leaving Jane alone with Matt. The silence in the room seemed to grow, demanding to be filled.

"I'm sorry about Manny," she said. "I wanted to come see you, in the hospital, but I was told you couldn't have visitors. Then Zoe took me to—"

"Hey," Matt broke in.

He stepped toward her, halting once he was two feet away. Jane could almost feel the strength emanating from him. Or was she recalling the way his arms had held her so tightly as she sobbed uncontrollably the last time she'd seen him?

"I've been out of the hospital for a year now," Matt said. "If anyone should apologize, it's me. I've been meaning to look you up, but—"

"*But,*" Jane interrupted. Embarrassed by where her earlier thoughts had wandered, and the weakness she'd shown that long-ago day, she went on quickly. "You've been busy putting your life back together. I understand how that goes."

Matt's jaw tightened. He knew Jane wasn't offering an empty reassurance. If anyone knew what it took to put a life back together—or create a new one out of nothing, for that matter—it was Jane Ashbury.

In the middle of May, nearly a year and a half ago, he and his partner had been called to the scene of a suspicious accident. A car had gone off a cliff near the ocean and burst into flames, but not before a young woman had been thrown onto the rocks. There were no skid marks to suggest that the driver had been speeding, and the wheel tracks on the grassy cliff indicated the car had come from an odd angle. Any identification that the woman might have been carrying had been destroyed by the fire, and her body and face had been shattered by the impact.

When a check of fingerprint files, dental records and missing persons lists all came up blank, the woman was tagged with the designation normally given to unidentified bodies—Jane Doe—and given the number thirteen to distinguish her from those who had come before and those who would follow. When she came out of her coma, in the middle of June, she had no idea who she was and didn't recognize the face the plastic surgeons had created for her.

He and Manny had elicited the aid of the media, and Jane's story was widely covered by newspapers and television. Numerous people came to see her, hoping she might prove to be their missing sister, daughter, wife. What few people knew, however, was how devastating both her celebrity and the subsequent disappointments had been for Jane. Matt knew, though. He had witnessed the last of such visits, had held Jane in his arms as she mourned the fact that, yet again, all parties concerned had been disappointed and she still was left without an identity.

However, when she pulled away from him that day and dried her eyes, a new Jane had emerged.

That quietly self-controlled person stood in front of Matt now—more or less. She wasn't as painfully thin as he remembered; the hair that had been shaved prior to the emergency operation on her bruised brain had grown out to frame her slender face in a chin-length cap of light brown;

and the scar at the left corner of her mouth had faded to the palest of pinks.

But her smoky gray-brown eyes held the same mixture of vulnerability and determination he'd seen the day she declared she was ready to move forward, that she would never search for her past again. However, from what the security guard had said, it seemed that today Jane's past had come searching for her.

"So," Matt said. "You remembered something."

Jane's eyes widened. "No. I didn't."

Matt gave her a small smile. "Jessup just told me you thought it was May. That was the month your car went over that embankment." It hadn't been her car, of course. The vehicle subsequently had proved to be stolen. Glossing over the inaccuracy, Matt got to the heart of the matter. "Don't you think there might be some connection?"

"No." She took a step back as she spoke, and broke eye contact. Her gaze fell on the scarf. "I was looking at this scarf one minute, then hearing some Christmas tune the next, and suddenly wondered why the store would play that kind of music so early in the year."

From the evasiveness in her whiskey-toned voice, Matt knew there was more to the story. He considered pressing the matter, then thought about Wilcox's attitude and decided to hold off, for the moment. Instead, as Jane slowly met his gaze again, he lifted the scarf from the center of the table.

"Good taste," he said, then let it fall back into a soft puddle as he looked into Jane's eyes. He tried to lend some lightness to his next words. "Well, for the record, I don't believe for one moment that you're some shoplifter making up a story to escape apprehension."

Jane stared at him. Her wide mouth began to twitch, as if she was fighting a smile. "You still talk like a cop."

Matt shrugged. Some of the tightness eased from his shoulders. "Force of habit. Besides, I'm still in law enforcement, sort of. I'm a private detective now."

Jane lifted one brow. "Did you come here thinking I might need your services?"

There was no missing the almost desperate note in that low, throaty voice of Jane's, a sexy quality that was the direct result of injuries sustained in a crime unsolved. *Temporarily* unsolved, Matt reminded himself. Now Jane Doe Num—Jane *Ashbury*—was no longer a half-forgotten part of his life. She was here, in front of him, a bit of unfinished business that had too long been pushed to the back of his mind by events that had turned his own life upside down.

His assessment of the crash made him doubt the theory that Jane had sent the car over the embankment herself, either accidentally or as a suicide attempt. When he and Manny were temporarily pulled off the case, they were certain that they'd eventually be able to prove that Jane's "accident" had been a murder attempt.

Matt frowned. It was obvious that Wilcox had done nothing with the case the man had inherited. And maybe it was just as well. No one had ever been punished for Manny's murder, or for the damage that had been done to Matt's body and life. The idea of justice denied ate at him daily. Maybe he would feel better if he caught the person responsible for the attempt on Jane's life and brought him, or her, to justice.

But first there was this matter of shoplifting to deal with.

"Well, to be honest," Matt said, "I don't consider this much of a case. I'd be very surprised if Mr. Jessup doesn't return with an apology for having doubted you."

Jane looked deeply skeptical, but before she could say anything, the door opened and the security guard entered the room. Wilcox followed him, but stopped just inside the door.

"Miss Ashbury," Jessup said as he approached Jane. "I'm sorry for the…misunderstanding."

Pure relief softened Jane's features as she came around the desk and faced the security guard. "I'm free to go, then?"

The man nodded. Jane gave him a wide smile, then opened her arms and gave him a quick hug. When Jane stepped back, the guard blinked and straightened the cap that had been knocked askew by her enthusiasm.

Matt fought a smile. The Jane he remembered had seemed to be far younger than her estimated late-twenties to early thirties. The doctors explained this was because she had no memory of the personal experiences that forge maturity. However, the Jane he'd met upon entering this room had seemed wary and suspicious in a most adult way. He was glad to see that she'd managed to keep at least some of the childlike openness he'd found so refreshing.

"And thank you, Matt."

Jane had turned toward him. Still smiling, she crossed the room and, before he could anticipate her intent, she went on tiptoe, threw her arms around his shoulders and drew him into a tight embrace.

Automatically Matt's arms went around her slender body. In an instant he realized this wasn't anything like the hugs he'd exchanged with Jane before, when she'd been as thin as an eleven-year-old girl. The woman he now held was still slender, but had developed gentle curves that seemed to melt into him, warming him, stirring him in ways he hadn't allowed his body to experience in far too long. Without willing them to, his arms tightened around her.

For the second time that day, Jane felt the life she'd spent a year carefully building shift beneath her feet. As she found herself drawn into Matt's embrace, a strange heat washed through her body, and although she had no memory of ever experiencing this particular sort of knee-weakening warmth, she knew what it was. It was the moment she'd read about in all those romance novels, when the woman's body responds to a man's. To *the* man. The one she is meant to be with, now and forever.

But real life, she heard a voice say, *isn't anything like a romance novel.* The voice was Matt's, she realized, echoing from a moment when he'd stood over her hospital bed.

He'd tried to explain that there were better ways to fill the blanks in her knowledge than watching movies and television or reading fiction, then he'd handed her a book about the science of the brain and another on world history.

But today proved that he'd been wrong all those months ago. This was *just* like those novels—a moment of breathless expectation, of heart-pounding joy, of...of absolute idiocy.

A chill slithered through Jane. Kyle Rogers had elicited similar sensations. As she reminded herself of the painful lessons she'd learned in the past year about confusing love with physical attraction, she released her hold on Matt's neck. As she stepped back, Matt's arms released her slowly. She found herself standing a foot in front of him, staring mutely into those dark-lashed green eyes of his. Embarrassed heat flooded her cheeks, and she forced herself to speak.

"It was super of you to come down and help me out of this mess. I really appreciate it." She paused. "I'm sure you have more important things to be doing. And Mr. Jessup here should no doubt be out looking for real shoplifters, so if he'll return my purse to me, I believe it's time I headed home."

"Not so quick—"

Jane had almost forgotten Wilcox. She turned to him as he finished, "I think the three of us have a few things to discuss."

Chapter Two

The security guard told Detective Wilcox to lock the door when they were finished speaking, then left the room. Neither Matt nor Wilcox had moved during all this. They stood on either side of the door, silently glaring at each other.

"You haven't done a thing on Jane's case, have you?" Matt asked the moment the door was shut.

"There hasn't been a thing to do," Wilcox replied. "I told her to call me if she remembered anything. Until today, I haven't heard a word from her."

The man turned to Jane. "You say you became confused downstairs because you suddenly recalled standing on a beach in the middle of May. Is that right?"

Jane nodded.

"Well, you could have been remembering a day from this past May, right?"

Jane was tempted to lie. It would make things far more simple. But the truth mattered more than convenience.

"No."

Wilcox's square features registered skepticism. "You sound rather certain of that."

Jane shrugged. "I didn't go to the beach this past May."

"Okay. What, exactly, did you recall today, standing in front of the scarves?"

"Just what I told Mr. Jessup. I heard the Christmas music playing, and for one second, I could remember standing on the beach and thinking how warm it was for May. Then I became irritated that a store would play Christmas tunes so early."

"Nothing more?"

Jane shook her head.

"Well, that's not enough to relaunch any investigation."

That was fine with Jane. She was releasing a slow breath of relief, when Matt spoke up.

"You have never believed that someone tried to murder her, have you. You still think she tried to kill herself."

Wilcox met Matt's accusation with one of his own. "You and Mendosa never put together a shred of real evidence to convince me otherwise."

"Oh, come on. Are you forgetting that the seat belt broke? It would hardly make sense to buckle up if one were intent on suicide. And do you really think Jane would know how to rig a car to explode?"

"That evidence was inconclusive."

"Wilcox, none of the evidence in this case, taken a piece at a time, is conclusive. But when you put together the fact that Forensics found scuff marks indicating that the car had been pushed off the cliff, that the air bag had been disabled, and that the steering wheel revealed only Jane's fingerprints—not even one belonging to the owner of the car—any cop with two brain cells to rub together could make a case for attempted homicide."

Jane tensed as Wilcox took a step toward Matt. Matt was a couple of inches taller, but the police detective's muscular form carried a silent, credible threat.

"If someone tried to kill her, why haven't they made

another attempt? Her whereabouts and the fact that she hadn't died in that accident were well publicized.''

"Exactly,'' Matt replied. "As was the fact that she had no memory and that several of her doctors believed the amnesia might have been caused by the trauma to her head, and thus be permanent. Why risk getting caught while making another attempt to kill her, when the media made it clear that there were no clues to her past, meaning the authorities had no idea who would have a motive to murder her?''

Wilcox shook his head. "Look, Lone Ranger. I know that you and your partner enjoyed tilting at windmills, solving the impossible cases. Me, I have enough to do pursuing criminals I have half a chance of catching.''

He turned to Jane. "You should go see that therapist person who was working with you, the one who hypnotizes people. If she manages to help you recall a fact I can follow up on, then call me.''

With that, Wilcox turned and left the room.

Jane drew a deep breath, then let it slide quietly through her barely parted lips. She reached for the purse Jessup had placed on the desk, then turned to Matt.

"Well, I think that was enough excitement for one day. I'd better be getting home.''

Matt turned to her, effectively blocking the path to the door. "First, we need to talk. I understand there's a coffee shop in the basement.''

Jane frowned as she placed her cup next to a small plate that was almost completely covered by an enormous chocolate chip cookie, then lowered herself into the chair Matt had pulled out for her. We *need* to talk, he'd said. It hadn't been a request. And what a good girl she was being, responding to the man's understated demand like a sheep stepping back into formation at the direction of a border collie.

Not that she didn't want to talk to Matt. She had a million

questions to ask him—over a year's worth, in fact. But something about the way his eyes had narrowed when he'd uttered those words suggested strongly that *he* wasn't going to be the subject of their discussion. Unless, that is, she moved quickly.

"No one ever told me why you left the force," she said.

Matt paused in the act of scooting his chair closer to the table and looked up sharply. His eyes met hers, a dusky shade of sea green, slightly wide with surprise. When he frowned, that color turned murky. Jane felt a tremor in her chest, but held his gaze as she continued.

"I tried to come see you at the hospital after you were shot," she said quietly. "But you were in intensive care for a long time, and I was told you weren't allowed visitors. Then it was time for Zoe and I to—"

"Leave for Maine," Matt said. "I know. I was the one who set that up, remember?"

Remember? How she hated that word.

"Of course I do. I remember everything that has happened to me since I woke in the hospital. For example, I recall the fact that I never got a chance to thank you for all you did for me. You, and Manny."

Her voice deepened as her throat tightened over the name. She swallowed as she gazed across at Matt, saw his expression go bleak, watched him glance away briefly before meeting her eyes once more.

"There wasn't anything to thank us for," he said softly. "We were doing our job. I just wish we could have finished it."

Jane shook her head. "You went far beyond just doing a job. Despite my lack of memory, which gave you a lack of motive, you and Manny stuck with me, did everything you could…"

Her words trailed off as she thought about all the times one or both of the men had sat in her room, explaining things she found confusing, making her laugh when the darkness closed around her. She drew a deep breath.

"You were needed elsewhere. And it was hardly part of your job to arrange for me to get a new identity. In fact, I realize now that you two spent a lot of time with me, in a case that was going nowhere. That could have gotten you into a lot of trouble."

With Matt's eyes gazing into hers, Jane felt an embarrassed flush heat her cheeks. The word *trouble,* when used with respect to Matt Sullivan and Manny Mendosa, was a woefully inadequate one. It would serve her right if Matt reminded her then and there just how inadequately.

A year ago August, the two detectives had been told to put her investigation on a back burner while they worked another case. Two weeks later, Manny had been killed by an unknown assailant. That was more than "trouble." That was tragic. And, until now, she'd been robbed of the opportunity to express her sorrow over Manny's passing to the man in front of her.

"I wanted to call you, after I heard about Manny," she said softly. "But—"

"I know," Matt interrupted. "I was undercover. In fact, I heard about Manny's death while driving up the coast, carrying some marked bills as the final step in flushing out the head of a money-laundering scheme. We got the guy, but not before he shot me."

He paused and glanced away again. Jane saw a frown drop over his eyes. It disappeared in a flash as he returned his attention to her.

"I got your card when I finally regained consciousness. It was good to hear from you. You know how it is when you're tied to a hospital bed—not much to do but read your cards and letters and catch up on your soaps."

He grinned as he finished speaking. Jane was quite familiar with the way Matt Sullivan used humor to deflect pain. It was a trait she'd adopted herself, finding it easier to laugh at life as she tried to dodge its slings and arrows than to let herself be swallowed up in the shadows lurking in the darkness of her unknown past.

"Soaps?" she said, taking the bait offered. "Aren't you the fellow who sat by my bed, telling me what a waste of time they were? How they distort reality?"

"Yep. Same fellow. Turns out that sometimes reality begs to be distorted, or at least ignored for a bit." Again he paused. Leaning forward, he looked meaningfully into her eyes. "Only for a while, of course. Then it's time to deal with whatever you've been handed."

Jane fought the temptation to look away. "It appears you've done that admirably. You mentioned that you're a private detective now. Do you like working on your own?"

"I work with my cousin, Jack. Also an ex-cop."

"Still trying to put the bad guys away?"

Jane recalled Matt and Manny trading jokes and insults about past cases, arguing over who had found what evidence, who had missed seeing something. It had been a comfort listening to them, not just because they made her laugh, but because she learned that the emptiness she found in her mind each time she tried to recall the past hadn't affected her ability to follow a conversation, to make the connections necessary to find things funny, sad, amusing or frightening.

"As many as possible," Matt replied. "Keeps us pretty busy. Not too busy, though, to take up old cases. Yours, for example."

Jane was aware that her smile had frozen. "You heard what I told Wilcox, Matt. Nothing has changed. I still have no idea who I used to be. And, without knowing who I am, there's no way of establishing who might have had a motive for trying to kill me. If that is, indeed, what happened."

"If you're referring to Wilcox's suggestion that you tried to commit suicide, forget it. And something *has* changed. Today your memory started to return."

"No." Jane reached blindly for the chocolate chip cookie, brought it to her mouth and said, "It didn't," then took a bite.

"Really?" Matt lifted one eyebrow. "How would you

describe the event that caused you to insist that it was the middle of May?"

Jane chewed slowly. She felt the combination of dough and chocolate soften in her mouth, but could taste nothing, as she thought back to the incident at the scarf counter. She shrugged as she swallowed.

"A moment of confusion. There was a lot of noise, and people and music..." She paused to fight a sudden chill. "It was my first real experience with Christmas crowds, actually. Last year, Zoe and I stayed with her family in a town that consisted of three square blocks surrounded by farms."

"What's that have to do with thinking you'd been standing on the beach yesterday?"

"I don't know. Maybe I had a subconscious yearning for somewhere quiet and peaceful. You know, a daydream."

"A daydream. Hmm. Tell me about this daydream."

The speculative expression in Matt's narrowed eyes made Jane uneasy. Or maybe it was remembering how she'd felt standing at the glass counter and discovering she had no idea what month it was, where she was, and worst of all *who* she was, that made her reluctant to discuss the fleeting but oh-so-real image that seemed to have thrown her into such confusion.

"It wasn't really anything," she said, then picked up her coffee cup.

Matt was aware that Jane was evading his question. He should know, being the self-acknowledged king of evasion himself. Remembering how transparent Jane had been when she first recovered from her three-week coma, he wondered if she'd learned this tactic from observing the way he and Manny joked around in an attempt to keep the particulars of her accident from her, hoping that she'd remember these things on her own.

Matt watched Jane take a drink, saw her mouth twist with distaste as she backed off from the cup.

"You don't like eggnog-flavored coffee?"

Her eyes met his as she lifted her chin. "Certainly."

Matt felt that her voice sounded a tad too defensive, but he wasn't going to let this minor mystery deflect him from going after the larger story.

"You told Wilcox you weren't at the beach this past May, right?"

Jane took another sip of coffee before placing the cup back on the table. She nodded, then picked up her cookie and began breaking it into tiny pieces.

"Okay. How about June?"

Matt watched as Jane turned her attention to the sliver of cookie between her fingers, then raised her eyes to his.

"No. And I didn't go to the beach in July or August, either. I've been too busy."

Matt couldn't miss the fear shadowing those unusual smoky eyes of hers. How could he have forgotten that haunted look, or the fact that Jane had always responded better to teasing than to police-type inquisitions? Maybe he'd been taken with the fact that she seemed so much more…grown-up, courtesy of the businesslike red jacket she wore and the sophisticated way her hair had been cut to fall in soft, spiky layers around her face.

"Too busy for the beach?" Matt purposely exaggerated his surprise. "Didn't you learn anything from me and Man—from that day we took you to Ocean Beach and demonstrated the fine art of surfing? I must say, whoever took over the job of educating you in the joy of living definitely fell down on the job."

Jane's smile was weak, but Matt took a great deal of satisfaction in having managed to get that much.

She said, "That would be Zoe. She's going pretty strong for a woman in her seventies, but I think surfing is a little out of her range."

"Okay. So you weren't at the beach this past May." He released an exaggerated sigh. "Well then, it seems clear to me that you must have flashed back to a day you spent at the beach a year ago May—before your accident."

Matt watched the tiny curve of the edge of Jane's mouth disappear. Her eyes seemed to darken as she stared at him, and her jaw visibly tightened before she said, "So?"

"So?" Matt's voice softened as he prepared to do battle. "Sooo, I would say that you have had your first honest-to-goodness memory in over a year. A matter worth celebrating."

With that he took a long drink of aromatic French roast. Savoring the rich, strong flavor, he placed his cup on the table, swallowed and grinned at her again.

"Matt, that brief image of sand and sea could hardly be considered a memory. And even if it was, I still don't have any desire to know who I once was. I've moved forward, just like I said I wanted to, and I have no interest in looking back."

Matt remembered the warm July day that Jane had made that particular declaration. She'd just returned to her hospital room, after meeting with a family who had come five hundred miles to see her, certain she would prove to be their lost loved one—only to discover they were wrong. He recalled the way Jane had dashed away the tears of disappointment, then declared she wanted nothing more to do with the past.

There was no sign of tears in her eyes now, but Matt recognized the same determination he'd seen on that day. The memory of that resolve had reassured him whenever he thought about Jane's unsolved case while battling back from his own injuries, then working tirelessly with his cousin Jack to build the sort of detective agency they both needed.

He and Jack had been determined to continue their childhood dream of catching the bad guys. It had taken a long time, and a lot of legwork to prove themselves, but they'd built a reputation for solving cases that the police had given up on, or were forced to let lie fallow as they pursued matters with more promise.

Like the case of Jane Doe Number Thirteen.

This had been his investigation. It was his again. Now he had the time, the autonomy and the resources to find out who had sent this lovely young woman over the edge of a cliff in a car rigged to burst into flame. And, it seemed that Jane just might be ready to provide the most important item in the equation—the memories that would lead him to the person or persons with a motive strong enough to set that horror in motion.

If, that is, he could get Jane to cooperate.

Changing tactics, Matt relaxed back in his chair. "You mentioned Zoe. How is she?"

Jane seemed to study him a moment before answering. "She's fine. I rent an apartment from her, and in case you're wondering, she has accepted my decision to forget about the past, and never bugs me about it."

Matt managed to keep his expression neutral at this news. Zoe Zeffarelli had come highly recommended by a couple of cops he and Manny knew. The therapist had used a combination of psychology and hypnotism to help crack several cases. Matt had found the woman to be a no-nonsense sort who had instantly gained Jane's trust and his respect. He had assumed that when he and Manny went to work on the money-laundering scheme, Ms. Zeffarelli would help Jane recover her memory and build a life for herself. For some reason he couldn't fathom, that hadn't happened.

Maintaining his casual attitude, Matt said, "Okay, we'll leave the distant past alone. Tell me what's kept you too busy to go to the beach."

"I started my own business."

"Yeah? What kind of business?"

"I make elves and fairies."

"Really? Would this be the one-wish sort, or three?"

As Matt watched Jane's eyes crinkle at the corners, he found himself smiling easily and naturally in a way he hadn't done since...

He let that thought go unfinished. Jane's stance on not

dwelling on the past was right, at least as it pertained to his past. Hers was another matter.

"No wishes, I'm afraid," she said with a sad sigh. "They just sit around and look magical."

"I see. How did you get into the business of magic?"

Jane grinned. "Zoe's cousin got me started, last October in Maine. She makes dolls. I tried to copy hers, but all the faces I carved looked more elflike, so that's what my creations became. I was looking for a way to support myself, so she suggested I put my things on consignment at the shop she owns, and they all sold. Somehow, almost magically, I've managed to build a thriving business."

She grinned as she finished speaking, then lifted her cup to take a sip of coffee. The grin became a grimace as she swallowed, then choked on the liquid.

After her coughing fit ended, Matt said, "I'm not sure why you insist on drinking something you obviously don't like, but for the moment, I'm more interested in another little mystery."

"And that would be?"

Jane looked so wary that Matt almost regretted what he was about to do. "That question," he said, "is why such an obviously intelligent and talented woman would be so determined to ignore the chance to look into her past, where she might discover the source of this magical ability of hers."

Chapter Three

She should have seen that coming.

Jane stared at the man who had just manipulated the conversation in the exact direction she'd been trying so very hard to avoid.

"You're good," she said quietly.

Matt's eyebrows rose in silent acknowledgment of her reluctant compliment. He continued to gaze into her eyes as his smile widened, increasing the depth of his single dimple.

Jane's shoulders sagged. She knew when she'd been outmaneuvered. She should have recognized the tactics. How many times had Matt and Manny started their visits to her hospital room with a series of jokes that got her laughing too hard to worry about the news they'd brought?

Perhaps some new reporter wanted to interview the celebrated amnesiac who had miraculously escaped death, or yet another person wanted to see if she might be the female who had disappeared from their lives a month, a year, a decade ago. And somehow, because Matt and Manny got her laughing, she'd always found a way to face these people, to give them what they wanted, so she might get what she wanted—answering invasive questions from reporters in the desperate hope that someone, the *right* someone, would read the story, see her picture and somehow recognize her, then give her a past, a family, somewhere to belong.

And when these people showed up—the ones Jane came to think of as "searchers"—she drew upon the lighthearted moments Manny and Matt provided, to help her smile while she covered her near baldness with a wig that matched the color of the missing person *du jour,* managed to hold hope in her heart as she prepared to enter the room where this newest searcher waited, and told herself that surely, this time, someone would find something familiar in the features the plastic surgeon had pieced together for her.

Considering that the lower half of her face had been smashed in, her nose broken and her jaw shattered, the plastic surgeon called in to make the emergency repairs hadn't done a bad job. Her nose was slightly crooked, her left cheekbone was not quite as prominent as the right and her jaw seemed a little too narrow. The tiny scar at the corner of her mouth and the larger one on her forehead were still noticeable, but the doctors had used the tiniest of stitches, and promised that over time they would fade to a pale white.

So, as faces went, hers didn't seem to vary too far from the norm. In fact, it was quite generic. And perhaps this was the problem, for each time she'd met with a searcher, it seemed she had lacked that special, unique or quirky thing that would tell them that Jane was their missing wife-girlfriend-sister-daughter.

And now Matt wanted her to go through all of that all over again. She'd seen the speculative glint in his eyes when he first asked her about the memory, or flashback, or moment of insanity that had gripped her on the department store floor. The very thought that she might have begun to remember filled her with fear, excitement, dread, hope and utter confusion, an impossible mixture of emotions that now led her to glare at the man who had pushed her into the corner of her mind where this cauldron boiled.

"What difference is it to you, if, indeed, I have finally remembered some little nugget?" She didn't give Matt a chance to respond before she went on. "The past is the past. No one claimed me, so whoever I was, I didn't matter to anyone. For all I know, Wilcox is right. Perhaps I did try to kill myself."

Matt leaned forward, looked hard into her eyes. "Forget Wilcox. First off, no one who had a death wish would have worked as hard on their recovery as you did. Secondly, toxicology tests revealed barbiturates in your system, which I believe indicates that someone had drugged you before placing you in that stolen car rigged to explode and sending it off that cliff. Whoever this was went to a lot of trouble not only to kill you, but to see to it that your body burned beyond recognition. I would say that whoever you were, you mattered very much to someone."

For a moment, Jane could only stare at the very serious expression in Matt's eyes, her mind playing his words back. This was his idea of being *important* to someone? The idea was so absurd that she laughed out loud.

The look on Matt's face made her laugh harder. She held her stomach as she rocked back and forth, then pulled herself up straight and sobered, only to collapse again, this time burying her face in her hands as her mind reverberated with the ridiculousness of Matt's statement.

A hand closed over one of Jane's wrists. Matt's hand, warm and strong. How many times had she fantasized back in the hospital about his touch—before she'd learned that it was typical, almost redundantly so, for victims of violent crimes to fantasize about their rescuers?

The mirth died on Jane's lips. She looked into Matt's eyes as she lifted her free hand to brush away a laugh-tear and took a deep breath. "Just what part of your statement," she asked, "is supposed to encourage me to care about my past?"

Matt grimaced. "Good point. How about this. The idea that you might have begun to remember your past matters because it's my job, my life's work, to go after the bad guys and put them away. Recently Jack and I have had some success in that area, but none of those can make up for certain personal failures."

Matt's features tightened. "I wanted to find who shot Manny. As soon as I was released from the hospital, I double-checked the extensive police investigation. The only evidence is the bullet that killed him, and it doesn't match any weapon in the system. I couldn't even get justice in my own case. The man who almost took my life, who did rob me of a career I loved, died when my cousin Jack shot the guy before he could finish me off. I don't equate death with justice, so that brings me to the matter of Jane Doe Number Thirteen."

Matt stared hard into Jane's eyes. "Hers is a case every bit as baffling and frustrating as the question of who killed Manny. Both continue to eat at me. Manny is gone, leaving no clues at the scene of the crime or in his past cases to point to someone who might have wanted him dead. You, however, are alive. And maybe, just maybe, your past is ready to speak to you. If so, I want to listen. I want a chance to find the answers to this puzzle, to get justice for at least one of the cases that means something—"

Matt broke off. His fierce expression reflected pain and bitterness. Jane blinked, stunned into silence at the sudden change in the man she had thought she knew so well.

But then, how well could she have known him? He'd been in her life a mere eight weeks before he and Manny were sent undercover. She could see now that she'd been a child at the time, at least figuratively. Without her memory, she'd had no experiences to draw on, to teach her how to behave.

And that is how Matt had seen her. After the doctors and nurses had finished poking and prodding her, he and Manny had appeared at her bedside. When she realized how disappointed the two detectives were to learn that she couldn't answer any of their long list of questions, she'd begun to cry. The only sound in that sterile hospital room had been her sobs, until Matt whispered, "Hush, now. It's okay," as he gently traced a cloth down the path of her tears.

She'd pulled herself together with a shuddering sigh, opened her eyes to see that Matt had twisted his slightly damp handkerchief around his hand and pulled the ends into two rabbit ears. The makeshift puppet bobbed and weaved as a high-pitched voice, unmistakably Matt's in origin, scolded Manny for browbeating the subject of their investigation and making her cry.

In moments she was laughing. After that, each visit from these two had made her feel stronger, even the times when they'd tried to coax her memory to life. As they included her in their teasing banter, she'd begun to feel less lost, less lonely, and discovered that although she might not have a memory, she wasn't without intelligence and wit.

So, did that mean, she found herself asking as she studied the serious lines etched into Matt's features, that all those jokes had been an act on Matt's part? Or had the loss of his partner and his own brush with death woken the grim expression she'd glimpsed when he first walked into the security office a mere hour ago—the one that tightened his features now?

Or was it something about her today, that had brought out an aspect of Matt's personality he'd previously kept hidden? Last year he would have used silly humor to coerce her into exploring the brief memory that had assaulted her. Had he dropped his mask of joviality because he recognized that now, after taking charge of her life, her education, her career, she was no longer a lost waif in need of coddling?

She would like to think so, but it really didn't matter. She recognized a challenge when she saw one.

"All right, Matt," Jane said softly. "You win."

"Win what?"

Gone were the tight, fan-shaped lines that had bracketed Matt's sharply narrowed eyes only moments before. Gone also were the deep vertical grooves that had been etched on either side of his lips. His smile wasn't particularly wide, but his green eyes were lit with anticipation. Someone who hadn't observed the relationship Matt had shared with his partner might wonder if he'd manufactured his earlier expression just to get her to this point.

"I did have some sort of memory," she replied. "I warn you, though, it was a very little one. I can't promise it will lead anywhere."

"Of course you can't." He got to his feet. "Let's go."

"Go where?"

"To Zoe's. If the door to your memory is finally unlocked, she's the one to push it open. Where's your car?"

"Car?" Jane asked as she got to her feet.

"Yes. I parked in the lot beneath Union Square. If you're parked somewhere else, I can drive you to your car, then follow you to Zoe's."

"I don't drive. I took the bus."

"Good." Matt's hand closed over Jane's elbow, and she let him steer her toward the escalator. "That will make things much easier."

Matt turned down the street Jane indicated and drove past a row of houses crowded next to each other. Most were some shade of off-white or tan, interspersed here and there with more boldly painted structures. Various styles were represented, from Mediterranean to English Tudor. Each rose several stories above garage doors, most with recessed ground-level entries protected by some kind of fancy iron gate.

"Nice," he said appreciatively as he braked at a stop sign. "The Marina District has always been one of my favorite parts of San Francisco."

When Jane did not respond to his comment, he glanced her way. She was staring straight ahead, her large smoky eyes wide and without focus.

He knew the signs. Something had frightened her. And he didn't have to ask what it was. Her past.

He could hardly blame her. If *he'd* gone through the horrors Jane must have faced at the hands of whoever had gone to so much trouble to end her life, he wouldn't be looking forward to searching that dark, shadow-filled memory, either. But he was aware, now even more than he had been when he was first assigned to her case, how important it was to pull the monsters out of the closet and defeat them.

"Jane."

She jumped and turned to him. He gave her what he hoped was a reassuring, lighthearted smile. "Do I go straight, or turn again?"

After a getting-her-bearings glance around, Jane said, "Straight. It's the four-story gray house on the left. You can park in the driveway."

Matt followed instructions, pulling his black Jeep up to a double garage door of the same color. By the time he switched the motor off and removed his keys from the ignition, Jane had already unbuckled her seat belt and opened her door. He got out and followed her up the curving staircase, with its ornate wrought-iron handrail. Before he could say a word, she had stopped within the arch of the second-story portico and was opening the bright pink door.

She turned as he started to follow, her eyes dark. For one moment he thought she was going to tell him she'd changed her mind, that she just wanted to leave the past alone—and then slam the door in his face. When he stepped into the foyer as a defensive tactic, however, she closed the door behind him and glanced at her watch.

"Zoe usually naps from three to three-thirty," she said, then moved toward a pair of French doors to her left. "She should be up by now. Wait in here, while I go up and tell her what's going on."

Matt followed Jane into a long, narrow room. To his right, a mahogany desk sat between a pair of bookcases. On his left, golden light spilled through an arched window onto a large tobacco-colored sofa. Two chairs sat on either side of the glass-and-iron coffee table in front of the couch, one a muscular wing chair covered in brown leather, the other a curvy, dainty thing upholstered in a tapestry flower print.

"Take a seat," Jane said. "I don't think we'll be long. Something tells me Zoe will be almost as excited as you to learn about what happened today."

Matt saw Jane's lips curve ever so slightly before she turned and left the room. The ghost of a smile was encouraging, Matt thought as he lowered himself into the leather wing chair. However, her eyes hadn't lost that haunted expression. It was almost enough to make him think twice about making her face the past she'd worked so hard to...well, put in her past.

After all, how often did anyone get a chance to start over, with a completely clean slate? No embarrassing mistakes to make you second-guess yourself, no old opinions to try to overcome, no emotional wounds urging you to lock your heart up, where it couldn't get tromped on again. Jane, it seemed, had taken full advantage of this freedom, had made a new life for herself, just as she'd vowed. And now here he was, stepping in to insist that she—

"Matthew?" A soft voice broke into his thoughts.

Matt got to his feet, stood and turned to greet the tall woman with the short gray hair who moved toward him.

"Ms. Zeffarelli," he said, taking her hand into his as she reached out. "It's good to see you again."

"Call me Zoe, please," she said with a smile and just the faintest hint of a French accent. "I am sorry you and I did not get to know each other better last year. But I am happy to see that you have recovered so nicely from your horrible ordeal. And now, according to our little friend here, it seems we will finally have a chance to work together."

Matt nodded, then glanced at Jane. Her eyes no longer looked haunted. Instead her eyebrows dipped beneath the uneven fringe of her bangs in an expression he recognized as pure determination. Her eyes locked with his briefly before she turned to Zoe.

"Well," Jane said, "I guess we'd better get down to it."

Zoe lifted thick black eyebrows. "You are suddenly excited now, after months of insisting you want nothing to do with your past?"

Jane shook her head tightly. "Hardly. I just want to get this over with. And I assumed you'd want to work with this memory, if you can really call it that, while it's still fresh in my mind."

"True." The woman nodded. "But I would prefer that you be at least a *leetle* bit relaxed when we attempt this thing. I suggest we all sit down and have a cup of tea, a cookie or two, and a tiny chat before we get down to business."

A half hour later, Jane sat in the center of the overstuffed sofa, with Zoe in the delicate chair the woman had proudly rescued from a thrift shop years before, and Matt looking right at home in the leather wing chair.

Although Jane had suspected that the combination of Zoe's strong tea and a sugar-laden sweet—make that *several* sugar-laden sweets—would render her even more keyed up, she was surprised to find that she was actually feeling calm. Maybe all that stomach-churning angst she'd experienced upon arriving at the house hadn't been due to dread. Perhaps she'd simply been hungry. After all, she'd actually only ingested a bite or two of that cookie in Maxwell's cellar, along with a few tiny sips of that eggnog coffee.

"The tea too strong, *ma petite?*"

Jane turned to Zoe with a smile. "It's always too strong. But loaded with milk and sugar, it is just perfect."

To prove her point and clear her palate of the remembered eggnog, Jane lifted her teacup and drained it of the bittersweet, milky contents. She then returned the cup to its delicate saucer and said, "In fact, I think I'd like a second cup."

Zoe's smile was gentle and she slowly shook her head. "I think not. I think it is now time for you to tell me what happened to you at Maxwell's. But first, get yourself comfortable. Take a deep breath."

As Jane leaned into the sofa cushions at her back, she glanced from Zoe to Matt. His expression was encouraging. Zoe wore a similar expression as she spoke again.

"Draw the breath deep into your belly, hold it, then release it very slowly."

Jane nodded. She knew the routine, had followed it each time Zoe worked with her in the hospital. All to no avail. Not one hypnosis session had brought forth even the tiniest scrap of memory.

"Jane."

Zoe's sharp tone broke into Jane's errant thoughts. She looked over to see that her friend was frowning.

"You are not listening to me, are you."

Jane shook her head. "I'm sorry. Let's try again."

This time Jane focused carefully on every word Zoe said, followed each direction carefully. After breathing deeply several more times, she closed her eyes as she was bidden and pictured herself back in Maxwell's Department Store. As instructed, she let herself recall the slightly perfumed air, the weight of her purse on her shoulder, the hard floor beneath the thin soles of her shoes. Then, when Zoe asked her to, Jane let her imagination put the image into motion, reaching toward the brightly colored strips of fabric draped from a metal rack sitting atop a glass counter.

"I'm examining a burgundy-and-tan plaid scarf," she reported.

"How does it feel?"

"Soft," Jane replied. "Cold and silky at the same time. Like the ocean."

The moment Jane uttered that last word, the image on

her closed eyelids changed. The fluorescent-lit department store was replaced by the sight of a wave curling toward her. No longer did hard flooring punish her feet. Instead, moist sand supported every arch and curve, and icy water slipped over her toes.

"I'm at the beach," she said.

"And what do you see?"

"White foam at my feet, pale green waves breaking farther out. Beyond that, sunbeams dancing on the dark blue sea. A cloudless blue sky above. The beach."

"Hold that image," Zoe urged. "Relax, then see what you can make out in your peripheral vision."

Jane did as she was asked. To her left there seemed to be nothing but foam sliding onto the damp sand. But— "I see cliffs, on my right."

"Close, or far?"

"Far, I think. I can only see the part where the cliff juts into the sea, not where it meets the shore."

"Do you know the name of this beach?"

Jane waited, feeling again the cold water over her toes. Nothing about the image changed. The same wave broke in exactly the same way it had a moment before, like some instant replay. No knowledge accompanied either the sensation of silky salt water or the image of curling, foaming green-blue water.

"No. I don't," Jane replied.

"All right," Zoe said. "Focus on your other senses."

As if by magic, Jane found she could suddenly smell salt—the briny scent that she knew, somehow, belonged to seaweed drying on the sand. "I smell the sea," she said. "And I hear birds—gulls crying and screeching and…"

Jane frowned as another sound intruded. "I hear music. It's too soft to identify the tune. It might be coming from a radio playing on the beach behind me. No. It's coming from above me, louder now. I can almost make out the melody. It's—"

Jane jerked straight up, her eyes flew open. Gone was

the sun-sparkled water, the crashing waves, the cloudless blue sky. What she saw now was Zoe, regarding her with an expression that blended excitement with concern. The woman leaned forward in her chair.

"The song I heard was 'Silver Bells,'" Jane said woodenly. "That was the tune playing on the department store sound system just before I harassed that salesgirl for rushing the Christmas season."

"And that was the tune that pulled you out of that moment from the past," Zoe said.

Every muscle in Jane's body had constricted. Her heart was racing, her breath was shallow as she stared at Zoe. Focusing on the woman's strong, angular features, she managed a stiff nod.

Zoe's black eyebrows formed a worried frown. "Jane, you understand, do you not, that it was this memory that confused you so, made you think that it was not November, but May?"

"Yes."

Jane wanted to say more, but at the moment it was all she could do keep from leaping to her feet, dashing up two flights of stairs to her attic apartment and shutting the door behind her.

"Why May?"

Matt's question brought Jane's attention back to him.

"Why did you think this particular sunny day was May?" he went on. "Why not July, or August? Or any other month, for that matter? This is, after all, California. Even up here in the northern regions, we have pockets of warmth all year long that draw people to the beach."

Jane couldn't answer. She knew only that her first thought upon hearing that music was that May was too early for Christmas tunes. She would have given that reply, if it weren't for the strange, insidious panic now clamping her jaws shut, holding her body prisoner. She could only stare into Matt's eyes, watch them darken as he moved from the chair to the floor next to her. Resting on one knee, he took her hands in his.

"You're afraid, aren't you," he asked gently.

Jane frowned. Yes, this tension gripping her was indeed fear. What was worse, she didn't understand what exactly had caused a memory of sea and sand to freeze her with terror. Now, crowds of people was a different matter. Add to that—

"Do you think," Matt was asking, "that you might have been abducted from that beach? You know you're safe now. There isn't anything to be afraid of."

Jane glanced at Matt's large hands sandwiching hers. The gentle strength in his grip returned sensation to her fingers, warming them. She looked again into his eyes—eyes that promised to bring her assailant to justice, to make sure she was safe.

Oh, how she wished it were as simple as that.

A shiver broke her paralysis. She shook her head. "That memory didn't make me afraid of whoever tried to kill me," she finally said. "It made me afraid of the person I was."

Chapter Four

Afraid of *herself?*

Matt tightened his fingers around Jane's icy hand, and wondered what in the hell was going on in that mind of hers. Of course, uncovering what was going on in her mind—or hidden in it—had been the point of this exercise in hypnotherapy.

He was surprised at the details Zoe had managed to draw out of what had to have been the briefest of flashbacks. Perhaps, with a little time, Jane might begin to recall larger pieces of her past, giving Zoe more than the image of an unnamed beach to—

The beach. If he could find that beach, take Jane to it, perhaps revisiting the sights and sounds she recalled so briefly would open her mind to further details. However, would Jane go along with his plan, such as it was? The fear plainly etched upon her pale features said not, but he knew how to take care of that.

Cocking his head to one side, Matt squinted at her in

exaggerated puzzlement. "You're afraid of the person you were?" he asked. "What, you recall being at the beach, and suddenly worry that you might have spent your past roaming the seashore, randomly destroying sandcastles built by innocent children? That you were once an evil surfer girl bent on mowing down unsuspecting swimmers with your ten-foot board?"

His ploy worked. Jane's lips twitched slightly, and some of the anxiety retreated from her eyes. "No." She sighed. "I'm frightened of what happened at Maxwell's, after I became aware of the music."

Matt squeezed her hand. "You thought it was May. Most people would be irritated by having the holiday buying season forced upon them in late spring. It's bad enough that Halloween is barely—"

Jane shook her head. "It wasn't just the timing. It was the idea of Christmas itself that irritated me. No. *Infuriated* me." She took a deep breath and squared her shoulders. "When the salesclerk suggested I might like to get a cup of coffee, eggnog flavored to be specific, I informed her that I hated the stuff."

"Then, why did you try to drink it later?"

"Because I don't *want* to hate anything about Christmas."

"What about last Christmas? Did you like it then?"

"I had a cold and couldn't really taste or smell it. Besides, disliking eggnog isn't the worst part. When I realized that it was indeed the day after Thanksgiving and that I had been Christmas shopping, I actually shuddered with revulsion."

As she finished speaking, a tiny tremor shook her slender form.

Matt smiled. "You zeem to have a very zerious zyndrome, young lady. You are afraid zat in your past you ver Ebenezer Scrooge, or ze Grinch Who Stole Christmas. Is zer a cure for ziz, Doctor Zeffarelli?"

He turned to Zoe, but she didn't look at him.

"Jane," the woman said softly. "I have spoken with many people who have issues with Christmas. Most feel overwhelmed at the idea of adding shopping, wrapping and parties to already incredibly busy lives. Some feel that commercial aspects overpower the spiritual meaning of the season. And many are plagued with childhood memories of Christmas involving deprivation or, worse, abuse. Sometimes, the effort to put on a show of good cheer is such an effort for these people that they end up resenting everything about the holiday."

Matt felt his smile grow tight.

"That makes no sense," Jane said, "I had a wonderful time last Christmas with your cousin's family in Maine, tromping through the forest to chop down the tree, then decorating it with the popcorn and cranberries I'd helped string, wrapping the gifts I'd made and walking over glittering snow on the way to midnight Mass."

Matt was relieved when Jane brought her Currier and Ives reminiscences to an end. With each new jolly image, his muscles had tensed further. The smile faded from his lips and he glanced away from Jane's features, where the glow of remembered joy warred with an expression of annoyance.

"Yes," Zoe replied. "But we were in a very small town, not a large city. She turned to Matt. "Does this description sound like any of the Christmases you remember?"

He forced his smile to widen. "Well, certainly not the snowy part. However, my McDermott cousins do have a party every year, where whoever wants to can string popcorn."

Zoe's sharp glance suggested she was going to ask him another question. Instead, she gave her head a little shake and turned to Jane.

"When you insisted on going downtown today, I warned you about the crowds. That might be what set you off, so it is best you put your worries out of your mind until you remember more of your past."

"I've got a question about that, Zoe," Matt said. "I think I might be familiar with the beach Jane described. Do you think it would help her to remember more if I took her there?"

"Well, the senses, that of smell in particular, are known to have a powerful effect upon the memory. Jane, how do you feel about a trip to the beach with Matt?"

Jane wasn't sure how she felt about anything at that moment. Other than completely exhausted. A profound sense of weariness had banished the tension in her muscles, leaving her with barely the strength to remain upright with her eyes open.

"That would be fine," she replied at last.

Matt stood. Jane managed to look up just as he smiled and said, "Good. I need to speak with Jack on a few matters in the morning, but I can be here at eleven."

On the one hand, Jane told herself as she pulled the door to her studio apartment behind her, it had been wonderful seeing Matt Sullivan again. Aside from the fact that he was every bit as handsome as she remembered, she'd yet to meet anyone with the same knack for making her laugh, even when she didn't particularly want to. But still, her insides were in knots over the idea of going anywhere with him.

Jane took a deep breath as she started down the flower-print runner that carpeted the stairway.

On the other hand, she wasn't sure she wanted anyone to read her all that well. When Manny's death and Matt's injuries had pulled those two men out of her life, she had looked for someone to take their place—someone she could trust with her thoughts, hopes, fears. The person she had chosen had used those things against her, so now the idea of trusting anyone made her stomach twist and brought a sour lump to her throat.

And, after the way she'd behaved in Maxwell's, she wasn't even sure she could trust herself.

When Jane reached the foyer, she moved to the small

window to the left of the front door and stared at the street below. She wouldn't want to even know the tense, dismissive person she had become for those few moments the day before, let alone *be* like that. How would Matt Sullivan feel about her if today's trip to the beach happened to bring out that "dark side" of her personality?

"Ah, there you are—"

Jane turned as Zoe stepped out of her office.

"You look like someone who was about to be led into the lion's den, or some other horrible fate, instead of what is supposed to be, as they say, a day at the beach."

Jane drew a deep breath and released it in a quick *whoosh.* "I know. I am looking forward to spending some time at the ocean again. It's just that I have some figures to finish, special orders I got when I stopped in at The Gift Box yesterday, you know, and I want to get to work on that new line of elves I started."

"*And* you are frightened of what you might remember, of what you might learn about yourself."

Jane hesitated, then nodded.

Zoe placed a hand on Jane's shoulder. "My girl, I see patients every day who are afraid of the same thing. People with perfectly good memories, you understand, who have nevertheless built up layer upon layer of fear and denial, until they no longer know where they begin or end—in other words, who they are. They come to therapists like me when they discover that ignoring their pain has become more frightening than facing it."

"How do they do that?"

"One step at a time. I tell them what I will tell you now. Life tests you only when you have enough strength to rise to the challenge."

The sound of a car engine drew Jane's attention to the window. In the driveway below, she saw Matt get out of his black Jeep. Her heart began to pound as he started up the stairs. She turned to Zoe.

"How do you know if you have that strength?"

The corners of the woman's eyes crinkled. "When life tests you, of course."

Jane surprised herself by laughing. "Dabbling in Zen, are you?"

"Whatever works," Zoe replied with a shrug.

At the solid knock on the door, Jane pivoted and pulled it open, then froze—just as she had when she'd seen Matt yesterday, framed in the doorway leading to Maxwell's security office.

He was, as the saying went, larger than life. Not just because his height topped six feet by several inches, that his shoulders were broad, or that his nearly black hair intensified the sea-green of his eyes. Those physical attributes were formidable, certainly, but the element that sent her heart racing had more to do with the quiet power in his stance, the undeniable cocky tilt to his mouth, and the sudden light of appreciation that swept her form, washing her body with heat.

"Looks like you've decided to rise to the challenge," he said.

"Challenge?"

Jane cringed inwardly at the breathless way the word came out, but Matt's simple nod suggested he hadn't noticed.

"You appear to be dressed for a day outside. I assume that means you've decided to accompany me and see if we can't track down the source of that memory of yours, and perhaps scare up some more."

Although Jane felt a shiver coming on, she found herself giving him a wry smile. "I guess so. *Scare* being the operative word."

Matt stepped forward and took her hand in one swift motion. As Jane looked into his eyes, she was aware of the strength of his grip, the warmth of his skin on hers and the reassuring determination in his gaze.

"No matter what happens today," he said quietly. "I have no doubt that you'll rise to the occasion."

"Have you and Zoe been comparing notes on how to handle me?"

When Matt looked quizzical, Jane explained. "She was just bolstering my courage with very similar words. So—" she drew a quick breath "—yes, I'm ready to see if we can find the gate leading to memory lane."

"All right. Get your jacket and we'll be off."

"A jacket? It's beautiful out."

"Sun or no sun, the wind on the coast can be quite chilly. You need a jacket."

With a nod, Jane turned. Matt watched her cross the foyer and start up the stairs, then noticed the way her sneaker-clad feet bounced off each step as she lightly ran up. It seemed like yesterday that he and Manny had escorted Jane, enveloped in a navy sweat suit that only served to emphasize her extreme thinness, to the hospital's physical therapy department.

Lying in bed for a month, comatose, had given the pelvic fracture she'd suffered in the accident time to heal, but the inactivity had left her as weak as a baby—she was going to have to learn to walk all over again. He and Manny had watched like proud parents as she gripped waist-high parallel bars, then wobbled like a newborn colt as she slowly made her way down the length of the track.

There was nothing spindly or wobbly about Jane now, Matt noticed as she neared the landing. The cut of her faded jeans hugged slender but shapely legs, and her hips had rounded into decidedly womanly curves.

"She has grown much in the past year."

Zoe's words made Matt realize where his thoughts had been leading. He turned to the older woman, aware his face had grown uncomfortably warm.

"It seems she has done exactly what she said she would," he said. "Created a life for herself, on her terms."

"Yes, she has. She has turned her lack of memory from a handicap to a strength."

"How so?"

"With no preconceived concept of what she could or could not do, she approaches each challenge with an open mind, along with the assumption that she can succeed."

Matt mulled this over. "After her accident, one of Jane's doctors told a reporter that the bruising her brain took may have resulted in permanent memory loss. Do you agree with that assessment?"

Zoe shook her head. "No."

"Well, Jane mentioned that you haven't been pushing her to regain her memory. Do you think it's wrong for me to encourage Jane to remember her past?"

"Not at all. Jane was disheartened when the hypnosis sessions in the hospital were unsuccessful. It would have been cruelty on my part to force her repeatedly to search her memory, only to encounter emptiness. But yesterday's incident indicates that her mind, and perhaps her spirit as well, has recovered to the point that she can access and, more importantly, accept whatever she remembers."

Hearing the sound of feet on the stairs above, Matt asked quickly, "Do you have any suggestions about how to handle this? Do I get her to relax, like you did yesterday? Or should I try to push her into remembering?"

Zoe seemed to consider his question for several seconds before she shrugged her shoulders and replied, "Try one first. If that doesn't work, try the other."

"All right, now," Matt said. "I want you to close your eyes and keep them that way until I tell you differently."

It had taken Matt and Jane over an hour to cross the Golden Gate Bridge and drive up Highway One. After turning on a road leading west, Matt had pulled onto the side of the road, then turned to face Jane before issuing his order.

"Close my eyes?" she repeated.

"Yes. And keep them shut."

"I thought we came here so I could identify the beach I

saw in my memory. I can hardly do that with my eyes closed.''

"No, the prime objective here is to provoke further memories. Although your description was pretty sketchy, I'm fairly certain I have the right place. Remember, I grew up surfing these beaches.''

"So, you think it will be more effective to lead me to the area, then spring it on me all at once.''

"Exactly. Ready? Close your eyes.''

Once Jane had obeyed his order, Matt put the Jeep in drive. Several minutes later, he turned onto the road that would lead them to Limantour Beach. It took him beneath a canopy of cypress trees, then wound down through a sea of golden grass and a crescent of sand that arched to the right, ending at the foot of a sheer cliff that jutted out to the sea.

"Tell me,'' he said, "just how do you create these magical dolls of yours.''

"Well, I sculpt the faces, hands and feet from a polymer clay, which hardens in the oven. The bodies are made of wire and stuffing, held together with fabric bodies. But they aren't meant to be played with, like dolls. They're collectibles.''

Matt glanced at her. "People collect elves?''

"People collect all sorts of things, it seems. Zoe's cousin Clara in Maine makes very realistic little men, women and children. She creates three or four new characters each year, and collectors from all over the country buy her numbered pieces.''

"Nice of her to teach you to do this.''

"Well, actually, she's published a book on her technique. I used it as a jumping-off point to create my own little world, and I assume others do that, too.''

Matt downshifted as he neared the dirt parking lot. "I had no idea there was such a market for…''

"Fantasy figures?'' Jane finished for him. "I didn't, either, but Clara took a few of my pieces to one of the stores that carry her things, and mine sold out right away. So, I made more when I got back to San Francisco, got a few specialty shops to carry them, then participated in a couple of craft fairs this summer, and the thing just mushroomed. Since July I've been really busy. I decided to adapt my faces to create special Santas and his little helpers in place of woodland elves and make angels instead of fairies. That's one of the reasons I was downtown yesterday. I delivered some of these to a place called The Gift Box, and they asked me to make even more.''

''It seems you've become quite the businesswoman,'' Matt said as he pulled into a parking space overlooking the beach, then added teasingly, ''I hope you have someone you trust keeping your books.''

He switched off the engine and turned to Jane.

''I suppose,'' she said in a mock huff, ''that crack was a veiled reference to my mathematical abilities.''

''No,'' Matt said as he opened his door. ''It's a direct reference to your decided *lack* of said abilities.''

Before Jane could respond to this allusion to what he and Manny had termed her ''numerical dyslexia,'' Matt slid from his seat and said, ''Stay where you are,'' before snapping his door shut and stepping around to her side of the car.

''I'll have you know,'' she said the moment he opened her door, ''that I have managed to master math. The important stuff, at any rate. I can add, subtract, divide, multiply and figure fractions with the best. The rest is superfluous. The idea of adding *a*'s and *b*'s and coming up with *x*'s is an exercise in futility, if you ask me.''

Matt hooked his hand over the top of the door's frame, noticing the way Jane's closed eyes wrinkled as she blindly reached for the buckle of her seat belt. That intense concentration of hers was a wonder to behold. It was the secret, he suspected, behind her swift recovery from the sort of injuries that had kept muscular linebackers out of commission far longer than they had this delicately boned girl.

Woman, he corrected himself when, freed of her seat belt, Jane pivoted toward him, slid out of her seat, then stumbled into his arms.

For the second time in two days Matt found himself holding her close to him. For one moment, he wondered if he could somehow absorb the joy that seemed to emanate from her, even when she was frightened. He had once responded to life that way, too, thrilled by the surge of adrenaline that came with walking the tightrope between safety and danger. He hadn't experienced that since leaving the hospital.

Until yesterday—when he'd walked into Maxwell's security office and gone to Jane's defense.

And now, the idea that Jane had begun to remember, that there was a chance he might solve a crime that had its origins back in the days before Manny died, before he had given up the career he loved, seemed to promise that he could reawaken the passion he'd brought to his old job.

Slowly, as Matt continued to hold Jane, he became aware of the awakening of a different sort of passion, the kind that heated his body, tempted him to tighten his arms around the woman he was holding, to lower his mouth to kiss lips that were still softly parted with surprise.

He just as quickly became aware of how inappropriate it was to feel this way toward the subject of an investigation.

After checking to see that Jane had gained her footing, he released her and stepped back in one quick motion. Instantly, her eyes flew open, surprised and tinged with hurt.

A second later she shut her eyes and muttered, "Sorry," in a voice more husky than usual.

Damn. Matt's jaw tightened. Keeping his distance from Jane Ashbury was going to be a challenge, and today it might even prove to be a conflict of interest.

Yesterday he had watched Zoe carefully. Today he'd planned to copy the therapist's methods, get Jane to relax in the hope that this would release those trapped memories of hers. Something told him that brusquely stepping away from her wasn't the best way to go about this.

Or keep himself sane.

Chapter Five

"I didn't see anything," Jane said. Not sure her tone was light enough, she smiled wryly and said, "Well, other than you."

A moment of silence followed Jane's words. Then she heard Matt chuckle before he replied, "Good. But if you had seen the beach, it would have been my fault for not thinking to guide you out of the seat. I'll do better now." His hands tightened on her shoulders as he went on. "I need you to step to the left—I'm sorry, that would be your right—so I can close the door."

Jane responded to his directions, sidestepping, then standing still when he requested. She heard the slam of the door, then the click of the key in the lock, all the while silently cursing herself for feeling so damn vulnerable.

She had to admit, it had felt wonderful, standing within Matt's strong arms for those few moments, feeling his warmth envelop her, his strength support her. Sometimes she got so blasted tired of taking care of herself, pushing to become a woman of independent means who needed to rely on no one.

Of course, when he'd pushed her away it had become clear that she couldn't afford to grow accustomed to that sort of feeling.

"Here—" Matt's deep voice broke into her thoughts. "Take my hand."

Matt's fingers had barely brushed hers when she pulled her arm away and said, "I can manage myself."

"No, you can't." Again he chuckled. "You remind me of my two-year-old cousin who's always insisting, 'Me do it.' The path down the beach is uneven. If you don't want to trip and fall, you'll let me hold your hand and guide you."

Jane hesitated. When she nodded, Matt's large hand closed over hers, gave it a tug, and she began to walk. It took a few moments to focus on the sound of his feet on the sand so she could walk beside him instead of being towed down the path. With each step she grew even more aware of the strength and warmth radiating from the man at her side.

"Do we have far to walk?" she wondered out loud.

"Not really," he replied. "You all right? Warm enough?"

His question brought Jane's attention to the brisk breeze ruffling her hair and cooling her cheeks. "Yes, thanks to your suggestion."

She touched the lapel of her dark blue fleece jacket to indicate her meaning. Matt didn't reply, and for several minutes the only sound was the crunch of the sand beneath their feet and the occasional crash of a wave some distance in front of her. The silence seemed to beg to be filled, and Jane asked the first question that came to mind.

"Why did Detective Wilcox call you the Lone Ranger yesterday?"

More silence. Then Matt replied, "It was my nickname

on the force. Until I was partnered with Manny, I preferred to work on my own whenever possible."

"Why?"

"Just a quirk of my nature, I guess."

Jane took a few steps before she said softly, "You miss him a lot, don't you."

For several seconds she heard only the sibilant whisper of waves breaking gently on the shore.

"Yeah, I do," he said quietly, then his voice drew stronger. "Fortunately, my cousin Jack understands how I work. And I understand him. He's always been drawn to the mystery aspect of law enforcement—tracking down the clues, hence his nickname—Sherlock Holmes—while I like the chase. We make a good team."

"Do you charge a lot?"

"We try to keep our fees reasonable."

"How much, exactly? Say, to find a murderer?"

Matt was quiet for a moment. "If you're thinking of paying me, forget it. I want to find out who tried to kill you for myself as much as for you. Now—" he stopped walking "—we're here. I want you to turn, like so. Take a deep breath, relax and take a look when you're ready."

Jane did as Matt ordered. When she opened her eyes, she was staring at a pale green sea beneath a watery blue sky.

"What do you think?" Matt asked. "Is this the place?"

Jane studied the seascape before her. "Well, the cliff over on the right does match the image I remember. But the colors of the sky and water are more washed out. And the waves were bigger, more aggressive than these."

"Yeah, well, the waves here tend to be pretty anemic, from a surfer's point of view," Matt said slowly. "The beach faces southwest, so they come in at an angle, instead of bowling right into the shore. But try just staring at the water for a while, relax and see if anything comes."

Jane gave him what she hoped was a cheerful smile. *Yeah, right,* she thought. Watching the curling surf was one thing. Relaxing? Now, that was another matter altogether.

How was she supposed to relax when she knew the man standing next to her was waiting anxiously for something to happen—something, moreover, that she wasn't sure she even wanted to come about.

However, Matt deserved her help in his quest for justice. Drawing a salt-laden breath, she released it, then repeated the action as she gazed straight ahead. She managed to breathe some softness into muscles tingling with awareness of Matt—but no memories came.

Finally she shook her head and turned to Matt. She caught his expression of disappointment before he had a chance to smile and shrug. Jane wasn't fooled. She knew she'd let him down. This man, who had cheered all her efforts to walk again, to recover knowledge she'd forgotten; who had held her as she sobbed when that last disappointment had made her vow to stop searching for her past, stop trying to figure out who people wanted her to be.

The idea that she had failed Matt made Jane want to cry, something she hadn't done since that day nearly sixteen months ago—something she wasn't going to do now. As she had so many times since, Jane hardened the ache in her heart to anger.

"I'm sorry," she said as she stepped away from him. "This isn't working. I really don't want to remember my past. For all I know, I was a thief, or a drug dealer, or something worse. After all, what does it say about the person I was that someone hated me enough to attempt to kill me?"

Matt was no longer smiling. In fact, as Jane glared up at him, his features twisted into an angry scowl. His hand reached out to close over hers with almost painful strength as he pulled her to him and bent his head toward hers.

"It doesn't say a damn thing about you," Matt said, his voice low, tight. "The fact that someone is driven to kill, only tells me about the perpetrator, not the victim. No matter what the crime, the victim is not at fault. And hey, we know you've never been arrested—or fingerprinted."

Jane's heart raced as his dark green eyes looked unwaveringly into hers. She watched as the deep vertical line between his eyebrows relaxed and his intent gaze softened to one of speculation.

"However," he said, "I'm not sure if I've ever met an injured party less deserving of the term *victim* than you. You, my friend, are the epitome of the title Survivor."

Matt's words surprised sudden tears to her eyes, tears that she was not about to shed. She blinked them away, to find that Matt was now grinning.

"So," he said, "your worries about what kind of person you were before you were injured? Forget 'em. It doesn't matter who you were. What matters is who you are now, the person you have made yourself into."

Jane thought her heart was going to pound itself right out of her chest. She could hardly believe this was happening. She'd dreamed so many times of a moment like this one. Even after Kyle Rogers had taught her, so very painfully, that her heart was not to be trusted, she'd held on to the belief that the one man in whose hands she *could* place the love she felt was Matt Sullivan.

She'd read all about her condition, knew that people who survived brain trauma often experienced bouts of hero worship, until their emotional states stabilized and matured. She believed that this explained how she'd fallen under Kyle's spell, but she knew her feelings for Matt were different.

And now he stood looking down at her, his gaze holding hers with all the tenderness she could wish for.

"You're wondering," Matt said, "if it's true that who you were isn't important, then why am I pushing you to recall your past."

Well, not really, Jane thought, but she wasn't about to reveal her true thoughts, so she let him continue.

"It's because the person you were is the key to the entire investigation."

Jane's heartbeat slowed. "Investigation?"

Matt raised his eyebrows. "The investigation into who

tried to kill you. Once I learn who you were, I'll be able to find out who knew you. Then, with any luck, I can determine which of these people had a motive to put an end to your life."

Turning, Jane stared out over the sea. *Great.* She had the starring role in Matt Sullivan's detective novel. Just what she wanted.

"You don't have to force your memory." Obviously misunderstanding her intent, Matt placed his hands on Jane's shoulders and swiveled her toward him. "It was a crazy idea to bring you down here and think that making you stare at the ocean would result in some sort of epiphany. Besides, I'm getting hungry. Are you ready to go?"

Jane shrugged. "Sure."

Matt took her hand, then turned and started back up the beach. Far ahead Jane could see a path leading to the parking lot above and to their left. She was surprised to realize how far she had come earlier with her eyes closed, conversing with Matt. The walk back now, in silence, seemed much longer. The wind was blowing harder, too, bringing bone-chilling moisture from the ocean. And beneath her feet, the uneven sand seemed to fight her desire to hurry away from this place of disappointment.

About thirty yards from the path, Matt stopped, bent forward and rubbed his right knee, then straightened and turned to her. "How about we take a little break before we head up to the car?"

It was on the tip of Jane's tongue to say she wasn't tired, when she connected his action to the injury he'd suffered. Uncertain just how sensitive he might be about the subject, she simply replied, "Sure," then followed him to the dune on their left. When he sat down and leaned against the hill, she followed suit.

The wind seemed less biting at this level. Between the warmth of the sand against her back and the rays of the weak winter sun, Jane felt almost toasty within her soft fleece jacket. Gazing forward, she noticed that the surf had grown rougher. Each wave created a large head of foam as it rolled and crashed. The hypnotic motion and rhythmic whisper slowly teased the tension from her muscles, calmed her mind and coaxed her to shut her eyes.

Matt glanced over, saw that Jane had closed her eyes, and released a quiet sigh. He rarely used his knee as an excuse, even if it truly was hurting. The tiny ache now pulsing in that joint made the discomfort he'd implied a few moments earlier a half truth. But even if it had been an out-and-out lie, it would have been a worthwhile one, if it gave Jane the opportunity to stare at the sea without feeling she was expected to perform.

It appeared his ploy had worked.

Matt recalled now the question she'd posed earlier. Just how would he feel if she regained her memory, only to learn something horrible about her past? It wasn't entirely outside the realm of possibility that the person she had been before the accident had been involved in some sort of illegal activity. Or, at least, involved *with* someone who worked on the other side of the law, someone who knew just how to set up a murder in a way that would leave no clue to their identity.

On the other hand, Jane might have been some rich heiress who stood between a fortune and some greedy miscreant. Either way, someone tried to kill her. And, if the strength she'd shown in the past year was any indication, he had no doubt that Jane would find a way to deal with whatever she learned about her former self.

So, yes, he was being relentless. And since his attempts to get her to relax enough had failed to produce any new memories, he was just going to have to try his other option—prodding.

"Jane," he said softly.

She opened her eyes with a start, blinked once or twice, then turned to him and said, "I think I remembered something."

Matt didn't move a muscle. He held her gaze and forced

himself to take several shallow breaths. "You want to tell me about it?"

Jane nodded, then frowned as if trying to bring some image to mind. "I didn't recall *seeing* anything new," she said slowly. "I dozed off, then I dreamed of the waves and the cliff off to the right. But this time I became aware of how I felt."

She paused.

Every muscle in Matt's body urged him to scream, *You felt what?* But he maintained silence.

"First there was anger—no, it was more like fury. Then I felt shame, or maybe embarrassment. That disappeared, almost like a door had been shut on it, and suddenly I was filled with this sense of determination, and a feeling of...of freedom." She sounded surprised as she said this last word.

Matt held his breath, waiting for her to speak again. When she did, it was with a wry twist of her lips.

"Not exactly hard evidence, is it."

"Nope. But it is another piece of the puzzle. And who knows? It might turn out to be important. However, for the moment, my leg is rested and now I'm truly famished." He pushed himself off the dune, stood and extended his hand to Jane. "Let's go find some food."

Once they were back in the car, Matt was so busy formulating a plan to prod Jane's memory further, he found it difficult to keep his attention on the road. It was after two o'clock by the time he found a parking space in Sausalito, almost three before he and Jane were sitting on a bench at the edge of the bay, unwrapping freshly made sandwiches from the deli on the opposite side of the street.

When his stomach was full and no longer emitting what had been an embarrassing set of growls, Matt sipped coffee from a plastic-domed paper cup and watched Jane follow the progress of the ferryboat gliding in the direction of Angel Island.

This respite suited his plans perfectly. Normally he'd be checking his watch, making sure to start for the city before the bridge became congested with cars full of folks on their way in to San Francisco for an evening of dining and entertainment. Today, however, there was no need to hurry, for the scheme he had in mind required two things—one, that Jane be unaware that there was a plan, and two, darkness.

So, when Jane turned to him, after tossing bits of bread to the circling seagulls, he suggested they stroll along the town's main street and check out the shops and art galleries. Along the way, Jane found a shop that sold various handcrafted items, and spoke to the manager about the possibility of placing some of her figures.

An hour and a half later, as they made their way slowly south over the crowded Golden Gate Bridge, Matt found himself wondering if the artistic abilities that had enabled Jane to find such success might be a clue to her past. He filed those musings away as they left the tollbooth. It was almost five-thirty. Dusk had fallen and the streetlights were coming on. The timing was right.

He glanced toward Jane. "Have you had a chance to see downtown San Francisco at night, all lit up for Christmas?"

"No. Yesterday, I had planned to stick around till dark to do just that, but..."

"I remember," he said. "Would you like to go down now? See the lights, look at the decorations in the windows?"

Jane gazed at him for several seconds. He held his breath, wondering if she would ruin his plan by saying she was too tired.

A moment later, when she said, "Sure. It sounds like fun," Matt relaxed. Step one was accomplished. The rest should be easy.

Chapter Six

The evening wasn't going at all as Matt had planned.

If this had been a date, things would be proceeding swimmingly. The night was black and clear, perfect to show off San Francisco in her holiday finery. And Jane was obviously having a good time, exclaiming with childlike enthusiasm at the wreaths that decorated every utility pole, was delighted with the strolling bands of carolers garbed in Victorian costumes, and positively enchanted with the blaze of green, red and white lights that twinkled, blinked and glittered everywhere.

However, as the strains of "O, Christmas Tree" battled with the jangle of "Jingle Bell Rock," Matt was beginning to get a headache.

He had counted on crowds. Knowing that large groups of people made Jane extremely uncomfortable, he'd figured that congested sidewalks, combined with the lights and the noise, would conspire to bring her to the panic state she'd been swept into yesterday at Maxwell's Department Store, and perhaps prompt another memory. But, although there were quite a few people milling about, checking out the decorated windows or hurrying along burdened with shopping bags, it wasn't nearly the mass of humanity he'd envisioned.

Matt released a frustrated sigh. Most likely the majority of the Thanksgiving weekend shopping fiends had already made off with their sale booty. The more sensible shoppers and the perennial procrastinators, like himself, probably figured that the big day was still weeks away, and were home enjoying turkey sandwiches.

He heard Jane echo his sigh. She stood next to him on the brick pathway in the center of the newly renovated Union Square, gazing at the blaze of light and color glimmering against the backdrop of the inky sky. Then her eyes met his and she smiled.

"I'm so glad you brought me down here. I was afraid I might get all Grinchy like I did yesterday. All the anger that boiled up must just have been a claustrophobic reaction of some sort, because I love all this. Even without snow, everything about Christmas is wonderful."

Matt gave her weary smile. "Even eggnog?"

Her lips took on a sour twist and she gave a shudder. "Hey, maybe I'm allergic. But everything else is truly magical."

Magical. Matt perked up. The work reminded him of something he hadn't shown Jane yet, something that usually attracted the crowds he'd been hoping for.

"Well," he said, "I've saved the best for last."

Her dark eyes lit up like a five-year-old. "What?"

"Come on," he said, taking her hand. "I'll show you."

As they made their way to the end of the square, then waited for the light to turn green, Matt became aware of just how many times that day he had held Jane's hand in his. It felt surprisingly natural—not to mention pleasant and a little more than that....

The light turned green, and he led Jane across the street,

then down one block and around the corner. And there, twenty feet away, some thirty people stood four- and five-feet deep in front of a huge plate-glass window.

"Isn't that Bertrand's Department Store?" Jane asked.

Matt nodded.

"What's going on?"

"The store's annual automated Christmas window. Bringing the kiddies to see it is the longest-running Christmas tradition in the city. Actually, of course, it draws people of all ages, even if they've seen it every year of their lives."

Jane stared at the throng. Light flooded out of the window to cast a glow on the shoppers' enthralled expressions. Her insides quivered at the size of the crowd, but something urged her to step forward and take her place in the back. Matt stood on her right, holding her hand, stepping forward each time a space opened up. In front of her stood a six-foot tall man with a small child perched on his shoulders. At frequent intervals the little fellow breathed an "ooh" or an "ahh," piquing Jane's curiosity and building her anticipation.

"Phillip. Ashley. Behave yourselves," a woman admonished directly behind Jane. "You have to wait your turn."

A shiver raced down Jane's spine as she realized how hemmed in she was, with Matt on her right, the man with the child on his shoulders in front of her, and a tall woman on her left. The not-so-gentle bumps against her fanny warned that Phillip and Ashley were directly behind her. Obviously, they were small, but still she felt as if she were stuck in some narrow, airless hole.

A moment later, Jane realized that the man in front of her had started to move to one side. She heard him mutter "excuse me," as he shuffled to his left. She immediately stepped into the space he'd vacated in front of the glass. There wasn't yet room for Matt to stand next to her, but he still held her hand, pulling her arm back at an awkward angle. She slipped her fingers from his as she began to study the glass-enclosed display area.

The first thing she noticed was the rug on the floor. Old-fashioned in a pattern of stylized flowers and vines of gold, green and red on a black background, it looked like something one might see in a Victorian parlor. Except…the images all seemed much larger than on any rug she'd ever seen.

Out of the corner of her left eye she caught some motion. She glanced over to see a gray mouse sitting just outside a hole in the pale green wall. Or perhaps, judging by the fact that the furry creature was the size of a small cat, it was a rat. It now sat motionless, its large liquid brown eyes gazing at something above. Jane had just decided this animal must not have been the source of the movement that had caught her attention, when suddenly its slender whiskers quivered, its tail twitched and its gaze lowered.

It appeared to be staring at something on the opposite side of the enclosure. Jane looked to the right. At the far end of the display, a huge leather chair stood at least six feet tall. The area beneath the seat was high enough for a small child to sit straight up, and within those shadows crouched a marmalade tabby cat the size of a Rottweiler. Its green eyes narrowed as it glared across the room, its tail snaked back and fourth as it obviously considered the mouse.

The cat edged forward as if preparing to pounce, only to blink and look up toward the back of the room. Jane did likewise. A breathless ''ahh'' escaped her throat as the meaning of the oversize animals and furniture became clear.

She was looking at a small child's view of Christmas morning. A mountain of toys, balls, dolls and stuffed animals, all at least three times larger than normal, nestled beneath the enormous evergreen branches that filled the back wall and upper portion of the display, rising a full three stories. Ornaments the size of beach balls hung from the lower limbs. As Jane watched, a slender oval of gold glass began to turn slowly, then to glow, finally becoming transparent to reveal a gossamer-winged fairy dancing within.

As more of the toys moved, Jane felt something brush her right shoulder. Glancing over, she saw Matt standing at her side, gave him a quick smile, then turned her attention to the magical sight beyond the glass.

She hardly knew where to look next. From the corner on her left, a black locomotive emerged from the tunnel formed by a large pile of wrapped packages. Murmurs of delight came from the crowd as a little train chugged around the perimeter of the assembled toys and colorful presents.

For some reason Jane felt compelled to look upward, into the dark green branches above. There, her attention was caught and held by a star-shaped ornament hanging from the uppermost branch. A combination of crystal and silver formed the star's eight arms, catching and reflecting the light as it rotated slowly. Jane gasped and started to point it out to Matt, but as she lifted her hand, she had the strangest feeling she'd preformed this action before.

That thought had barely crossed her mind, when the scene before her eyes changed. As if in a dream, the ornament seemed to dangle just above her. Two slender arms clad in red velvet sleeves rose in front of her, as if they were her own. A small hand extended from lace cuffs, reaching for the crystal star. The crystal star was held by perfectly manicured but gnarled fingers. Above and behind the aged hands, she saw a woman with deeply wrinkled features framed by a mound of snowy white hair. The woman smiled widely and more wrinkles appeared, especially at the outer corners of her crinkling blue eyes, and suddenly the uplifted arms were reaching for the woman, not the glittering star. A glorious warmth filled Jane's heart as the old woman—

Disappeared, along with the star, as Jane fell forward and struck her cheek against the cold plate-glass window.

She felt the pressure on her lower back only seconds

before it was removed. She heard "*Phillip!* I told you to wait your turn," as she placed her hands against the glass and tried to straighten. Behind her, the woman hissed, "Stop that, Phillip. Don't you dare kick me. I'm going to have to—"

Jane lost interest in whatever punishment was in store for the little brat. She only knew that he *had* started kicking. One of his shoes had connected with the back of her left knee. Now, as she fell, she pressed her palms against the window. They squealed across the cold surface.

Time seemed to slow. Jane found herself wondering why no one was standing on her left, thinking it would be preferable to collide with the relative softness of a stranger's shoulder than the granite sidewalk. Then her heart began to race as she thought about the people surrounding her, the shoes that might trample her, the—

Something—some*one*—grabbed her right arm. Fingers bit into her flesh, tugging her upright. She'd barely regained her footing, when a strong arm encircled her waist and another slipped beneath her knees. A second later she was lifted into the air, cradled against someone's broad chest.

Jane knew the "someone" was Matt even before she looked into his worried face. She saw his lips move, heard him mutter "excuse me," as she was carried through the smothering crowd. Once free, he strode on, stopping at the corner of the building beneath a streetlight. His eyes met hers, narrowed with anger.

"Are you all right?"

Jane nodded. "Yes. Thanks to you."

"Blasted kid." Matt lifted his head to glare over her head, in the direction of the crowd. "I should go back and—"

"No," Jane broke in. His eyes met hers. "It wasn't his fault, not entirely. It's late. He's probably tired, and got impatient waiting while I stood there…"

As her words trailed off, Jane again envisioned the star ornament and the wrinkled, kindly face of the old woman.

It faded just as swiftly. A bittersweet ache filled her chest, and Matt's features began to blur. By the time she realized that warm tears had filled her eyes, one of them had spilled onto her right cheek, then another onto her left. She blinked and two more followed.

"You *are* hurt. Is it your leg, or did I pull your shoulder when I grabbed—"

Jane shook her head. She drew a deep breath and forced words past the odd lump in her throat. "I'm not hurt."

Matt paused, then said, "I'm going to put you down."

Only half of Jane's mind registered Matt's words. The other half was reaching for that image of the old woman, wondering who she was and why the thought of her should have made Jane cry. Then she became aware of Matt again, felt the arm around her waist tighten as the one beneath her knees slipped away. She was lowered slowly until her feet reached the ground, was held in his arms, breathing in his musky scent several seconds, before Matt released his hold on her waist. She slowly raised her head. He looked into her eyes for a long time, his full of concern and some other emotion she couldn't quite decipher.

"Everything okay?" he asked at last.

Other than the fact that you're no longer holding me, came her silent reply.

Jane forced away the sudden feeling of abandonment and made herself smile. "I'm fine. Really."

Matt continued to look into her eyes. She felt something warm brush gently across her cheek. Matt's thumb, she realized as his hand reached across to wipe the tears from the other side of her face.

"Then, why were you crying?"

Matt's features were tight, his eyes warm and caring. Jane felt a rush of emotion—happiness, hope, longing. A nervous giggle escaped her chest. Then she shook her head and replied, "I had another memory."

Matt raised his eyebrows. Jane hurried on. "It wasn't

much. Just the image of an old woman handing me an ornament.''

"But it made you cry."

Jane frowned. She stared at the front of his sweater for a moment, then looked back up at him. "Yes, I guess it did. I don't understand why, though. I never cry."

"Really?"

Jane made a face. "Only when I'm with you."

The right side of Matt's mouth lifted. The dimple appeared in his cheek, but Jane couldn't tell if his smile actually reached his eyes.

"Maybe that's because you know you can trust me," he said.

The words *trust me* sent a quick shiver through Jane. Then she remembered that it was Matt Sullivan saying those words, not the man who had used her trust to trick her into giving her heart unwisely. It was Matt Sullivan whose large hand rested on her waist, ready to give support if she needed it. Matt Sullivan who wanted so much to see that someone paid for all the pain she'd suffered.

She gave him a small smile and said, "Probably."

"Then, you'll believe me when I tell you that we should go back to Zoe's and see if she can help you discover more about that memory?"

She nodded. "Sure. Considering it was obviously a happy memory, I'd love to know more."

"That's it?" Jane asked an hour later. "I thought for sure I'd remember more under hypnosis."

Zoe shifted in her tapestry-covered seat and shrugged. "You did manage to give us a few details. It appears that the moment you shared with the old woman actually did occur within the display window at Bertrand's."

"True, but I thought perhaps hypnosis could help me expand that memory—tell me who the woman was, or the significance of the star."

"Well," Zoe said, "I can tell you that a large crystal-

and-silver star decorates each side of the columns inside Bertrand's this time of the year, and that image is imprinted upon the store's dark blue holiday shopping bag. You wouldn't have any way of knowing that, since we weren't here last Christmas and your first visit downtown this year was two days ago.''

Jane glanced at Matt, who appeared to be studying the gold-and-brown rug beneath the coffee table's glass top, and didn't respond.

"Jane, dear," Zoe said quietly, "you must be patient. It is obvious that your subconscious has finally started to release the memories it has been hoarding. More will certainly follow."

"The question seems to be," Jane said, "just how many memories will be released, and when?"

"I wish I knew."

Jane sighed. She turned to the man who seemed so intent on getting answers to these questions. "Matt?" When he looked up with a jerk, she said, "I'm sorry."

He looked confused. "Sorry?"

"Yes. For not being much help. No help at all, now that I think about it. We have no more idea who I might have been now than we did when I came out of that coma." She drew a deep breath. "I'm sure you and your cousin have more important matters to investigate—cases that will help you pay your bills. You should probably forget about me."

Matt got to his feet and smiled down at her. "I don't think that's likely to happen. I have some things to look into, though. I'll call you as soon as I have anything to report."

As Jane watched Matt leave the room, she wondered just when she had begun to hope that his prodding questions might actually uncover the secrets of her past.

Chapter Seven

When Jane hadn't heard from Matt by Tuesday morning, she couldn't decide if she was disappointed or relieved.

She'd used her time well, finishing all the figures she'd started Saturday morning and sculpting even more faces. She'd also visited her favorite thrift stores to purchase clothes in red, greens and gold velvets, to be recycled into costumes for her Santas and Christmas elves. But, as she'd stitched bodies and limbs, stuffed them, then fitted them onto the wire frames that gave them shape, she'd grown aware of a sense of loneliness that she'd never experienced before.

She didn't understand how, after going without seeing Matt for over a year, she could suddenly miss the aura of strength that he wrapped her in when she was frightened, the way he made her laugh when she was taking things too seriously, the warmth in his eyes when he looked at her.

She had assumed that after escaping the media storm that had swirled around Jane Doe Number Thirteen, along with the prodding of well-meaning professionals, she would be happy going about her anonymous life, alone. And yet, after two days of being the center of Matt's attention, she found she missed that terribly.

Jane scrutinized the dregs of her coffee as she sat in Zoe's yellow-and-blue kitchen. She was going to have to put an end to this infatuation. It wasn't healthy, and it was pointless—

"I see you have some appointments today."

Jane jumped slightly at the sound of Zoe's voice. Meeting the woman's gaze, Jane told herself there was no way Zoe could have read her silly thoughts. Fighting off a blush, she managed a light smile.

"Yes. I have to fill the orders I got the day after Thanksgiving. The owner of The Gift Box said that she'd sold most of my figurines the moment they went into the window. And the manager at The Crystal Cave in the Embarcadero Center called yesterday and needs more things, too. Amazing."

"Not really, *petite*. Your work shows a combination of artistry and whimsy that makes people believe in magic, and want to have some in their lives."

Jane could only blush and say "thank you."

Zoe turned from filling her kettle with water and walked toward the stove. "You still haven't heard from Matt?"

Jane said a quick "no," then got to her feet. She picked up her breakfast dishes, then started for the sink. "I think he's probably decided I'm a hopeless case and moved on to something less frustrating."

She turned on the tap to begin washing up, but easily heard Zoe's comment over the sound of the running water.

"I doubt that. I think not only that Matt Sullivan is determined to uncover the wretch who attempted to kill you, but that he is utterly fascinated with you."

Jane felt the heat rise in her cheeks as the sink filled with suds. Fascinated with her? She wondered. She knew she wasn't beautiful, by a long shot. The scar at the left corner

of her mouth had faded, but it gave her a somewhat lopsided smile, which was enhanced by the slight twist of her
narrow nose and the fact that one cheekbone was just a bit
lower than the other. But the romance novels she'd read
promised that a true hero saw past those things, to a
woman's inner beauty. Not that this gave her all that much
hope.

Jane began rinsing her dishes, thinking that if a person
was truly the sum of their parts, she didn't add up to much.
After all, how much could reading books and watching
movies really add to the barely one year's worth of experiences that she'd managed to piece together to form what
she considered her personality?

Jane switched the water off, sighed, placed her coffee
cup on the wooden rack to dry and turned to Zoe.

"You're right about Matt's determination to solve this
case. But I doubt that his interest is personal. It has something to do with his need to get justice for what happened
to me, and in some way, for the death of Manny Mendosa."

"His partner?"

"Yes." Jane finished drying her hands, then lifted her
backpack from the floor. "Matt probably will call again,
when he has something new to tell me, or more likely, to
ask. In the meantime, I have to deliver these pieces, then
get over to the hospital."

Matt almost strode right past the children's occupational
therapy area. When his mind registered the tiny white words
etched into the black plaque hanging on the wall to the right
of the open door, he stopped walking, took three steps back
and looked into the large room. He spotted Jane almost
immediately, and just as quickly some of the tension eased
from his shoulders.

It had been a busy, frustrating couple of days. He'd spent
most of Sunday on the computer, searching the *San Francisco Chronicle* Web site for any reference to Bertrand's
Department Store. He'd downloaded a bunch of stuff about

the family that had owned the place for nearly a hundred years, along with articles concerning a recent deal to sell the store to some large conglomerate. But if the woman Jane had recalled seeing was a member of the family, there were no pictures of her published in the past five years, which was as far back as the Web site went.

To check farther into the past, he would have to go to a university library and search the microfiche on file there. By the time he learned that, the place was closed. Yesterday, both he and Jack had spent the day in court, testifying on a case their agency had helped crack three months earlier. He'd planned on hitting the library first thing this morning, but remembered that Jack wouldn't be in till noon, leaving him to run the background check on a prospective employee for one of their oldest clients.

Out of desperation, he'd sent the agency's newly hired secretary, Paula, off to the university with instructions to locate and copy any and all articles and photos connected to Bertrand's—the store or the family. Just as he finished giving their client the go-ahead on the new employee, Paula had returned with reams of paper.

A quick look through the information revealed several photos of a particular white-haired woman. Immediately he'd left the office and rushed off to Zoe's. She had informed him that Jane was at the hospital.

Playing with puppets.

Matt watched as Jane spoke with a small red-haired boy in a wheelchair. Rather, the puppet in Jane's hand spoke. The elf bobbed and weaved. When the little boy laughed, Matt stepped away from the door. He wanted to see more of Jane relaxed and laughing, but that little boy needed her right now, and he didn't want to distract her.

Twenty minutes later, Matt watched from his station near a vending machine as a nurse wheeled the redheaded kid past. The puppet was on his little hand now, cajoling the nurse into making the chair go faster.

"Matt? Is something wrong?"

Matt turned to meet the concern in Jane's smoky eyes, gave her his brightest smile and a wink, then said, "Not now."

Her cheeks seemed to grow slightly pinker as she asked, "What are you doing here?"

"Looking for you. I've got something I want you to see."

"Oh. Of course. What?"

"Well, it's actually several things. And they're back at the office. I went to Zoe's to get you, but—"

"She told you that I was here."

"Right." Matt placed his hand on her shoulder. "I caught a bit of your session with that little kid. I didn't know you did puppets, too."

"They're not something I sell. I just use them with the kids. They seem to get a kick out of having their own elf or fairy."

"When did you start working here?"

"I don't. I volunteer one afternoon a week. This place helped me a lot, so I thought I should give a little back."

Matt frowned. "Do they know who you are?"

Jane looked surprised. "What do you—? Oh. You mean, do they know that I am, or was—" she lowered her voice "—Jane Doe Number Thirteen? Only Joyce Abernathy, the head of the department, and she understands that I don't want anyone else to know. From time to time I've seen some of the nurses who cared for me last year, but none of them seem to recognize me now that I've gained some weight and have some hair."

Matt wondered if the situation was safe. True, there hadn't been any attempts on Jane's life when she was hospitalized, possibly because of the well-publicized interview in which her neurosurgeon stated that Jane's memory loss was most likely permanent.

Then, more urgent news items had taken the edge off the media attention, even before he and Manny had arranged for Jane to get a new last name and leave town for a while.

Still, if he was right, there was someone out there who knew who Jane was, and would probably just as soon get rid of her, should they stumble onto her new life.

"You said you had something to show me."

Matt smiled at Jane's half reluctant, half curious tone. "I do, indeed. Will you come to my office?"

The office of McDermott and Sullivan was located south of Market Street, in an area known as SOMA. Once a collection of abandoned warehouses and clothing factories, the neighborhood had been revitalized in the past several years, resulting in a mixture of light manufacturing, nightclubs, restaurants and artists' lofts.

Matt parked in front of an aged brick structure that rose three stories to a sharply pitched roof. Inside, light spilled into the first-floor hallway from a large bank of multipane windows in the wall at the opposite end.

"This was a commercial bakery throughout the first part of the twentieth century," Matt explained as he led Jane to a ten-foot by ten-foot metal door set in the wall to their right. "It stood vacant until the 1990s, when it was divided into a combination of loft and business spaces. There's a travel agency, an interior decorating firm and a small café on this floor."

Matt pushed a button. The door parted in the center with a *clang*, then slid open. He continued speaking as he and Jane entered the cavernous elevator.

"Jack and I were able to get one of the two spaces on the third floor." Matt pulled a switch and the doors closed. "We had a hell of a time finding office space we could afford. This loft also has a living area, saving the small fortune required to rent an apartment in the city."

Jane nodded. "I know what you mean. I've been incredibly lucky there, too. Zoe insisted that I live in her attic studio, rent free, until I started making money, and still she charges much less than most places that size are going for." She paused. "So both you and Jack live here?"

"Lord, no." Matt grinned as the elevator stopped. He flipped the switch again and the door started to open. "I love the guy, but living together would be...not a good idea. Besides, he's married. Haven't I ever told you about Libby?"

Jane shook her head as Matt led her out of the elevator.

"Oh, right. Jack didn't meet her until after I was sent undercover last year. Now that I think about it, they met *because* I went undercover. When I introduce you to Libby, you'll have to ask her about the night I killed her."

Jane stopped walking. "Killed her?"

Matt's grin was positively devilish. "It's too long a story to get into right now. We have work to do. First a quick tour, so you don't get lost."

Jane's thoughts were still bouncing back and forth between *killed her* and the suggestion that she would eventually meet this mysterious, presumably not-dead woman. Matt's fingers tightened over hers, and as she was pulled forward, she turned her attention to the enormous room surrounding them.

The ceiling soared at least fifteen feet high. Light spilled through several skylights as well as the tall windows set in the brick wall to her left. In front of this, a huge, timeworn table appeared to have been called into service as a desk. Jane could see several metal filing cabinets beneath the table, and a telephone, computer and a mug holding pens on the top. To the left of the desk, a brown sofa and two armchairs sat atop a dark oriental-style rug.

"That's our reception area," Matt said. "Until a month ago, that table was sitting against the wall, where we'd found it when we rented the place. Libby thinks it may have once been used to roll out and knead dough. Anyway, we finally got busy enough to afford a secretary. Paula immediately claimed that monster as her desk and got the decorators on the first floor to help her set all this up. For the moment, however, it appears that she's absent from her post."

Matt guided Jane toward the right-hand door in the brown stucco wall in front of them. "Jack and I originally operated in the middle of this big empty room," Matt explained. "Eventually the need for private time with clients forced us to partition off two offices and enclose the area beneath my loft."

Jane glanced at the dark blue wall on her right, rising halfway to the high-pitched roof. There was an open archway in the center, and to the right of that, an intricate wrought-iron staircase led up to an iron railing that separated the edge of this area from a long white wall.

"Through the doorway," Matt said, "we have a small kitchen, a bathroom and a storage area."

"*And,*" a voice rang out, "a secretary."

The woman who stepped through the opening was perhaps five foot one. She had a cap of short black hair and a small round face with a surprisingly pointed nose. Jane was reminded of an elf—an elf who appeared to be somewhere in her mid-twenties, wearing a purple jacket over a very short skirt of the same color. She held a large green mug in her right hand, which she transferred to her left as she stepped forward.

"My name is Paula O'Shea. And you must be Jane Ashbury."

Jane numbly reached out to shake hands. "How did you know?"

"You match the description Matt gave Jack late Friday." The woman gave Matt a saucy smile. "See? I've been boning up on my Sherlock Holmes—using my 'deductive reasoning.'"

"What, by order of Jack?"

"Well, he is my boss."

"Only one of them."

"Hey. Didn't I spend hours in a musty old library, fighting with rusty old microfiche machines and copiers for you this morning?"

Matt chuckled. "Yes, you did. And speaking of that, Jane

and I are going to be in my office looking at the stuff you brought back."

"Have fun. I have some messages for you and—" The ringing of the telephone interrupted Paula. She glanced at her desk. "And a phone to answer, it seems."

"Hold those messages until we're done in here," Matt called out to her as the young woman scurried away. Then he stepped into his office. Jane followed.

The room was long and narrow, spanning nearly twenty feet from side to side and only ten feet from the doorway to the brick wall that formed the back of the office. The area beneath the multipane window was lined with wooden shelves crammed with books, file folders and slovenly stacks of paper. The scarred oak desk on her left was as neat as a pin, but a table that nearly filled the right-hand wall had papers scattered every which way. A gray armchair stood in the corner.

"Excuse the mess," Matt said as he walked over to the table.

He began sorting through the papers, quickly placing them in one of three stacks. Two contained printed matter that appeared to have been copied from newspaper articles. The third, a smaller stack, was of black-and-white photographs.

"Now, where did that thing go?"

As Matt swept up a stack of pages, revealing a slender laptop computer, Jane saw several pieces of paper fall onto the floor. She bent down to retrieve them, then glanced at them as she stood.

"Is this what you're looking—"

Jane's question stuck in her throat as she stared at the photograph in her hand, saw the white upsweep of hair framing the small, wrinkled features.

"That's her," she breathed.

Matt moved to Jane's side. "The woman from your memory? The one who was handing you the star?"

Unable to make her mouth move, Jane simply nodded.

"Thank God."

Jane looked up at him. "Why? Does this tell you who I am—who I was?"

Matt looked into her eyes. "Do you recognize her?"

"Well, from the memory."

"Nothing else? No name?"

"No."

Matt stared at Jane a moment, then said, "Well, damn."

She drew a deep breath. "Are you telling me you don't know who she is, either?"

"Of course I know who she is—or, I should say, *was.* She was Louise Bertrand, wife of Jean-Philippe Bertrand, the founder of Bertrand's Department Store."

"And she is connected to me how?"

Matt shook his head and gave her a twisted smile. "I'm sure you'd tell me if you could. I had hoped that springing that picture on you would unlock something in your memory and, *voilà,* you would recognize the woman, then remember everything else."

Jane couldn't decide whether to laugh at what he seemed to consider a joke, or to hit him over the head with the papers she still held in her hand. She settled for slapping them down on the table.

"Well, I'm sorry to have disappointed you."

The words were barely out of her mouth before she realized they weren't just a half-teasing retort. She really didn't want to disappoint this man. One of the reasons she'd worked so hard when she first started rehab was to see the pride and elation on Matt's face when she exceeded the expectations of her physical therapists. And, if she was going to be completely honest, a major reason she'd pushed herself to succeed at creating an independent life for herself was so that, if their paths ever crossed again, he would be proud of her.

But she wasn't going to be that honest. In fact, now that she'd brought that thought to light, the idea of living her life for anyone's approval filled her with sudden anger.

"I'm not disappointed," she heard Matt say. She looked up to see a sheepish grin crease his face. "Okay, maybe a bit. It just means I have to dig a little deeper. No, make that a lot deeper."

"Dig what?" she asked tightly. "Where?"

"I have to dig for how you might have been connected to that old lady, and to Bertrand's. You apparently recalled a moment when Louise was handing you an item that I have since learned was a treasured family heirloom, so I researched the family. Louise Bertrand died eighteen years ago at the ripe old age of ninety-one. She was survived by her grandson John Phillip, who passed away a little over two years ago, and his children, Noelle, Phillip and Aimee. The oldest girl would be around thirty now, the youngest twenty-six. Since the doctors could only guess your age, I figured you might be one of Louise's granddaughters. However, Noelle died last December, and Aimee and her brother are currently running the department store. So my missing-heiress theory seems to have gone…amiss."

He paused. "The other day, Zoe mentioned a Bertrand's holiday decorating tradition. I discovered that every year, except this most recent one, the employees did gather each Thanksgiving Eve to get the store all decked out for the Christmas shopping season. This included setting up the window display. A buffet supper was served and entertainment was provided for the children of the employees. My guess is that you may have been one of these. I just have to figure out which one."

Jane's anger was replaced by incredulity. She stared at him for several moments before she said, "Are you nuts? That would be like looking—"

"For that old needle in the haystack," Matt finished. "Yep. But Paula unearthed an article about the tradition, and discovered that a group picture was taken each year. I'm sure the store has copies."

Jane shook her head. "I'm not even going to bother asking how you plan to get a look at these fabled photos. I'll just skip to the question of what it is you think you'd find. Some little girl who looks like me? Crooked jaw, slightly twisted nose and all?''

Jane expected Matt to frown. Instead he reached out and ran his thumb down her nose. ''It isn't all that twisted, you know. Besides, it's the eye area that counts when a forensic scientist ages a photo. The trick part will be figuring out approximately when the scene you recalled with Louise took place. You said your hands were small in the memory, yet you were being entrusted with a priceless crystal ornament. I figure you had to be at least six, and nine at the most. Sound right?''

Jane dredged up the image of the small outstretched hands, then nodded.

''Then, I just need to look for a girl in that age bracket. As to how I'm going to get a look at the photos, it seems that Bertrand's is in the process of being purchased by a company called Bestco. In a recent article, employees of Bertrand's complained about the cancellation of the Thanksgiving Eve decorating party. A few speculated that once the store is in the hands of this conglomerate, all the old traditions will go out the window—excuse the pun— including the famed Christmas window. Bestco denied this, of course. I thought I'd approach Bestco, posing as a free-lance reporter, and propose an article featuring the store's history and the way that Bestco intends to keep the best of the old while bringing in the new and improved. If they bite, I can set up a series of interviews with some of the longtime employees, and make my request to see the photos taken at previous decorating parties seem completely innocent.''

''That seems like a lot of work. Can't you just ask to see the pictures?''

Matt looked into her eyes, suddenly serious. ''Jane, I've always believed that no second attempt was made on your life because as long as you have no memory, you don't pose a threat to the perpetrator. And you've kept yourself out of the public eye for the past year. But there's a chance that the person, or persons, who engineered that accident are somehow connected to Bertrand's and might get suspicious if a detective starts nosing around.''

A prickle danced down Jane's spine. She shook it off.

''What makes you think Bestco will go along with this?''

''Well, first off, my proposed article is just the sort of double-speak that corporate people…speak. Second, I have a friend at the newspaper who will vouch for me, assure Bestco of the quality of my work and all that. Of course, I won't really write this article.''

Matt walked over to his desk, removed the telephone receiver and punched in some numbers. Holding the receiver to his ear, he said, ''Ted will make up some lie about why the thing doesn't run. He'll probably have to fire me.''

Jane shook her head. ''What was it you said about double-speak?''

Matt grinned, then said, ''Ted McPherson, please.''

A moment later he hung up. ''Gone for the day. I'll have to get him tomorrow. You ready?''

He stepped toward the door. Jane pivoted as he passed her. ''Ready?'' she asked.

Matt stopped and turned to her. ''Yeah. To go back to Zoe's.''

Jane shook her head. ''Not until you tell me what my part is to be in all this.''

Matt lifted one eyebrow. ''What do you mean, your part?''

''I'm not exactly sure,'' she replied. ''Two days ago, the thought of looking into my past filled me with terror, but I realize now that if I don't face that fear, it will be like turning and running from a wild animal—it will chase me. So, I think I should go along on these interviews, and see if anything, or anyone, sparks some new memories.''

Matt stared at her for a moment, then nodded slowly. ''I guess you could come along, as my assistant or something.

I'm just concerned that someone might recognize something about *you,* and— What is it, Paula?''

He turned to the secretary, who was standing at the door.

''Remember those messages I mentioned earlier?'' she said. ''One of them is on the phone now—Tasha Nichols.''

Matt and Jane instantly looked at one another.

Chapter Eight

"That's right, Tasha," Matt said. "Anything I might know about the location of Jane Doe is confidential, and that's all I have to say."

Jane leaned against the table, muscles tense, watching Matt carefully. He stood on the other side of the room, cradling the receiver to his ear, frowning as he listened to whatever Channel Fifty-Four's reporter was saying.

Jane knew just how persuasive Tasha Nichols could be. The other San Francisco stations had aired brief stories about the attempt on her life and the questions surrounding her identity, but Tasha had run in-depth segments entitled "Woman Without a Name" almost every night.

Jane crossed her arms. Tasha had convinced her that someone would recognize something about the way she spoke—despite the permanent hoarseness that had resulted when the tracheotomy tube nicked her vocal chords after she was first brought into the emergency room—then see beneath the facial changes wrought by the plastic surgeons.

But that never happened. Eventually Jane had began to suspect that no one was going to identify her as a result of this publicity. Some of the ''searchers'' who came to see if she was their missing loved one seemed sincere. But others seemed more interested in the interview with Tasha that followed their disappointing visit with Jane.

The final straw had come following the visit from the Harpers, the very last people Jane had agreed to meet. The couple had driven seven hundred miles to see if Jane might be the daughter who'd disappeared fourteen years earlier at the age of sixteen. Tasha's interviews following this heartbreaking meeting showed no sensitivity to the painful disappointment that any of her subjects might be feeling.

''I know you're not accustomed to this, Tasha,'' Matt was saying, ''but you're going to have to take no for an answer. If you're really interested in Jane's welfare, as you insist, leave this alone— No, I won't. Now, goodbye.''

When Matt hung up the phone, Jane said, ''She never gave a damn about my welfare. Not really.''

Matt straightened from the desk. As he crossed the room, his expression caught Jane by surprise. He looked, suddenly, much as he had when he'd first walked into Maxwell's security office—mouth set in a hard line, eyes grim. He stopped a mere two feet in front of her, looked into her eyes and said, ''I know. I'm sorry.''

Jane shrugged. ''It wasn't your fault she turned out to be a blood-sucking bitch in sheep's clothing.''

''Yeah, it was.'' Matt gave her a tight smile. ''I'm not claiming responsibility for her actions, mind you. But I was the one who convinced you that speaking to the press might bring forth someone who knew you, then recommended Tasha for the job.''

''Why wouldn't you? You said you knew her.''

Matt glanced away. ''In the biblical sense, yes.'' He returned his gaze to Jane. ''Tasha and I were...involved for a short time about a year before you showed up. It didn't last long. The attraction was purely physical, and both of us recognized that we were too involved in our careers to put in the time required to make it into anything else. We parted friends, and moved on. Our jobs caused our paths to cross from time to time, when she was assigned to report a case I was investigating. She turned over any clue she encountered, and I tried to see to it that she got first crack at breaking information whenever possible.''

He paused, then shook his head once and went on. ''Anyway, that's why I suggested you give your first on-air interview to her. But it didn't take me long to realize that she was much more interested in how your story could promote her from local to national news than in helping you.''

Jane held his gaze. ''Why didn't you tell me this back then?''

Matt placed his hand on her shoulder. ''Because you seemed so anxious to learn who you were, so grateful for Tasha's help. I didn't know how you felt about her until after the Harper incident, when you told me that being interviewed by her made you feel like you were being stripped naked in front of the entire world.''

Jane glanced down at her tightly crossed arms as she managed to shake off a shiver, then forced herself to say, ''I remember. Then you promised I'd never have to do that again.''

Matt's finger was warm beneath her chin as he urged her to look back up at him. ''And if I have anything to say about it, you won't. But this call changes everything.''

It was on the tip of Jane's tongue to ask what ''everything'' he was referring to, when she thought of another question. ''What prompted Tasha's call, anyway?''

Matt's hand fell to his side as he replied, ''It seems the salesclerk at Maxwell's overheard you trying to explain to the guard that you hadn't been stealing that scarf. You apparently mentioned that you were Jane Doe Number Thirteen, and had been confused by a sudden memory.''

Jane remembered the salesgirl coming into the security

office to identify both her and the scarf she'd run out of the store with.

"Yes. I might have said something like that." Sudden fear made Jane straighten. "So, Tasha knows I came back to town and have a new last name. She'll track me down and want to ask me what I'm doing, how I *feel* about this, just like—"

"Whoa." Again Matt placed his hand on her shoulder. "First off, Tasha doesn't know what that name is. I called the security guard the next day and asked him not to release your name to anyone. Before he went to work for Maxwell's, Mr. Jessup was a cop, so he understood the reason behind my request. From what Tasha said just now, I gather he's protecting this information with his life."

"But he made a report on Jane Ashbury. I'm sure Tasha wouldn't think twice about bribing someone to look it up."

Matt smiled at her. "I thought about that. Jessup agreed to file that report in a place only he could locate."

Jane felt some of the tension ease from her muscles. "Good," she said. "Then, what did you mean when you said Tasha's call has changed things?"

"I meant that you can't come along when I go to Bertrand's to interview the employees. I'll have to make up some reason for getting copies of Thanksgiving Eve photos so that you can look—"

"Wait a minute—"

Matt scowled at Jane's interruption. She mirrored his expression as she went on, "Would you mind explaining just *why* I can't go to Bertrand's with you?"

"Because, I know Tasha. The fact that she *has* no facts won't keep her from running a story about you, something along the lines of 'Where Is Jane Doe Number Thirteen Today?' The last thing I want is for anyone to be looking for you. I certainly don't want to take you to a place where someone might recognize you."

"Matt, do you actually think that there's one person who works for Bertrand's who didn't see those interviews last year? If anyone there had recognized me, they would have said so then.''

"Okay, but what if the person or persons who tried to kill you works at Bertrand's? They've been feeling very safe, believing their intended victim has permanent amnesia, and suddenly Tasha goes on the news and suggests that Jane Doe may be regaining her memory.''

Jane gazed up at him as if considering his words, then gave her head a quick shake.

"That's providing that he, she or they are actually connected to Bertrand's. Matt, if I'm going to overcome my fear of remembering whoever I used to be, I need to feel somehow in control of this process. I think that might make it easier for me to access those memories.''

It would have taken a blind man not to see how Jane was battling fear with determination. Her eyes had a dark, haunted look, while her lips were set in a tight line. Matt didn't want to argue with this woman. He wanted to pull her into his arms, hold her close and promise to protect her, to chase away the dragons in her past, to promise that everything would be all right.

His jaw clenched. Where the hell had those thoughts come from? None of those actions would be appropriate. And too much was at stake to let emotions cloud his judgment.

Placing his hands on both of Jane's slender shoulders, he held her away from him to keep his resolve from weakening.

"And you might be right about that," he said. "But taking you to Bertrand's, with your story suddenly fresh in the public's mind, could put you in harm's way. I won't do that.''

He watched Jane carefully, saw her look down, then slowly raise her face to his again.

"Matt," she said quietly. "In all the time that you and Manny worked my case, coming to check on me and my memories every day, you never once made me feel like a helpless victim. Please don't start now.''

She paused. ''Besides, has it occurred to you that if I go to Bertrand's with you, I might be the one doing the recognizing?''

Matt shook his head, started to say that his gut told him that taking her to Bertrand's was a bad move, when a deep voice broke the silence.

''She has a good point.''

Matt turned to find his cousin Jack leaning against the doorjamb, hands crammed into the pockets of his tan jacket. His brown hair looked windblown, and beneath Jack's thick mustache, his lips curved. Two long, deep dimples creased his cheeks.

''Actually,'' Jack went on, ''she made several good points, if you ask me.''

''Well, I didn't.''

Jack raised his eyebrows. ''Touchy this evening, are we, cuz?'' He gave Matt no time to respond before turning to Jane. ''I take it that I'm in the presence of the famed and mysterious Jane Doe Number Thirteen, am I not?''

''I am,'' she replied. ''That is, I was. I'm now Jane Ashbury. And you must be Jack McDermott, Matt's cousin, partner and—''

''And terminal buttinsky,'' Matt finished. ''Someone who has no idea what's at stake here.''

''Not at all true,'' Jack said as he pushed away from the door. ''If you recall, you filled me in on the situation yesterday, while we were waiting for court to begin. It seems to me, since Miss Ashbury is in possession of the memories you need to break this case, that you have little choice but to take her to Bertrand's with you. I completely understand your desire to protect her, but as we both know, there are just some women who refuse to be confined to the damsel-in-distress role.''

He turned to Jane. ''I'm married to a woman like that,

so my little cousin is aware that mine is the voice of experience, and should therefore be listened to."

Matt felt the sudden urge to knock his cousin onto his self-assured butt, then inform him that the situation he faced with Jane was nothing like the circumstances Jack had found himself in with Libby. But before he had a chance to make a total fool of himself, he recalled how Libby had insisted on lying motionless in a morgue, pretending to be dead so that one Matthew Sullivan wouldn't end up on a similar slab for real.

It wasn't at all the sort of thing a man liked to see the woman he loved put herself through. But this was where his situation differed from Jack's. Although he wouldn't deny that he cared about Jane, there was no question of a romance here. She was the victim of a horrible assault. It was his job to see that she received justice, make sure that the person responsible was put away so that she could live her life without fear.

And, he was forced to acknowledge, this just might demand some risks, on her part as well as his.

Matt released a sigh as he fixed his cousin with a glare. "All right, *Mother*. I'll consider your suggestion. And discuss the matter with Miss Ashbury."

He turned to Jane. "Over dinner, if it's okay with you. I know it's not quite five o'clock, but my lunch consisted of a candy bar from the hospital vending machine. I'm starving."

Jane seemed to hesitate before replying. "I ate something before my puppet session with Robbie, which seems like aeons ago, so dinner sounds great."

Matt glared at his cousin. "You aren't invited."

Jack laughed. "I would have turned you down, anyway. Libby's in the car, anxious to get home. She's been shopping all day while I followed up on the Mayfair investigation. I just stopped in to pick up my messages and see if *someone* might want to see the latest picture of his niece or nephew-to-be."

"A new sonogram? You bet."

Matt stepped toward Jack as his cousin reached into the breast pocket of his jacket and drew out a white rectangle. As Matt examined the image, he could feel his eyes opening wider.

"My God. The detail they get on these things now is amazing. Jane, come look at this little doll."

As Jane came over to stand by his side and examine the black-and-white image, Matt turned to Jack. "Still don't want to know the gender?"

"Nope. Libby wants all the excitement and suspense she can squeeze out of this experience. So do I."

Matt looked at the sonogram again, then turned to Jane. She was still staring at the image on the card, her expression a strange mixture of intense longing and dawning surprise.

"What is it, Jane?" he asked.

She looked up at him, eyes moist. "I just learned something about myself. It seems I very much want to have children."

Matt switched the windshield wipers on to clear away the fog. He spotted Zoe's house and pulled into the driveway.

"You sure it's okay to park here?"

"Zoe never drives at night," Jane said. "The restaurant is several blocks from here, but I doubt we'd find a closer spot on the street."

Matt opened his door. "I'm sure you're right. And I could use the walk."

The stroll, past the tall narrow houses that made up the Marina District, was as silent as the drive from the office had been. Matt glanced at Jane, who seemed lost in thought, hands stuffed in the pocket of her black coat. Whether this was due to her intense concentration or to protect them from the chilly moist air, Matt wasn't sure. He had issues of his own to work out. Like why a sharp pain had pierced his heart at Jane's wistfully stated desire to have children.

On second thought, maybe he should leave that question unanswered.

If ever he'd needed to be completely focused on the facts of a case, it was now. Granted, the facts didn't amount to much, but if he hoped to collect any more, he had to be alert, ready to spot any change in Jane that might indicate a new memory was coming to light.

But that was *all* he should be focused on—not Jane's feelings or her longings or even her fears. Certainly not the way her throaty voice felt like a caress, or how her eyes lit up when she was amused, making him want to tease her every chance he got, or the way her cheeks bloomed pink whenever he touched her.

Matt jammed his hands into his pockets of his jeans. The case, dammit. Focus on the case.

There were plans to be formulated and agreed upon, rules of behavior to be set up if he was going to yield to Jane's demand that she be allowed to participate in his fact-finding visit to Bertrand's.

With that clear in his mind, Matt led Jane across the street to Osome, the Japanese restaurant she'd recommended, held the door open for her, then followed her in. They were led to a small room, where they stepped down to a low booth containing a table for two. He waited until they'd ordered before initiating conversation that didn't involve fish, seaweed or rice.

"I want to talk about this Bertrand's situation."

Jane nodded. "I do, too. I noticed that you gathered quite a bit of information on the place."

"I couldn't get a picture of Louise Bertrand until Paula went to the university library for me today, but I was able to find an article on the *Chronicle* Web site from a couple of Christmases ago—one of those half information, half advertising pieces."

Jane grinned and asked, "Like the one you're going to propose to Bestco?"

Matt lifted a small, square cup and took a sip of hot sake,

then leaned toward her and responded in a conspiratorial whisper. "That I'm going to *pretend* to propose." He straightened, took another sip. "Anyway, I learned that Bertrand's has been owned by the family of that name since 1906."

"The year of the earthquake."

Matt smiled. "I love the way people say that, like San Francisco has only had *one* of those. Anyway, the store was under construction when the quake hit, so the damage was relatively minor. The original owner, Jean-Philippe Bertrand, came from a wealthy French family, and he managed to open the store the day after Thanksgiving of that year. And as a special gift to the still-recovering city that had welcomed him when he arrived eight years earlier, he unveiled a spectacular automated Christmas window."

"The same one we saw the other night?"

"More or less. The mechanics have been updated over the years, of course. Apparently, when anything needs to be replaced it's copied faithfully from the original."

The waiter arrived with their food. Jane picked up her chopsticks. "You said the woman in my memory was named Louise, that she was married to Jean-Philippe."

"Yes. Jean-Philippe I was twelve years older. He was seventy when he died. Louise lived another thirty-three years, dying at the age of ninety-one, having witnessed the death of her son, Jean-Philippe II, and his wife. She raised her grandson John, who died two years ago this past September, at which point Bertrand's passed into the hands of his three children, Noelle, John and Aimee. Bestco tried to purchase the place at that time, but apparently the oldest girl, Noelle, had controlling interest and refused to sell the family business."

Matt paused to sample some sushi. While he was enjoying the combination of flavors, Jane asked, "I wonder what made her change her mind."

Matt shook his head. "She didn't. Noelle died just about this time last year, in Paris."

"Paris."

Jane's pensive tone made Matt look up. She seemed to be studying the California roll that she held inches from her mouth.

"Yes, Paris. Does that mean something to you?"

"I'm not—" Jane shook her head, but continued to stare ahead as she said, "I have no idea. I just found myself wondering if I've ever been there, or anywhere else. So, anyway, Noelle died, and now the store has been sold?"

"In the process. Bestco got the remaining two siblings to sell, but there's been a legal struggle. It seems a group of employees banded together and made an offer that would have created an employee ownership. They lost their battle, but the delay means that the store won't actually change hands until sometime in February."

Jane took a sip of hot sake, then frowned. "It's interesting that these employees should have felt so strongly about the store."

"I'm glad you mentioned that. Unless I want to get bogged down listening to complaints about both the new and the former owners when I interview the employees, I'm going to have to make it clear that the focus of my article is to be Bertrand's holiday traditions."

Jane placed her cup back on the table. "And while you're doing that, provided you get permission to write this fictitious article, what will I be doing?"

Matt sighed as he placed his chopsticks on the plate, then met Jane's determined gaze. There was no point in arguing with her. He could see she was determined to play a part in this. And, he had to admit, she had every right to do so. It was her past they were searching for, her future that was at stake.

"It depends," he said. "I suppose I could introduce you as my assistant. Someone to keep my tape recorder in batteries or some such thing."

"You said, *It depends.*" Jane's eyes narrowed. "Depends on what?"

"On whether I feel fairly certain we can maintain your anonymity. I'm still concerned about Tasha snooping around. Tell me, how many people besides me, Zoe and my cousin Jack know who you are?"

Jane shrugged and her eyes seemed to darken. "Only Joyce Abernathy, who runs the volunteer department at the hospital. And she would never tell anyone."

"That's it? What about your friends?"

Jane suddenly seemed very interested in the black design on the outside of the pottery cup that held her sake. She reached for it, took another drink, then stared at the container as she placed it back on the table. Slowly her eyes met his. They looked empty.

"I don't have any friends," she said. "Not any close ones, that is. I sometimes go thrift-store shopping with a woman I met at a quilting class I took last year. Her name is Georgia. And I have coffee with a couple of people following the mystery readers' group that meets on Wednesdays. And these people only know that I make elves and fairies, that I like to read and that I just moved here from Maine. That's the story I made up after Zoe and I returned."

Matt reached over to take her hand. "I'm sorry."

He watched her stare at his hand before looking at him again. She lifted her chin.

"Don't be. I'm incredibly busy. I love what I do, and I'm learning new skills all the time. Zoe and I go to the movies or to a play at least once a week. Actually, I enjoy solitude. I sometimes have little moments of *déjà vu* that catch me by surprise, then fade before I can get ahold of them. When I'm alone I can wonder about them without someone commenting on my silence, asking me to explain, forcing me to make up yet another lie. Being alone is easier."

Matt ran his thumb over Jane's wrist. He knew just what it was like to feel alone in the midst of a crowd, how hard it was to pretend to fit in, to live a lie because the truth was too painful. If sharing this information with Jane would make life different for her, he would do it in a heartbeat. But until he caught her assailant, Jane needed to go on as she had been.

"Oh, I forgot about my work at the hospital," Jane said suddenly.

Her gaze warmed.

"That's the best part of the week. I help the kids make the bodies for their puppets. The act of making something seems to help translate the hard work they do in physical therapy into progress that they can see."

"Well, I can't say enough about that hospital's physical therapy department," Matt replied. "I was impressed by how quickly they built your strength back up and had you walking again. Of course, I know that your stubbornness had a lot to do with that."

Matt stopped speaking for a moment, allowing Jane to come back at him with a saucy remark. Instead, the joy disappeared from her eyes and her smile suddenly looked forced.

He didn't know why this should surprise him. His own days in the hospital were hardly his favorite memories.

"Hey," he said. "In that case, your stubbornness was a virtue. I should know, I needed quite a bit of that myself— along with some heavy-duty prodding from my physical therapists. They were pretty good, but I'd been hoping to get that guy who worked with you. I had my doctor ask if Kyle Rogers could take on a patient in another hospital, but he was told that…" Matt slowed down as he noticed that Jane was no longer even trying to smile. "Kyle no longer worked there," he finished.

Jane drew her hand from his, pulled her napkin from her lap and placed it on her plate. Then she reached for the check. Matt grabbed her wrist.

When her eyes met his, he asked, "What's wrong?"

"Nothing."

Jane's eyes were wide, blank, as if she wasn't seeing him.

"Right," he said. "Jane, you're talking to me—Matt Sullivan, private investigator. Do I have to break out the rubber—"

She cut him off with a shake of her head. "I'll explain, if you insist. But not here."

With her mind on other things, Jane made a halfhearted attempt to pay for her part of the dinner, but lost the minibattle. She watched Matt close the black folder containing the money to cover the check and a generous tip, then followed him outside.

The air was still bracing, but since the fog had lifted to form a soft gray ceiling several stories above the street, it wasn't as bone-chillingly moist as it had been earlier. Or maybe the hot sake had warmed her.

Aware of Matt's close attention as he walked next to her, she turned and asked, "Do you mind if I hold off on telling the story? The sake seems to have made my head a bit fuzzy."

"Take as long as you want," Matt said. "I'll wait."

Jane nodded, then turned north, toward the bay. She walked quickly, her stride brisk, as she fumed at herself. She had accomplished so much this past year. But it seemed that she wasn't much better at hiding her emotions than when she'd first woken from her coma—when amusement had resulted in unrestrained laughter and sadness had brought instant tears. Her neurosurgeon had said this was a normal response to a brain injury—a short-circuit of sorts. Zoe had said this made her refreshingly spontaneous. Jane had felt it made her seem like a child—like that helpless creature who had woken up with no idea who she was, who seemed to be ignorant of so much.

She didn't want Matt to see her that way now.

He and Manny had each done a wonderful job of playing the part of her "big brother" when she first came out of her coma. Then she'd begun educating herself, building up her brain as the physical therapists worked with her weakened body. It hadn't taken long to cast Matt in a far different role, to see him as the hero in every romantic story she read or movie she watched. The books made it clear that heroes didn't fall in love with overemotional children— they fell in love with women who were as strong-willed as they were.

Before she'd had a chance to become that woman, Matt had been placed undercover. Then he'd been shot, and when she'd tried to reach him at the hospital, she'd been told he was in intensive care, unable to take calls or have visitors. Manny was dead. And she…had felt utterly lost.

Only one person seemed to understand how alone she felt. And that man had been in the perfect position to take advantage of those emotions.

The feel of Matt's fingers tightening around hers brought Jane's attention to her surroundings. She was surprised to find that they had reached the large grassy area that made up Marina Green, on the edge of a harbor filled with private boats.

"You okay?" Matt asked.

"Sure," Jane replied. "I love walking down here. There's something soothing about the motion of the water."

With that, Matt tugged on her hand and drew her across the grass to the part of the path that bordered the water. There was no wind at all. The only sound was the lapping of tiny waves against the rock wall that led down from the sidewalk to the water, and the occasional squeak of a boat pulling at its mooring.

After a few moments of walking beneath the gauzy fog, listening to the whispers of the marina, Jane stopped walking beneath the filtered beam of one of the park's streetlights and turned to Matt.

"The therapist you mentioned, Kyle Rogers. He's in prison—convicted of raping a patient."

Chapter Nine

Matt's fingers closed painfully over Jane's. His features hardened. Before he could say a word, she spoke.

"I wasn't that patient. It was someone Kyle had worked with several months before I started physical therapy. But I... He..."

Jane took a deep breath. She didn't want to talk about the man who had used her loneliness, her dreams and her needs to weave a trap that could very well have destroyed her. But she knew Matt needed to know about this.

"As we worked in the physical therapy room every day," she said, "Kyle told me how brave and strong-willed I was. He made me feel like the heroine of some adventure story, overcoming all odds. I...needed to hear that. I felt very much alone after you and Manny went undercover. Everyone was very helpful, but the doctors had other patients to see, the nurses were too overworked to spend time chatting with me. Zoe visited a couple of times a week, but I saw Kyle every day. He never tried to make me remember anything. He encouraged me to look to the future. As time went on, I began to believe he was talking about a future with him.''

Jane paused. Matt placed a hand on her shoulder. ''Jane—'' he started.

She shook away his next words and hurried on. ''It's all right. There really isn't much more. After you were shot, Zoe explained to me that your leg had become infected. I knew you hadn't abandoned me. And, of course, Manny…''

Jane swallowed the tight knot in her throat and noticed the way the muscle in Matt's jaw bunched.

''Anyway,'' she said, ''after all this, Kyle seemed to take extra care with me, making time at the end of our sessions just to talk. Then one day, he decided I was strong enough to walk outside the hospital. It felt good to be away from those walls. Scary, too, like leaving home for the first time. I had just learned about your second knee replacement surgery. Kyle listened to my concerns about you, and when I started crying, he held me. Then he kissed me.''

Jane turned to stare at the black water, her face hot in spite of the chilly air. In the embarrassed silence, she could almost feel Matt gearing up to ask questions. She didn't want to go through an interrogation. She wanted to say what had to be said, and get it over with.

''That sort of thing happened a couple more times,'' she said. ''He told me that we needed to keep this *our secret*. Then, one day, he wasn't there. Zoe came to visit that day and explained that Kyle had been arrested. A former client of his had finally told her psychiatrist that Kyle had…raped her. The doctor reported this to the police, who'd found two other women willing to testify that he'd either molested them or attempted to molest them while acting as their physical therapist.''

Jane paused, fought off a shiver as a slight breeze sent a small wave rippling toward the seawall at her feet. ''I didn't want to believe he could do such a thing, but Zoe arranged for me to listen to the women's taped statements. As I heard them describe the same pattern of secret meetings and stolen kisses, how these suddenly led to something horribly ugly, it became clear that I would have been his next victim.''

Jane stared at the ground beneath her feet and emptied her lungs in a slow exhale. That was it. Nothing else to say. She'd been stupid, foolish, and no matter what anyone—

''Did you have to testify against him?''

Without looking up, Jane said, ''No. Neither did the other women. He took a reduced sentence for pleading guilty.''

Her words were followed by a moment of silence, broken only by the slap of water on rock.

''Look at me, Jane.''

For a second she resisted the quiet demand in Matt's voice, then gave up, turned and raised her head to meet his gaze. His features were still tightly set. His eyes were dark within the shadows formed by the overhead light. She could see no expression in them, but she was sure he was going to remind her that before he and Manny had gone undercover, they'd both warned her to watch who she trusted.

Jane took a step back from him. ''I know what you're thinking,'' she said. ''That I should have been more careful. You don't have to say it. I've learned my lesson. I'm very careful now.''

Jane stuffed her hands into her coat pockets.

''I believe you,'' Matt said slowly.

A strong, warm hand came to rest on her right shoulder as he leaned toward her.

''But it's one thing to be careful, another to become a virtual hermit. You mentioned a few women friends. What about guys? Have you been on any dates this past year?''

Jane recognized the ''big brother'' tone in his voice. That quality had once had the power to soothe her, to make her feel safe. Tonight it made her angry. She looked up as she replied. ''Lots of them.'' She paused. ''Well, a couple, anyway. Enough to know that I'm not ready to trust anyone.''

"Because of what happened with Kyle Rogers? Jane, I told you, the victim is—"

"Not at fault. I *know* that. But when guys meet a woman who appears to be in her late-twenties or early-thirties, they expect a level of experience in certain…areas. I've read a lot of romance novels, remember. I know how things are supposed to progress. What I don't know is how to allow that to happen, when I can't really let a man know me. I can't tell anyone about the person I was, because I have no idea. And the person I am now is just…making things up as she goes along."

"And doing a damn fine job, if you ask me."

Matt now had a hand on each of her shoulders. He leaned forward. Jane could see his eyes more clearly. Tonight they were the murky green of the sea on a stormy day.

"But," he said, "no one can, or should, go through life not trusting anyone. You can trust yourself, Jane. You have good instincts. And you know you can trust me."

Jane saw his lips form a tiny smile, his gaze soften slightly. She became aware of some force, some magnetic pull, that had her leaning toward him, lifting her face to look more closely into his eyes. Or was it his mouth she was interested in? Firm lips that had always told her the truth. Lips that had never spoken promises they didn't deliver on, at least until a bullet had made it impossible for him to carry them out. Lips that were now moving closer to hers.

Suddenly it was her lips that Jane was aware of, parting softly, tingling, wanting. It was her heart she heard, beating loudly, quickly. It was the heat of Matt's chest she felt beneath the palm of her hands as they rested on the front of his jacket, the pressure of Matt's fingers on her shoulders as he drew her closer to him.

Then, slowly, gently pushed her away.

She saw him frown, then give his head a tiny shake.

"Janey," he said softly. "I can't tell you how sorry I am

that I wasn't around to protect you then, to help you learn who else you could trust.''

He didn't want to be the one who taught her about kissing, Jane thought, just about trusting. She swallowed the disappointment clogging her throat, nodded slowly, then forced herself to smile.

''I'm sorry I couldn't have helped you, too,'' she said. ''When you were first wounded, I begged to be transferred to the hospital you were in. I had this wild idea that in between my own therapy sessions I could sit by your bedside and nurse you back to health. It probably sounds silly, but—''

''No,'' Matt interrupted. ''I would have liked that. It would have been far preferable to the harassing I got from Jack at every turn.'' He grinned, then grew serious again. ''Actually, you were with me, in some ways. My right leg was pretty messed up. Recovery was a long, hard battle, to say the least. More than once I thought about giving up any attempt to walk and ordering the fanciest wheelchair available.''

Slowly his smile returned. ''Then I'd remember watching you—so thin it seemed a stiff wind would blow you out to sea—gripping the parallel bars, sweat streaming down your face, as you forced yourself to take one more trip down that path than you'd taken the day before. I realized I could hardly allow myself to do any less. The doctors weren't sure I'd ever be able to walk without a cane, but with your example egging me on, I proved them wrong. My leg isn't perfect...''

He touched his forefinger to the top of her nose, then traced the slight curve down to the tip as he finished. ''But then, perfection is highly overrated, if you ask me.''

''Well, I guess turnabout is fair play,'' she said. ''You were there for me all those times I faced the 'searchers,' only to learn I wasn't the one they were searching for. You understood my decision to stop trying to find out who I had been, and encouraged me to discover who I could be, even though that wouldn't help you catch whoever had been responsible for my accident. I can't tell you how good it felt to focus on creating a new life for myself instead of worrying about the past."

Jane paused and the smile faded from her lips. "After the situation with Kyle, I was even more determined not to look back. But now, with you popping up in my life again, asking all your questions, urging me to remember, I think I'm beginning to realize just how much I lost in that car wreck. And how much I have to gain now by trying to recover my memory."

Matt chuckled. "Well, it seems that my skill at being an 'aggravating pain in the butt,' to quote my cousin Jack, isn't such a bad thing. If I can badger you into exploring your past, I should have no trouble getting the information I need out of the employees at Bertrand's."

"They'll never know what hit them." Jane smiled, then asked. "You're still planning on taking me along, right?"

Matt hesitated. "I don't like the idea that someone might recognize you, but given how different you look these days…"

"You mean with hair?"

He turned from the bay and stepped onto the grass. "I want to think about this. In the meantime, I think it's time to get you home."

Jane walked silently at his side as they crossed the green. She wanted to argue with him, but she was just too tired. The next few blocks seemed like miles to legs that threatened to buckle at any moment. By the time Matt had accompanied her up the stairs to Zoe's door, she barely had enough energy to dig out her key and fit it into the lock.

With her hand on the doorknob, she turned to Matt. "Thanks for the dinner."

"Thanks for introducing me to the place."

Matt's hand was once more on her shoulder, warm, strong. One side of his mouth was lifted in that half smile of his. Her own lips curved. She felt suddenly free, as if telling him about Kyle had banished the experience from her past. Wanting to thank him, yet unable to think of the right words, she rose on tiptoe to give him a quick kiss.

The contact was brief, but her reaction to it was intense. Her lips and her entire body heated up, as if she'd taken another sip of sake. She wanted more than anything to place her arms around his neck and deepen the kiss.

Her face flamed. *That's right,* she thought, *throw yourself at him, make a complete fool of yourself.*

Jane dropped to her flat feet, breaking off contact, then forced a smile and managed a weak "Good night." As she stepped inside, Matt's hand slipped from her shoulder like a caress. Heart pounding, she pulled the door shut.

Matt's arm fell to his side. He stood staring at the pink door for several seconds after it closed, then turned and started down the stairs.

What had he been thinking just now? He'd been a second away from wrapping Jane in his arms and kissing her for all he was worth. He'd assured Jane that she could trust him, yet if she hadn't stepped away, he certainly would have violated that trust, taking advantage of a simple good-night kiss to gratify his desires.

The problem, he told himself as he got into his car, was that he hadn't been thinking. He had been feeling, and he knew all too well where that sort of thing led—to disaster and disappointment. Jane had faced enough of both. The last thing she needed was for him to add confusion to the mix.

So if he knew better, why had he found it so difficult to restrain his longing for contact of an undeniable romantic sort? Maybe there had been something in the sushi, he thought as he started his car. Or something about the way the fog blurred the edges of everything, making him forget that Jane Ashbury was a victim of a crime that he was investigating. That no matter how much she'd matured, she was still vulnerable. That she had very good reasons not to trust people.

And some of this was his fault. He'd encouraged Jane to trust Tasha Nichols, to believe the reporter when she promised that taking Jane's story to the public would give her the past, the family that she so desperately wanted.

He and Manny had agreed that getting Jane's image in newspapers and on television was their best hope—only hope, actually—of obtaining any leads to solve the crime that had been committed against her. But nothing had come of this, nothing but heartbreak and disappointment for Jane, and, as she'd said, the feeling of being stripped naked in front of the entire world.

Matt slowed to take a left turn, downshifting with far more force than necessary.

With the best of intentions, he and Manny had helped Tasha expose Jane to all of this. And then, when they were out of the picture, leaving Jane completely vulnerable, Kyle Rogers had stepped in, built up her trust in him, only to shatter it completely.

Matt took the turn faster than he should have. Shoving the shifter back into third, he tromped on the gas, moving up the dark, deserted street at a speed above the posted limit. After a block, he braked, slowing the car as he took control of his anger. No point in getting a ticket or, worse, running over some homeless person who happened to step into his path. Now, if that person happened to be Kyle Rogers...

Matt shook his head as he pulled into the parking lot on the side of his building. No, that would only get him charged with vehicular homicide. It wouldn't change anything. Wouldn't fix the past year of Jane's life—a year spent walling herself off instead of making new friends, or even falling in love.

With no life experience to fall back on, Jane had done what wounded animals do—holed up in a cave of her own creation. The thought filled Matt with anger as he entered his building. No matter how much work it took, no matter how much Jane resisted, he was going to shine a light into that cave—solve the mystery of who had put her there and bring him, her or them to justice. He was going to give Jane some sense of security so she could open up to life.

As the elevator rose to the third floor, he recalled the desire that had pulsed through him when Jane gazed into his eyes. He'd seen longing in her face. Succumbing to the urge to pull her into another, deeper kiss would have given him a few moments of pleasure, might have granted her a temporary sense of safety. But both would have been fleeting.

He couldn't give in to these urges, Matt told himself as he stepped out of the elevator. A single low-watt bulb lit his way across the deserted space leading to his private office. He stood in the doorway, staring into the dark, narrow room. Jane trusted him, and might very well misinterpret the intent behind even the briefest of kisses. And he doubted he had the control to stop at brief.

What, then? He couldn't remember the last relationship he'd had that went beyond purely physical attraction. He'd scoffed when Manny had warned that Jane had cast him in the role of romantic hero. The look in her eye tonight suggested Manny had been right. He had to be careful not to do anything to encourage that. For more years than he wanted to remember, he'd made sure he kept anyone from getting close enough to be disappointed by him. He needed to be doubly careful with Jane.

Turning on the light above the paper-strewn table, Matt finished sorting his research into piles. He had been Tasha Nichols's unwitting accomplice once, offering Jane empty hopes. He wasn't about to breach her trust by offering anything else that wasn't real. He needed to stick with what he knew—examining clues, pinning down facts.

Yes, he told himself a week later as he stood next to Jane on the bow of the ferry headed toward Sausalito, no matter how much he enjoyed her company, how intrigued he was by the woman she had become, he had to keep his association with Jane Ashbury strictly business.

A stiff breeze tugged at his hair as he rested his arms on the railing and gazed at the sunbeams dancing on the water ahead. His hands were cold, but he was warm within his brown leather jacket. The sound of the waves slapping the hull soothed his muscles. His eyes drifted shut; he'd had scant sleep the night before.

"You know," Jane said, "you didn't have to come with me. I can take care of myself."

Matt opened his eyes and turned to Jane. She wore a pale blue turtleneck, jeans, a heavy gray sweater and a blue backpack. Her cheeks were pink, and her bangs fluttered back from her forehead as her dark eyes met his, then shied away to stare out over the water.

Jane seemed nervous, unsure of herself. He'd caught a hint of those emotions in her hesitant words when he'd called her at noon, but had attributed them to the fact that his call had caught her just as she was about to leave the house. She needed to catch a bus for the wharf, she'd explained. She had contacted one of the galleries they'd visited on their last trip to Sausalito, and the owner had agreed to consider carrying some of her figures. She wanted to get those elves of hers over to Sausalito, then catch a ferry back to the city before it got dark.

The dark. He'd forgotten that Jane was almost as uncomfortable in the dark as she was in crowds. When he'd offered to drive her over the bridge and back, Jane had hesitated, then said no. She'd spent the past several days working in her room. She needed some sunshine and fresh air. Riding the ferry would give her that.

A day in the sun had sounded good to Matt, especially since he'd spent most of the past week in front of a computer. This morning had been more of the same, interspersed with a series of telephone calls setting his plan in motion. With that completed, there was nothing to do but wait, something he did poorly, so he'd asked Jane if she would mind some company on her jaunt.

Now, seeing the way Jane stared resolutely over the water, he wondered if her hesitant "Uh…sure" in response to his offer to accompany her shouldn't have told him that she would have preferred to take this trip alone.

"No," he said quietly. "I didn't *have* to come with you. I wanted to. I hope I'm not messing up some plan—"

"No," Jane broke in. "I have no plans to mess up. But what about you?" Jane turned to him, her face set. "You're a busy man. I'm sure you and Jack have other cases that could use your attention. I can't believe you have time for a ferry ride, unless you're here just to keep an eye on me. To make sure I don't suddenly say the wrong thing to the wrong person."

She paused to glance around, then locked eyes with him before going on in a softer tone. "I don't need a babysitter, Matt. I may not have past memories to draw upon, but believe me, this past year has taught me a lot about keeping to myself, about revealing only what I want to reveal. I don't need you to protect me from myself."

Matt could only stare at her troubled eyes, wondering what had ever made him think that this strong woman was in need of protection. A second later, she broke eye contact to stare ahead, blinking into the wind.

Matt recognized the gesture from his childhood. How many times had he fought tears or found some way to hide them or make them dry before they fell? How long had it been since any of that had been necessary, since he'd learned to brush away emotional pain before it could even surface? He placed his hand on Jane's. He didn't know what to say, how to offer sympathy for feelings she was trying to deny.

She turned to him and, before he could say a word, spoke quickly. "I don't know what made me say that. I…I'm not used to being able to talk to anyone about all this. Here you are, the one person besides Zoe that I feel safe enough to speak my mind around, and I take a year of biting my tongue out on you. I'm sorry."

Matt shook his head. "Don't be. I'm the one who should apologize. If I'd suspected how difficult all this was on you, I'd have followed up on your case long ago." He paused. "But that isn't why I wanted to come along today. You were right when you said that Jack and I are busy. At the moment, things have reached a standstill, on your case and several others. So, I thought that riding a ferry across the bay with you would give me some downtime, a commodity I've allowed myself very little of this past year. I also figured it would give me a chance to tell you how our plan to learn about Bertrand's longtime employees and their offspring is progressing."

Chapter Ten

"*O*ur plan?" Jane asked.

As Jane stared into Matt's eyes, she became aware of his hand holding hers, of the connection that flowed between them. Her heart began to race wildly, her cold cheeks to flame.

Careful, a voice warned. *Don't imagine for one moment that when Matt Sullivan holds your hand or looks into your eyes, there is anything the least romantic about his actions. He's made it clear that he sees you as the victim of a crime. His use of the word* our *means he's accepted you as a partner in this investigation. Nothing else.*

"Well," Jane managed to say. "How is our plan going?"

"Good, I think."

Matt released her hand and shoved both of his into his jacket pockets. He turned toward her, resting one elbow on the railing. Missing the warmth of his hand over hers, Jane mirrored his actions.

"I looked through all the information I had gathered on Bertrand's, and wrote up a proposal outlining my plan to get quotes from longtime employees regarding the store's dedication to making each Christmas magical for both workers and customers. I suggested that the article would include comments from Bestco management, explaining their plan to…I think I said 'bring these traditions into the new century.' That's corporate-speak for 'get by as cheaply as possible without losing too many customers.'"

When he paused, Jane asked, "Aren't you being a bit pessimistic, not to mention cynical?"

Matt gave her one of those half smiles that never failed to make her heart race.

"I like to think of it as being realistic. And perhaps, preparing myself for disappointment. My only really nice memories of Christmas are connected to the first time I saw Bertrand's window. I'd hate to see it go the way of the dinosaur."

For one moment, Jane could almost swear she was looking at the wistful features of a five- or six-year-old boy. His mouth took on an ironic twist.

"Anyway, I e-mailed the proposal to my friend at the *Chronicle*. Ted called back to say it wasn't bad for an amateur like me, then promised to doctor it up, get it over to someone he knows at Bestco. Today the public relations guy for the company called to say the idea is under consideration. He'll let me know if and when I can start interviewing Bertrand's employees."

"You mean when *we* could talk to the employees."

"Exactly."

"And if Bestco doesn't agree to the article?"

Matt gave her a mock scowl. "I think I mentioned I was looking for some relaxation today. Let's pretend you didn't ask that question, deliver your little people, then get off the tourist track and enjoy the sunshine. Okay?"

It sounded *very* okay to Jane. The first stop was the gift shop, where the owner, Robin Jones, exclaimed excitedly over each piece as Jane brought them out. Along with figures in Christmas crimson and emerald green, she'd brought several of the woodland creatures garbed in shades of olive, brown and burgundy.

After they worked out a pricing system and percentage deal, Jane left, with Matt at her side. They turned right, heading toward the bay. Several feet from the door, Matt released a low whistle.

"Jeez," he said. "I had no idea the price that fantasy commanded."

"I was surprised, too, when I learned how much my first little people had sold for in Maine. The market out here seems even better. I'm both surprised and thrilled to find I can make a living at something I love doing."

"It's going to be interesting to find out where these talents of yours come from," Matt said.

Jane considered his words. "You know, I never thought about that."

"Well, after seeing the work you do, I'm guessing you must have been a rather accomplished artist. I figured your little people would all look alike, other than variations in the clothes they wore. But each face is so lifelike...and they're all completely different."

"Of course. Each one has its own personality. Most of them are very nice and helpful, but others are just a bit mischievous."

Matt lifted his eyebrows. "I see. And just what sort of mischief do these elves get into?"

Jane felt her face grow warm. "You're laughing at me."

Matt stopped walking and turned to her. "I am not. Look at this face. Do you see even a hint of a smile?"

Jane studied his features. He was the picture of wounded innocence, with not one twitch at either corner of his lips. She started to shake her head, then caught the gleam in his green eyes.

"I'm not some nutty old lady, talking to her dolls," she said.

"Of course you aren't."

"It helps me to form their faces if I make up little stories about them."

"Of course it does."

This time the corners of Matt's mouth did twitch. He turned, as if to hide his expression, then pointed to the concrete stairway leading up to their right. "Want some exercise? I'll race you to the top."

Jane raised her eyebrows at the length and steepness of the stairway, then accepted the challenge. "Looks like a good workout. You're on."

They turned at the same moment, each choosing one side of the iron railing that ran up the center of the steps, and began to climb. Feet pounding, Jane reached the first landing only seconds behind Matt. She was already hot from exertion, but didn't want to lose time removing her sweater, so she started up the next flight.

The stairway narrowed here, with no railing to hold on to. Trees grew on either side of the path, forming a canopy that rustled in the wind as Jane found her steps slowing slightly. Her lungs began to ache, but she was determined to keep up with the man at her side, the man who didn't seem to be having any trouble at all catching *his* breath.

As they neared the top of the rise, the stairs gave way to a ramplike stretch of concrete, no less steep than the steps. Jane's mouth was dry from pulling air into lungs that now burned as if demanding that she stop. When Matt pulled farther ahead, she realized that she would never catch up with him, and finally let her aching legs slow.

A moment later, Matt reached the top of the hill and turned toward her, removed his jacket, hooked his finger into the collar and draped it over his shoulder. As Jane drew closer, she was pleased to note that he had the decency to appear as if he was also fighting to regain a normal breathing pattern.

"Okay," she said, drew in another breath and went on, "you are officially…king of the hill." She slid her nearly empty backpack off and removed her sweater as she forced herself up the last few feet. "What," she panted, "made me think this would be a good idea?"

"Maybe—" Matt took two quick breaths as he grabbed her hand and pulled her to him, then twirled her around to face down the hill in one swift motion "—it was this."

Jane knew he was referring to the view. The stretch of blue-green water below, with the lush Tiburon Peninsula rising in the distance, was a postcard shot of outstanding beauty. But to Jane "this" referred to standing so close to the man behind her that the heat of his body warmed her back. She could actually feel the beat of his heart against her shoulder blades, was acutely aware of the forearm he'd casually draped across the front of her, of the hand resting on her shoulder, of his warm breath caressing her ear.

In spite of the wind blowing down the hill behind them, Jane was still hot from the climb. Being so close to Matt raised her temperature to a truly uncomfortable level, but she wasn't about to move. She was going to enjoy the moment, bask in his embrace, no matter how impersonal it might be, store up the memory for the next time she woke in the darkness, alone and terrified.

"This is good."

Matt's words so perfectly expressed Jane's feelings that she simply nodded. Afraid to do or say anything that might break the mood, she continued to gaze ahead, watching a pair of seagulls perform a slow, lazy circular dance below, mere feet above the rippling water.

But when Matt drew a deep breath and said, "You're good for me, you know?" Jane slipped from his light embrace and turned to look at him in surprise.

"How's that?"

Matt gave her one of those lopsided grins. "Well, for the first time in all the months since Jack and I started the business, I've actually gotten outside to enjoy a bit of nature. Until I took you to the beach last week, my life had consisted of hours interviewing clients and suspects, searching the Internet or sitting in court. Of course, from time to time I'd be out on some sort of surveillance, but even if that takes you to a park, your attention is on the subject, not…"

Matt's hand came to rest on the side of Jane's face as he looked into her eyes. She realized she'd stopped breathing, waiting for him to finish.

"Not on the beauty around you."

Jane could feel her cheeks grow hotter. She saw Matt's eyes darken, saw his head bend toward hers. Then, just as her lips were parting of their own accord, he straightened. A small vertical line formed between his eyebrows as he suddenly looked past her.

"So," he said, "this is a true luxury. Since I'm discussing a case with a client, the workaholic in me is happy, but I'm still getting a chance to appreciate things I've been missing. Like a certain bookstore I haven't visited in years. Let's see if it's still there."

With that, he turned. Jane stuffed her sweater into her backpack, then slung the pack over her shoulder. She matched Matt's leisurely pace, telling herself with each step that her imagination was getting out of hand. Matt Sullivan had not been about to kiss her.

A quick sideways glance showed that he was still frowning. As she wondered why, it suddenly occurred to her that unlike those last two incidents, in which the darkness of night had undoubtedly obscured her willing anticipation of the kisses-that-never-came, today her longing must have been as clear as…the nose on her face. Or, to be more exact, her parted lips and half-closed eyes.

The last thing she wanted was to give Matt an impression of her as hopelessly love-struck. Well, she supposed that would actually be the *correct* impression. She was certainly feeling *something* struck. Whenever Matt stood near her and looked into her eyes, her heart raced and her knees grew weak.

But she didn't want Matt to see her as needy, or silly.

Or worse, to be embarrassed by whatever he may have seen in her eyes back there. And walking silently along next to him wasn't likely to erase whatever impression he'd formed. Searching for something to talk about, she jumped on the first subject that came to mind.

"You know," she said, "you didn't strike me as the workaholic type when you were working my case last year."

Matt gave her a tight smile. "I'm sure I wasn't. I loved my job, and threw myself into each case I was assigned to. But it's completely different when you work for yourself. The long days aren't a problem, at least for me. The paperwork, however, is another matter altogether."

At the end of the street, they started downhill.

"Thank God we found Paula," Matt went on. "She keeps that stuff organized, freeing us up to reap the benefit of the time we put into building our reputation. Though, sometimes it seems all the work coming our way is too much of a good thing. It's getting hard on Jack. He has to commute between the city and San Rafael. Me, I sleep at the office and have no personal life."

No personal life? Jane smiled at that, then immediately frowned.

"What's wrong?"

Matt's question took her by surprise. She turned to him as they neared the bottom of the hill. "Wrong?"

"Yeah, you're frowning. Something I said?"

No, she thought. *Something I was feeling. Some selfish part of me that took comfort from knowing I wasn't the only one living a lonely life this past year.*

Jane caught herself before she could give voice to these thoughts. As they reached the bottom of the hill and turned onto the quiet street that ran parallel to the busy main road into town, Jane again fumbled for something to say.

"Oh, I just was thinking about all the hours I put into my business," she lied. "I can't think of anything I don't like about working for myself, even the uncertainty. It keeps me busy—planning new and fresh designs. Fills my mind.''

"That's important to you, isn't it?''

"What's important?''

"Keeping your mind filled. It just occurred to me what it must have been like for you when you woke up and didn't remember anything.''

Jane shrugged. "That's why I spent so much time reading.''

"Well, then, this is the perfect place for you,'' Matt said as he stopped walking. He pointed down a wide set of stairs leading from the sidewalk to the basement level of the building on their left. "This is one of my favorite used bookstores. Haven't been here since…I can't remember when. We have about a half hour before we need to head back to catch the ferry.'' He gestured with his left hand toward the store's entrance. "Shall we?''

The place was a book lover's dream. Rows of shelves were packed with used books, arranged and labeled by category from automobiles to zoology. Jane shuffled between the shelving units, carefully stepping around the overflow arranged in stacks on the floor.

She slowly became aware of the soft tones of an instrumental version of "God Rest Ye, Merry Gentlemen.'' Out of the corner of her eye, she saw that Matt was watching her. No doubt checking to see if the music was going to trigger some memory.

Fighting off her annoyance, she stepped behind a bookcase and began to browse. Her irritation completely dissolved when she discovered two out-of-print titles she'd been searching for. As she made her way to the cash register in the front, she sidestepped a tall stack of books nearly blocking the aisle. The cover of the top one caught her eye. A surfer, balanced on a bright red board, slid down a gray wave, white foam curling behind him beneath the title *Surfing Northern California*.

Jane grabbed it, then hurried to the wooden counter to

the right of the door. She managed to pay for her purchases and get them into her backpack before Matt came up to buy five paperbacks.

She waited until they were up on the sidewalk and halfway down the block before she said, "I got something for you."

"For me?" Matt looked surprised, pleased and suspicious, all at the same time. "What? And more important, why?"

"Well, the answer to *why* is that you won't let me pay you for all this work you're doing."

Matt was frowning now. "Look, I told you, this is about unfinished business, not about making money or making a name for myself or any—"

"I know," Jane broke in. "I just…saw this and thought of you."

She drew the book out and handed it to Matt. He stared at the cover. When he didn't say anything, Jane asked, "Do you already have a copy?"

Matt shook his head. His features softened. "This was really thoughtful of you."

"Well, I'm sure you already know the best places to surf in the area, but the subtitle mentioned *secret beaches,* and I thought maybe…"

Jane stopped speaking when she noticed how taut Matt's features had grown, how closed his expression had become. Her stomach twisted as she said, "You don't surf anymore—do you."

Matt shook his head. "No. The doctors warned that the twisting motion required to keep me on the board could screw up my knee all over again."

"I'm sorry. In the hospital I met several people recovering from knee replacement surgery. They seemed to think it was this miraculous procedure, that they were going to be as good as new."

"Yeah. That's the promise—partial bionic men and women." Matt attempted a smile. "Well, the surgery works that way in most cases. However, I suffered permanent damage to the nerves and tendons that control the knee's stability. No matter how good my new joint is, I have to watch how I move. Recovering from a ripped tendon is a long and painful process, one I'd rather not go through again.''

By the time Matt finished speaking, Jane's face felt hot, her throat tight as she recalled his joyful exhilaration the day he and Manny had taken her to the beach.

''I'm sorry,'' she managed to say.

Matt flashed her a look that appeared almost carefree. ''Don't be. I get in some bodysurfing and boogie-boarding from time to time, so I'll definitely be able to use this book.''

Just not like the guy on the cover, Jane finished silently.

''Hey, we'd better hurry,'' he said briskly, ''if we want to catch that ferry.''

With that, he turned and stepped forward. As Jane hurried to keep up with him, she glanced at his face and saw him grimace slightly, then noticed this happened almost every time he placed his weight on his right leg. As she recalled their slow descent from the hill after they'd raced up the steps, she felt slightly sick, and completely embarrassed that she hadn't realized how Matt's injury might have changed his life.

Slowly, though, she began to feel defensive.

How was she supposed to have known about his continuing problem? It wasn't as if the man ever spoke about himself. Every time something came up about his personal life, whether it be how he felt about family, or Manny's death, or if he was in pain, or...*anything,* he always brushed her off with that wide, dimpled smile of his, then changed the subject. Yet, she was expected to tell him everything about her life, past and present, no matter how reluctant she might be to reveal these details.

Jane was still fuming when they reached the boarding area on the dock. She followed Matt onto the ferry. The

wind had picked up, the sun was setting and the temperature
had dropped, so she wasn't surprised when he led her to a
table inside the boat, next to a wide window on the star-
board side.

Jane assumed he'd commandeered this spot so they could
watch the sun descending through a tattered bank of clouds
forming beyond the Golden Gate Bridge, far out to sea. The
sunset was a magnificent blend of oranges, pinks and pur-
ples, but Jane took scant pleasure in it. Occasional glances
in Matt's direction revealed that he wasn't enjoying the sunset, either. His attention appeared to be focused on the ever-
darkening gray-green water just past the ferry's railing.

Neither of them said a word until they had disembarked
near Fisherman's Wharf, when Matt asked, "Do you feel
like dinner? We could—"

"No, thank you," Jane said quickly. "I have some other
pieces I need to finish for a place called The Crystal Cave
in the Embarcadero Center."

In the fading light, Jane could just make out Matt's
frown. "Hey," he said as he placed his hand on her shoulder. "I'm sorry for being such lousy company. I got to
thinking about your question."

"Yeah? What question would that be?"

"What I was going to do if Bestco doesn't buy the idea
of my writing that story."

Jane shrugged. "You know, Matt. Maybe that would be
all for the best. It's a long shot, anyway, to hope that these
interviews might unearth whatever I might have had with
the place some twenty or so years ago. And, frankly, I just
don't think I'm up to any more mind probing."

With that she turned, breaking his light hold on her
shoulder, and began walking west. It was about two miles
to Zoe's house, but most of the trek would be on level
ground and along well-lit streets. The walk would be safe
enough, and maybe by the time she got home she would
feel calm enough to work.

It didn't surprise her at all to find Matt striding along

next to her. She was surprised, however, when he stopped, grabbed her arm and turned her to face him. She gasped when he bent toward her and asked, "What the hell is wrong with you all of a sudden?"

Jane stared into his suspicious eyes as the words built up in her chest. "Nothing at all is wrong with me, Matt. I think that anyone in my position would be a tiny bit ticked off."

"And just what position would that be?"

"Oh, I don't know. A tree that's been picked clean, perhaps. You have repeatedly questioned me about every aspect of the life I've made for myself in the past year. Nothing seems too unimportant in your eyes. I suppose I should feel flattered, but, of course, you aren't interested in me as a person, you are obsessed with Jane Doe Number Thirteen."

She held up her hand when he started to speak. "Look. I know you want to get justice for what happened to me. I can even accept that I might be in danger at some future date from whoever tried to kill me. What I can't deal with is feeling like I'm some bug lying on a slide beneath your microscope."

When she finished speaking, Matt was silent for a moment, then asked, "Is there anything more?"

Jane shook her head, then said, "Wait. Yes, there is. Do you remember my telling you that being interviewed by Tasha made me feel like I was being stripped naked in front of thousands of television viewers? Well, you make me feel exactly the same. It's less public, but in some ways worse. You don't reveal one thing about yourself. Other than the fact that you have a cousin named Jack who has a wife named Libby, I know nothing about your family, nothing about how you really feel about the shooting that almost killed you. You stand there in full armor, with your bright smile that says everything is fine with you and it's none of my business if it isn't. Yet I'm supposed to reveal every secret I ever had."

With that, Jane pivoted from him again. Matt continued

to hold her elbow. He stepped in front of her, took hold of her other arm and stared darkly into her eyes. They stood, gazes locked for several heartbeats, then Matt breathed, "Damn," before pulling Jane toward him.

Then he lowered his head and his lips closed over hers.

The kiss was not gentle. Matt's mouth held hers firmly; his right hand released her arm, then cupped the back of her head. But Jane found nothing painful about the increased pressure. As the contact increased, she leaned into it. Her left hand lifted, came to rest at his waist. Her fingers found his belt and closed over it, holding on tightly as his lips parted and closed again over hers, as if to claim them more fully. Her heart raced, her mind froze, her lips pressed up to his, her breasts rejoiced as they came into contact with the heat of his chest.

And then, the kiss was over.

Matt straightened. Only five inches separated their lips, a scant two their chests—just enough for the chill wind to blow between them. Jane went from pleasantly warm to icy cold in the second it took to open her eyes and look into Matt's.

She was hardly surprised to see that they gave no hint to his feelings. He turned, pulling her with him as he said, "I'm going to take you back to Zoe's."

Jane had no energy for arguing. Or for thinking, for that matter. Feeling as if she'd somehow been swept up by a tornado and dropped off in some foreign land, she sat silently in the passenger seat for the short drive.

When Matt pulled the car to a stop in Zoe's driveway, he turned to Jane. His eyes were still unreadable.

"Listen," he said, "you can continue to help me with the case, or ignore the whole thing. It's up to you. I'll call you when I get a date for those interviews."

Jane didn't say a word. She only wanted to escape Matt's presence and get up to her room, where she could be alone with the mixture of anger, wonder and embarrassment that gripped her stomach, burned upon her lips and threatened to bring tears to her eyes.

Chapter Eleven

Jane forced herself to work that night. But as she sculpted clay, forming noses, mouths, delicately etching the wrinkles and lines that gave each face its distinctive personality, a part of her mind strayed to the subject of Matt Sullivan. And that kiss.

She knew what had led up to that moment, at least her part of it. She'd been infatuated with Matt practically from the time he walked into her hospital room, over a year ago. Her adolescent state of mind at the time had led her to picture Matt as the hero in the books she read, even if the character had blond hair.

Zoe had helped her see that this emotional inexperience had also prevented her from recognizing Kyle Rogers as a sexual predator. And as frightening as that experience had been, it had forced her to grow up—taught her not to take people at face value, and had put an end to the need to please that had underscored her earlier interactions with people of all genders. She had learned to take control of her life.

Or, Jane wondered, had she just learned to manage it into a small, safe circle?

When Matt Sullivan came back into her life, he'd asked just that—then all but dared her to step out of the secure, predictable world she'd locked herself into. And, she told herself, she'd accepted the challenge. A bit reluctantly, perhaps, but she hadn't run away completely.

And she wasn't going to now, Jane told herself as she placed the finished faces onto a backing sheet to dry before their trip to the oven. She hurried into her pajamas, then got into bed, determined to go to sleep. But when she closed her eyes, all she could see was Matt's eyes, shadowed with pain, even as his lips curved into a smile.

The kiss they had shared, she realized, was just like that seemingly carefree smile of his—a way of dealing with frustration, of shutting off the emotions that their argument had cued up. She doubted it had anything to do with any romantic feelings he might have for her.

Jane had read about a lot of conflicted heroes. The actions of these men seemed so understandable in the pages of a book, but she had no narrator to tell her what was going on in Matt's mind. No guide to assure her that he really was one of the good guys, someone who was capable of returning love, rather than just inspiring it. No clue to the source of his pain. Only her heart whispering to trust.

On Friday, Matt hung up the telephone and glanced at the clock. Would an hour be enough notice? It was going to have to be, he decided as he lifted the telephone receiver and dialed.

Jane answered on the third ring. Matt heard the sleep in her voice as she said, ''Hello?''

''I found a message on my machine last night,'' he stated without introduction. ''My friend at the *Chronicle* says

Bestco will have several of their employees assembled today at eleven for me to interview. Do you want to go?''

Matt listened to five seconds of silence before Jane replied, ''Yes. I can meet you there. There's a bus that leaves
at—''

''I'll pick you up at ten,'' Matt said. ''You'll be playing
the part of my assistant. Dress accordingly.''

When Matt pulled up in front of Zoe's, a storm was
creeping into town on a drizzle. Through the gray mist, he
saw Jane standing on the bottom step, wearing a navy-blue
jacket, matching trousers and a white blouse. Her features
were obscured by a huge black umbrella, but as Jane
crossed in front of the Jeep, Matt noticed she was wearing
narrow black-framed glasses.

His muscles tightened as he noticed the solemn set of her
features. He should probably say something about that kiss
that he'd given her—no, more like forced upon her—last
night. But what could he say? That he was sorry?

That wouldn't really be true. The memory of her lips on
his had stayed with him long after he'd dropped her off at
Zoe's—a sweet, searing sensation that left no room for regrets. Besides, he was fairly certain that she had kissed him
back. At least, it had seemed that way when he'd finally
come to his senses and realized he'd broken the first of his
self-imposed rules: Never get personally involved with a
client.

He leaned over to pull on the passenger side handle and
push the door open for Jane, as she collapsed her umbrella
and hurried into the seat. She hadn't looked at him yet. Matt
made a split-second decision. Unless Jane brought the subject up, the best way to avoid any further personal involve-
ment was to focus on the case.

As she pulled the door shut, he searched for a neutral
subject. Jane reached for the seat belt. He saw her glance
at him once, her smoky eyes unreadable behind the narrow
glasses. He decided her eyewear was a safe subject and
jumped on it.

"Good idea," he said.

Jane paused in the act of fastening her shoulder belt to lift her eyebrows. "It's the law."

It took a moment for Matt to follow her train of thought. Then he grinned. "I wasn't talking about buckling up, I meant the glasses."

"Oh." She shrugged. "Well, I kept insisting that no one at Bertrand's would recognize me, since I don't look anything like the bald, starving refugee that appeared in the paper and on the news last year. Then it occurred to me that since my features have filled out a bit, I might actually bear some resemblance to the person I once was. After all, the plastic surgeon did say he was guided by a computer projection based on the facial bones that weren't completely smashed."

Matt finished backing out of the driveway, turned the wheel to get the car pointed in the right direction, then shifted into first. "So the glasses are a disguise?"

"Yeah. You said something about the eye area not changing much. I figured that since I have twenty-twenty vision, I probably didn't wear glasses before. These are dime-store reading glasses with a really low correction level. I use them when I'm doing detail work, and they only blur my distance vision slightly. But if you think they're a silly idea, then—"

"Not at all." Matt turned onto Fillmore. "For one thing, they make you look very assistant-like."

"Well, thank you. And I suppose you look, very... writerly. Or maybe professorial."

Matt glanced suspiciously at the suggestion of a smile lurking at the corners of her mouth, then briefly down at his attire. Earlier in the week he'd gone to a thrift store, where he'd purchased a brown tweed jacket with suede patches on the elbows and a dark green sweater vest. Along with a white dress shirt, tan necktie and a pair of brown pants he already owned, the outfit, he thought, gave him the appearance of a casual intellectual.

Now he wondered if he hadn't gone a bit overboard.

"Something wrong?"

Jane shook her head. "No."

"You're laughing at me."

"I am not. It's just…"

"Just, what?"

"Well, if you were wearing the right kind of hat, you'd look very much like Professor Higgins."

Matt glanced in the side mirror, searching the left lane for an open space. Seeing nothing but an unbroken line of cars, he looked at Jane again. "Who's Professor Higgins?"

Jane looked at him like he'd asked who Santa Claus was. "Rex Harrison, in *My Fair Lady.* You've seen that movie, haven't you?"

Never one to miss the chance to get the most comic value out of a conversation, Matt responded with an elaborate shudder. "Oh, of course. It was my cousin Sharon's favorite movie. I can remember coming home from high school football practice to strains of 'I could have *dahnced* all night.'" His features took on a wounded expression. "Are you saying that people will take one look at me and start singing, 'Just you wait, 'Enry 'Iggins, just you wait'?"

Jane laughed out loud. "I doubt it," she said. "After all, you don't look anything like Rex Harrison. And you don't look like a detective or a cop, either, and that's good. Right?"

That wasn't the only thing that was good, Matt decided. The discussion of disguises had gotten them past any awkward discussion of the kiss they'd shared.

"Right," he replied. "So, now that we've gone over our wardrobes, let's get down to how we're going to play this charade today. I'm using the name Matthew Simpson. I'll introduce you as Jeanette Martin. Now, see that briefcase sitting on the back seat? I want you to carry it. Once we've met the employees, you'll set the tape recorder up. You'll also find a notebook in there. Your job…"

He paused to evaluate a spot that had just opened up in

the left lane. As he maneuvered into it, he heard Jane mutter the *Mission Impossible* refrain, "Your mission, if you choose to accept it..."

Matt grinned. "...is to sit next to me and appear to take down everything that's said."

"Appear to?"

"Right. I'll say that I like to have a backup transcription, in case something happens to the recorder or the tape. However, what you're really going to do is watch how people react and to note down any unusual behavior or expression you might see."

Matt stopped for a red light as he finished speaking. When he glanced over at Jane, she met his gaze and nodded.

"Okay. Anything else?"

"Sure. Cross your fingers. The more I think about this plan of mine, the bigger the haystack begins to look, and the smaller the needle."

A little over an hour later, Matt glanced around the pale green room that served as the employee's break room on Bertrand's mezzanine level. His back ached from sitting on a narrow stool, and he was growing frustrated.

Just as he'd feared, for the first twenty minutes he'd been forced to listen to the employees argue. Roughly half of the fifteen people felt things would change for the worse once Bestco took over, and the rest thought things would improve. This second group seemed particularly unhappy about the way things had been managed the past few years of John Bertrand's life as well as the year that his daughter, Noelle, had been in charge. They didn't seem to have any problem "speaking ill of the dead."

This discussion came to an abrupt end when Joshua Miller, Bestco's public relations manager, entered the room along with Bertrand's current owners, Aimee and Phillip Bertrand. However, Matt was still having trouble steering the discussion in the direction he wanted.

"The Bertrand star?" Wanda Hassock was saying in response to his most recent question.

The woman had worked in the store's lingerie department for forty-four of her sixty years. From her seat at the edge of the U-shaped front row, Wanda ran long, peach-toned fingernails through short dark hair teased to amazing heights. She glanced at Phillip Bertrand sitting across the room, as if checking for his approval before she answered.

"Well, the star has been the store's Christmas symbol ever since I started working here. I believe the crystal ornament was part of the dowry that came to Jean-Philippe, Senior...that would be your grandfather, wouldn't it?"

Phillip Bertrand was slender with a narrow face and medium-brown hair. Matt knew the man was twenty-seven. The cut of his charcoal-gray suit indicated expensive taste. Matt had also observed that Bertrand seemed rather bored with the proceedings, especially for someone who was going to continue on as the store's general manager once Bestco took over.

"No, Wanda." Phillip shook his head. "Jean-Philippe I was my *great*-grandfather. He didn't marry my great-grandmother until the year 1911. Five years earlier he'd commissioned the crystal piece to mark the opening of the store at the beginning of our first Christmas season in 1906. And, in consideration of the earthquake that had devastated the city eight months earlier, he had the star reproduced to become the store's primary holiday decoration, serving as a symbol of hope and renewal."

"As it will continue to do in the future."

This last was stated in a smooth tone by Joshua Miller. The thirty-something Bestco executive wore a gray suit that was several shades lighter than Phillip's. Matt figured it also cost several hundred dollars less. And where Phillip seemed bored, Miller appeared filled with boundless enthusiasm, anxious to make it clear that nothing would change when his company took the reins in several months.

Way too anxious, to Matt's mind. But then, he'd experienced enough bureaucratic posturing on the police force to recognize it when he saw it in a corporate setting. However, at least the conversation had moved on to the subject of the star. Perhaps he could salvage something of the day's work, after all.

"I'm confused about this ornament," Matt said. "I understand that the first year, the original star hung from the topmost branch in the store's window display. After that, it was replaced by a copy. Is that true?"

"Oh, most certainly," Aimee Bertrand replied.

Matt's research told him she was twenty-six, but she gave the appearance of being older. This probably had something to do with her perfectly applied eye shadow and bright red lipstick, along with the pale blond hair that curved around her slender face in a style reminiscent of Marilyn Monroe. The fire-engine-red suit trimmed in matching ostrich plumes that hugged her rail-thin body also lent an air of world-weary sophistication that was rare among the twenty-somethings he knew.

"The original ornament was far too valuable to leave hanging about in public," Aimee said, looking vaguely amused. "It's now in a safe-deposit box, along with several other priceless family heirlooms."

"Has it always been?"

Aimee's bored half smile disappeared, her bright red lips tightened. "No, actually. For years it hung near the top of the Christmas tree in our home. The year my mother died, however, someone dropped it while we were decorating the tree. Fortunately it caught on a lower limb, which prevented the crystal from shattering. My father decided it could no longer be trusted to clumsy hands, so he put it in the bank, where it is safe." She paused. Her lips curved ever so slightly. "Why do you ask?"

"Well…" Matt's mind raced, grasping for a way to move the conversation forward. "When I was researching Bertrand's Christmas traditions, I came across a picture of an old woman handing the star to a child. I believe the caption identified the woman as your great-grandmother, Louise, and said that the hanging of the Bertrand star was the highlight of the employee party, where the employees and their families helped decorate the store.''

"Oh, really?" For the first time, Aimee's green eyes showed some genuine interest. "I would love to see that article. Do you remember what year it was from?"

Not likely, Matt thought, considering he'd just made that tale up, hoping to direct the conversation toward any photographic record the store might have kept to chronicle these gatherings.

He shook his head.

"Oh." Aimee sighed and glanced at her brother. "That's a pity. We have very few pictures of Grandmere—that's what we called our great-grandmother. Actually, we hardly have any pictures of the family at all. Most of them were destroyed eleven years ago, when we had a fire in our home."

Matt remembered seeing a story on that fire, recalled that it had been started by Paul Bertrand's second wife, who'd apparently been smoking in bed. The woman died in the fire, which destroyed parts of the second and third floors of the family's Pacific Heights mansion.

"I'm sorry to hear that," he said. "Didn't the store keep photographs of company events on file?"

Aimee shrugged. "I never thought of that. I've been so busy performing my duties as head buyer that I've given little thought to the administrative details. Phillip?"

Her brother shook his head. "I'm afraid all my attention has been directed toward the financial aspects of the company. Graham might know if we have any old pictures."

He turned to a round gentleman with thin white hair, wearing a brown tweed suit and a green tie. Earlier, Graham Carmichael had introduced himself as the office manager and explained that he'd worked for Bertrand's since arriving from England thirty-four years ago.

His voice still held traces of a British accent as he replied. "We certainly do, sir. I shall be happy to show the gentleman what we have."

Having obtained this information, Matt was more than ready to bring the interview to an end. He'd hoped to learn more about the pre-Thanksgiving decorating parties themselves, but his questions had been answered by vague praise for the buffet dinner that had been served, and the pride the employees took in making the store ready for the holiday buying season.

"Well, then," he said, "I think I have what I need for my article. I'd like to thank you all for coming and for sharing your memories with me. And Mr. Miller for outlining Bestco's plans for the future."

Around the room people began to stand. Over the sound of scraping chairs, a deep voice echoed. "You don't have the whole story, Mr. Simpson."

Everyone in the room seemed to freeze. Matt looked in the direction of the voice. A man in a brown security guard uniform stood just inside the door, removing his cap to reveal graying red hair.

"I'm Harold O'Malley. I've been working for Bertrand's since I was eighteen years old, forty-seven years now. I know quite a bit about the place, as you can imagine, and I want to clarify a few things. No matter what has been said about Noelle here today, it should be made clear that she was the one who kept the holiday traditions going as long as they did. Nothing has been the same since Noelle's death. She never would have agreed to canceling the Thanksgiving Eve decorating party without giving us a decent explanation. I think this is something Mr. Simpson should know."

The man stood, hat in hand, as proud and as tall as his slightly paunchy five-foot-nine frame would allow, chin up as he looked first to Aimee, then to her brother. As the rest of the employees slowly sat down again, Phillip remained standing.

"Harold, I know my sister treated you as some sort of

uncle,'' he began softly. ''But you know that Noelle was acting…irrationally before she left for Europe. Since she insisted on running the store following our father's death without my help, or Aimee's, I assume that the stress finally got to her. That, plus the fact that the store was losing money.''

Phillip paused. ''I believe we did explain that in preparing to sell the store, we determined it would be a considerable saving to hire laborers to install the decorations, rather than putting on the elaborate buffet we served in the past. And if you recall, we took the matter to the employees. The majority said they no longer wanted to be forced to spend Thanksgiving Eve decorating the store.''

''Forced?'' Harold said as he stepped farther into the room. ''No one was ever forced. People looked forward to it.''

''Some, perhaps,'' Phillip replied with a smile, but his dark eyes were hard. ''Others, like Michelle Stewart here, felt she had to attend, or it would appear that she wasn't a loyal, committed employee.''

He indicated a tall woman with short brown hair. Matt recalled that she, like so many in the room, had gone to work for Bertrand's directly out of high school. In Michelle's case, this had been fifteen years ago.

Without rising from her chair, Michelle swiveled to face O'Malley. ''Harold, I know you loved Noelle. She and I were great friends, too. Once. We worked together when I first started here, and had a great time, until she went away to college. When she came back and became her father's assistant, she was different—cold and uptight, just like Mr. Bertrand. The store was everything to them. They were devoted to a version of the place…of the world…that no longer exists, and they were determined to keep that alive, no matter what.''

The guard shook his head. ''Noelle was not like her father. She wanted to please him, yes, but at the same time she wanted desperately for things to be as they had been in her grandparents' time. Noelle was the heart and soul of the company, just like Louise had been. And since Noelle's death, Bertrand's has been dying, as well—no matter what sort of pretty picture you paint for Mr. Simpson here.''

"Heart and soul?" This came from Aimee.

Matt could only see the woman's profile, but he could tell that her expression had grown as stony as her tone of voice.

"Try cold and grasping. And as to the decorating party…Harold, you of all people know how my sister felt about—''

"Hey!" a male voice broke in. "What's going on here?''

Chapter Twelve

Jane studied the man who had just entered the room. A chill danced down her spine. She shivered, then decided the door closing behind him must have just let in a cool breeze, for there was certainly nothing wrong with his looks.

Tall and built like a linebacker, he wore a dark blue suit and maroon tie. His thick sandy hair and wide smile gave his features a boyish charm that seemed to be at odds with the air of command in his bearing. He strode confidently forward, nodding to Phillip Bertrand as he passed the man. When he reached Aimee Bertrand's side, he took her hand.

"Is there a problem?" he asked.

Jane had arranged her stool several inches behind Matt's, where she could inconspicuously study the employees as Matt interviewed them. Now she watched Aimee Bertrand smile back at him and shrug.

"Not really," the young woman replied. "We were answering Mr. Simpson's questions about the holiday traditions here, and it seems Harold is still upset because we canceled the pre-Thanksgiving decorating party. I…I'm afraid I got a little defensive about it. You know how Phillip and I agonized over the decision. And we do realize that the turkeys we gave the employees aren't as personal as the dinner was, but—''

''It had to be done,'' the man finished.

He turned to Matt. Jane could see now that his eyes were a very pale blue. His smile was warm as he extended his hand. ''Mr. Simpson, hello. I'm Glen Helms, a member of the law firm that represents Bertrand's Department Store. It sounds like you're getting more than you bargained for here. I'm afraid that emotions always seem to run high this time of the year.''

''Of course,'' Matt said. ''It's a very busy period. I was just about to thank Phillip and Aimee for allowing me to spend this time with the employees.''

Behind Mr. Helms, Jane noticed several people glancing at one another nervously.

''We were thrilled to contribute to your article,'' Aimee said brightly, then turned to the group. ''It's time for all of you to get back on the floor. However, I must tell you what a good job everyone is doing out there. Don't you agree, Mr. Miller?''

The representative from Bestco stood at the back of the room, holding the door open as people began making their way out. ''Excellent job,'' the man replied. ''The sales figures thus far are phenomenal. If this keeps up, those bonus checks we mentioned are going to be quite hefty.''

Aimee turned to Glen Helms. ''We told Mr. Simpson about the bonus program Bestco is initiating.''

Helms squeezed her hand as he gave Matt a wide grin. ''That's an amazing show of good faith, you know. The corporation has no actual obligation to these employees until February, when the sale of the store becomes final.''

Matt turned to Jane. ''Are you getting all this down, Miss Martin?''

The expression in Matt's innocently widened eyes

seemed to suggest he found everything the handsome lawyer was saying to be a load of baloney. Or maybe she was just projecting her own assessment of the man.

"Yes, Mr. Simpson," she managed to respond.

Matt turned to face Helms and Aimee again. "I'd like to see those pictures, if your office manager can unearth them, Miss Bertrand."

"Pictures?" Helms asked.

"Mr. Simpson would like some shots of former Thanksgiving Eve functions," Aimee replied. "Graham seems to know where they are." She turned to Matt. "Would you like to follow me to the office?"

"Most definitely." Matt rose from his stool, then turned to Jane again. "Miss Martin, gather up the recorder and your notes and meet me at the store entrance."

Jane glanced at him sharply. The pictures he was going off to see might very well contain some image that would spark a memory. Shouldn't she be going with him? Matt seemed to read her thoughts, for his eyes held hers in a way that said *Trust me,* as clearly as any words.

"Certainly, Mr. Simpson," she replied, then watched Glen Helms and Aimee Bertrand escort Matt to the back of the room, where they exited with Phillip Bertrand and Joshua Miller.

The moment the door shut, Jane experienced a sense of abandonment. As she glanced around, this feeling changed. She felt suddenly and inexplicably anxious. Her shoulders tensed, her heart began to pound so loudly she could almost hear it in the eerie silence. Moving quickly, she placed the tape recorder and her notebook into the briefcase. The *click* of the lock as she shut the case echoed softly. Responding to her irrational but growing need to escape the room, she hurried out the door.

She didn't feel much better in the hallway. It was wide, bordered by beige walls, yet Jane felt as if she were walking down an ever-narrowing corridor as she made her way toward the service elevator that Joshua Miller had brought them up on earlier. The feeling that she was being watched prickled at the back of her neck. When the elevator doors opened, she stepped in and pushed the down button. Staring at the diamond pattern on the elevator's steel floor as the door slid shut, she took several deep breaths as the car slowly descended.

By the time it came to rest, her heart was no longer racing. The fear and depression had almost completely dissipated. When the door opened, Jane stepped into the loading area at the rear of the store. Waiting as a cart full of boxes was pushed by, she wondered just how long Matt was going to be. She moved toward the door that would take her to the department store's main floor, and decided to use the time to get in a little shopping. Christmas was getting nearer, she reminded herself as she pushed the door open and stepped onto the shiny black-and-cream harlequin-patterned floor, then made her way toward one of the gleaming oak counters. She still hadn't found the perfect scarf for—

Jane's thoughts froze as she became aware of the sea of humanity swirling around her.

The ornate turn-of-the-century ceilings that soared high above did little to ease her sense of claustrophobia, as a stream of people crossed in front of her, while still more shoppers made their way in the opposite direction behind her. As her breathing became difficult, she was poised to turn and run through the door she'd just left, until she remembered the electronic keypad that opened it. She hadn't been able to see the code Miller had punched when he guided her and Matt to the loading area earlier, so she was trapped, helpless to do—

No. The fingers of Jane's left hand tightened around the briefcase handle, her right hand grasped the purse strap hanging from her shoulder. *You are not helpless,* she told herself. *Nor are you trapped.*

Jane glanced to her left. Between two tall marble columns, each bearing a swag of evergreen that held a two-foot version of the Bertrand star, she caught sight of the revolving brass-and-glass door that led outside, twirling endlessly as a stream of people entered and departed the store. When she saw that more were streaming in than going out, her chest tightened, her heart again began to race.

She clenched her jaw. She was not going to give in to this ridiculous phobia. She had a gift to purchase, and she had the time to do it. All she needed to do was negotiate the crowds. Jane rose onto her toes to see if she could spot the accessories section, and she caught sight of a display of purses.

Scarves should be in the same general area, she told herself. And it wasn't that far off, she decided as she began walking in that direction. It shouldn't take her long to get there. That is, she fumed a few seconds later, if it weren't for the clump of people that had stopped right in the center of the aisle to discuss what to get for Uncle Joe. She sidestepped Uncle Joe's family, muttering a tense apology when she bumped into a package-laden woman moving in the opposite direction.

Moments later she reached the aisle that separated the perfume counter from the makeup section. She spotted a rack of scarves twenty feet in front of her and was halfway there when six teenage girls came out of an intersecting aisle and began marching, double file, in front of her. Slowing her pace to match theirs, Jane ordered the muscles in her shoulders to relax. The tension had just started to ease, when suddenly one of the girls in the front exclaimed, "Oh, dear. I dropped one."

All six stopped, bent down and began searching the floor. Jane had no idea what had been dropped, and didn't really care. She just wanted to get to the scarves, see if Bertrand's carried any that would suit both Zoe's taste and her own budget, then get herself safely on the other side of those revolving glass doors.

However, blocked by the giggling girls in front of her and the grumbling crowd of people behind her, Jane was now truly trapped. Her heart began to race again in spite of her attempts to breathe slowly and deeply. Her mouth grew dry, and she felt far too warm to be in the Winter Wonderland suggested by the song playing overhead.

Realizing that her panic was building toward the irrational irritation she experienced at Maxwell's, Jane pulled her attention from the music. As she focused on the star hanging on the column at the end of the aisle and tried to draw a calming breath into her chest, she became aware of a conversation in progress on her right.

"Are you sure you don't have it?"

"I'm sorry" came the not-so-apologetic reply. "I've been working here three months now, and I've never come across a perfume called *Fleurs de Rochaille*."

Jane glanced toward the perfume counter on her right, as a girl of about eighteen with long blond hair asked, "Do you think you could ask another salesperson? It's the one gift Great-Aunt Jessica asked for, and I'm leaving tomorrow to spend the holidays with her."

The salesgirl was tall and thin with brown hair that fell straight to her shoulders. There was absolutely no hint of compassion either in her stony features or her voice as she responded, "There isn't anyone else to ask. You still have eleven shopping days before Christmas. Perhaps you can locate the perfume once you reach your destination."

Jane felt the muscles in her shoulders grow more tense. She frowned as she watched the customer shake her head.

"My aunt lives in this tiny town in Montana. I think they have a Kmart, but I really doubt they would carry this scent. It's an old brand, but my mom said Bertrand's always has some. Are you sure you've looked everywhere?"

"Yes, I have," the clerk replied with barely disguised impatience.

Jane felt something snap, as if she'd suddenly been split in two. One moment she was standing silent witness to this little drama and the very next she was crossing the three feet to the counter and leaning forward to glare into the salesgirl's surprised brown eyes.

"You have *not* looked everywhere," Jane said. "If you had, you would have located several bottles of *Fleurs de Rochaille* in the back of the cabinet beneath the cash register. Go find it."

The clerk's wide eyes expressed a mixture of surprise and fear.

"Do it now," Jane said. "You've kept this person waiting far too long as it is."

The clerk turned, stepped to the register and hunkered down to open the oak cabinet door. Jane watched, jaw clenched, one hand grasping the briefcase handle, the other curled into a fist atop the glass countertop, as the clerk peered into the cabinet, then slid her arm in. Her straight hair formed a brown curtain that hid her features until she stood slowly, staring at something in her hand. She turned to walk back to where Jane and the customer waited.

"Is this what you wanted?" the clerk asked as she handed the blond woman a four-inch-tall white box.

Jane noticed the spray of flowers printed on the front of the package. As the customer breathed a relieved, "Oh, yes," Jane felt the room begin to spin.

She closed her eyes. When the sensation stopped, she opened them again. She stared at the open shelves on the other side of the counter, then noticed the woman staring back at her from behind the array of perfume bottles. As she slowly realized that the face she was seeing was her own, reflected in the mirrored backing, Jane felt someone touch her hand, then heard, "Thank you so very much."

Jane spun to find the blonde smiling at her. Whatever alien energy had brought about that sudden burst of knowledge and command had completely faded, leaving her feeling slightly drained, barely able to manage a weak smile in acknowledgment of the girl's gratitude.

"How did you know where that was?"

This question came from the salesclerk. Jane shook her

head slowly and pushed herself away from the counter. Turning, she discovered that the teenagers had gone, leaving the aisle relatively clear. Moving as if in a dream she weaved in and out of slower-moving people until she at last stood in front of the four glass doors revolving within their ornate gilded cage.

She remembered entering the store this way, hesitating as Matt strode forward, slowing to a stop as she watched the doors go round and round in a way she found somehow threatening. Matt had stopped in front of the door, turned and stared into her eyes for several seconds before walking back to her. Wordlessly taking her hand into his, he'd gently drawn her forward. When they'd reached the door, he'd released her hand and slipped his arm around her waist, then smoothly eased her into the next open space that swung by.

A moment later, they'd stepped out of the gilded cage and into the old-world feel that was Bertrand's. At the time, Jane had found it a wonderland of oak, marble and crystal that she longed to investigate. Now, she only wanted to escape the crowds, the music and that confusing confrontation at the perfume counter.

The revolving doors moved even more quickly than they had this morning, as people flooded through them. But Jane barely hesitated before stepping forward as one brass-edged door swung past. Once inside the open triangle, she kept moving, then stepped quickly out on the other side.

Directly into the driving rain.

Blinking, Jane made her way to the side of the building beneath a five-foot awning, where several people stood shifting their packages so they could open their umbrellas. She had just turned to stare through the rain at the huge Christmas tree in the center of Union Square, when she heard a man say, "Good job back there."

Jane looked up as Matt pushed his dark, damp hair back from his forehead. Jane wondered how he could have known what happened at the perfume counter. Apparently noting her confusion, he jerked his thumb toward the entrance to the store.

"I was heading for the door myself when I saw you walk through, smooth as a hot knife through butter."

"Oh, that."

The lost, only-half-here tone in Jane's voice made Matt go suddenly still. He studied the gray-brown of her eyes and saw that although they appeared to be looking directly into his, there was something decidedly unfocused in them.

"What's wrong?" he asked softly.

Jane's expression didn't change at all. "I'm not sure, exactly. I apparently had another memory."

"Apparently?"

He saw Jane blink. Her eyes suddenly looked frightened. She opened her mouth, but before she could say a word, Matt said, "Not here."

He glanced at the people crowded around. In spite of the rain pounding on the awning, it would be too easy for someone to overhear anything Jane had to say.

"Where's your umbrella?"

Jane moved slowly, as if half her mind were somewhere else, reached into her shoulder bag and fumbled around before drawing out an eight-inch bundle of black nylon and metal. Matt took the umbrella and opened it. Holding it aloft, he placed his other arm around her waist and drew her close to his side as he guided her across the street.

When they reached the parking area beneath Union Square, Matt collapsed the umbrella, then took Jane's hand and led her toward his Jeep. Once they were both in their seats, he turned to her.

"Okay," he said. "I want to hear all about this 'apparent' memory of yours. What happened?"

Jane shook her head. "I'm...not sure I know."

Tension tempted Matt to shout at Jane, shock her out of the mental fog that seemed to be holding her in its grip. But years of conducting interrogations with reluctant, confused or drugged-out individuals had taught him a certain kind of patience.

He watched Jane stare at the V of his knit vest. Her look of concentration suggested she was putting her thoughts together. Then she took a deep breath and lifted her eyes to his.

"I got stuck in the middle of an aisle near the perfume counter," she said. "I heard a young woman ask for some special brand of perfume, and the salesclerk wasn't being particularly helpful. The customer was practically in tears, begging the clerk to look again. When the salesgirl adamantly refused, I…became furious. Without thinking, I walked over to the counter, told the salesperson where to find the boxes the customer was looking for, and ordered her to get it."

Jane stopped speaking and glanced away, then met his eyes again before saying, "Matt, the perfume was right where I'd said it would be."

Matt slumped back into the corner formed by the car door and the driver's seat. "Wow."

Jane hadn't moved. She stared at him, eyes wide.

"That's not all," she said.

Matt raised his eyebrows. Jane hesitated before she went on.

"When I looked at the mirrored display on the other side of the counter, I didn't recognize myself."

"What do you mean?"

"I saw this woman with short brown hair framing this narrow face, and felt a moment of…surprise, I guess. Then suddenly I knew I was looking at my own reflection, and I became aware of everything I'd said to the salesgirl. And worse, *how* I'd said it."

The sudden tears that filled Jane's eyes took Matt completely by surprise. He could only watch as Jane blinked rapidly, before turning her head to gaze out the passenger window. Matt stared at the back of her head as he tried to make sense of what she'd just told him. Realizing that the picture was too incomplete to make sense, he reached across and touched her arm gently.

"It's okay, Jane."

She swiveled toward him so quickly that he pulled his hand back, as if it were in danger of being bitten.

"No, it's not okay."

Jane brushed away the tears that had fallen onto her cheeks. "You weren't there. You didn't hear the way I spoke to that clerk. I sounded even bitchier than I did that day in Maxwell's."

Matt again placed a hand on her arm. "You did say the salesclerk wasn't being helpful."

"She was being downright rude. But that didn't give me the right to order her about like I was the Queen of Bertrand's, or something."

For the second time in less than fifteen minutes, Matt felt himself go completely still. His brain, however, worked furiously, connecting the story Jane had just told him with several other things he'd heard that day. Slowly a theory began to form. An almost impossible blend of speculation and half-recalled facts that needed verification as soon as was humanly possible.

Jane looked both confused and scared. Taking both of her hands in his, Matt looked deep into her eyes. "Who are you?" he asked softly.

Her frown told him she had no idea what he was asking. He rephrased his question. "What is your name? Right here, right now?"

She drew a shaky breath. "Jane Ashbury."

"That's right. And you chose that name, didn't you?"

Jane nodded.

"You have also chosen the kind of work you do, the kind of people you associate with and way you interact with them, right?"

"Yes, but—"

"Jane," Matt broke in. "Nothing that you discover about

the person you were in the past will change the person you've created. The person I've come to—"

Matt stopped speaking. Had he been about to tell Jane that he *loved* her?

He was aware of Jane's slender hands in his, her eyes gazing up at him, still glistening with unshed tears. His arms ached with the urge to pull her to him, to cradle her against his chest; his lips longed to feel hers beneath them. But that wasn't love. It was sympathy. It was desire. It was a need to connect with someone that went so deep that it burned the pit of his stomach.

It was an impulse he couldn't allow himself to give in to. He knew the kind of disappointment this would bring about—the promises that couldn't be kept. Love existed for other people—Jack and Libby, Jack's parents.

But not for him.

He refused to speak of something he didn't believe in, to someone as vulnerable as Jane, so he searched his mind for some way to finish that sentence that would give Jane the assurance she so richly deserved.

"The person I've come to think of as one of the most courageous people I've ever met," he said. "On or off the police department."

Jane glanced away and sighed. "If I'm so courageous, why do I feel so scared?"

Matt squeezed her hands. When her eyes met his again, he grinned. "Haven't you ever heard that courage isn't the absence of fear, but going forward in spite of it?"

Jane attempted a smile. "I don't know. You'll have to ask that person I became at the perfume counter. The one with my memories of the past and the lack of people skills."

"Well," he said as he released her hand and reached for the key. "When we finally drag the Queen of Bertrand's to the surface again, I'm sure she'll be able to teach you all sorts of things. And you can give her a lesson or two in civility."

After checking his mirrors, Matt backed out of the parking space, then turned the car toward the exit ramp.

"Where are we going now?" Jane asked.

Matt considered sharing his newly formed hypothesis with Jane. She had, after all, insisted upon being a partner in this investigation. But he recalled all the times in the past when she'd gotten her hopes up, only to have them dashed. This time, he wanted to be sure of his facts—as much as possible, anyway—before he even hinted at what he was thinking.

"We're going to my office," he replied. "And then, to a party."

Chapter Thirteen

"What do you mean, a party?"

Matt took his change from the woman at the parking booth and pulled forward. When he reached the street, he turned on the windshield wipers, then glanced at Jane as he waited for an opportunity to move into traffic.

"It's the annual McDermott wrapping-paper-making and popcorn-stringing get-together. This year it's going to be held at Jack and Libby's."

Something he wouldn't have remembered at all if he didn't need Libby's assistance to prove his recent half-formed theory.

"Well, if it's a family thing, maybe you should drop me back at Zoe's after we go to the office."

Just as Jane finished speaking, Matt pulled onto the street, only to be stopped by a red light at the end of the block. He turned to Jane. "I thought you wanted to know about my family."

It was the first time that day that either of them had

referred to the battle of wills that had culminated in that kiss. Just touching on that memory made Matt suddenly warm, forced him to remind himself that kissing Jane had been the single most stupid thing he'd done in his entire life. And the most dangerous. He'd been in many a tricky spot as a cop, taken chances with his life in the name of justice. He'd cheated death on more than one occasion. But he couldn't remember the last time he'd risked his heart.

Jane's gaze danced away as color flooded her cheeks. But before he had time to decide if this meant she was also remembering those moments they'd held one another, kissed one another, a horn sounded behind him.

Matt peered through the rain to see that the light had changed to green. Stepping on the gas, he focused on the traffic as he drove and directed his thoughts to more practical, and more controllable, matters concerning the woman sitting next to him.

Once he got to the office, he would need to look through the information he'd collected regarding the Bertrand family. Not the stuff Paula had collected at the library. This time, he would concentrate on more recent family history, check a couple of dates that would help confirm the suspicion that was growing ever stronger. Oh, and he would also need some photos. He could download and print—

"Perhaps it would be better if you just told me about them."

Jane's words completely confused Matt. Dragging his attention back to the present, he asked, "Tell you about who?"

"Your family."

Matt glanced at Jane. Her cheeks were no longer pink. In fact, she was looking quite pale.

"Well, I suppose I could do that," Matt started slowly. "But why learn about them secondhand?"

"Because, this party tonight is a family gathering. I would be an outsider."

"Hardly the only one."

Matt only realized how bitter these words sounded when Jane's eyes widened. He returned his attention to the road and spoke quickly. "The McDermotts are always taking in strays. I was seven when my uncle and aunt took me in— even though they already had a full house with six kids of their own. And when they hold barbecues and holiday gatherings, their belief is that there's always room for one more."

"They sound like nice people."

Matt replied warmly, "They are. You'll like them."

Several minutes of silence followed. Matt watched the oncoming traffic as he waited for a chance to turn left, into the loft parking lot. But he was very aware of Jane sitting next to him, conscious that the conversation was quickly moving in a direction he preferred to avoid. The issue of how and why he'd come to live with the McDermotts was bound to come up eventually—maybe even at Jack and Libby's tonight.

That was fine. It would be easier to allow his aunt or uncle or one of his cousins to talk about what had happened. However, he knew Jane well enough to bet that any minute now she was going to ask for just such an explanation.

Unless he gave her something else to think about.

"Hey," he said. "You haven't asked about the photos I went to look at."

A space in the line of cars coming toward him opened up as Matt finished speaking. Giving the steering wheel a quick pull to the left, he shot across the street. After parking next to the building, he turned to Jane.

"By the time I got to the office, Graham Carmichael had gone through the files and found the pictures that had been taken at various Thanksgiving Eve decorating parties, bless his efficient little soul. He let me take them so I could decide which one should go with the article I'm supposed to be writing. Oh, and speaking of the article, when I got off the service elevator, Harold O'Malley was waiting for me."

"The security guard?"

"Yeah. He seems to want me to do a real, in-depth story about the department store. He told me I should speak to a woman named Vivian Norman, who worked for Bertrand's from the time she was eighteen years old, until last year, when she was retired."

"*Was* retired?"

"That's how O'Malley put it." Matt reached into the back seat to retrieve his briefcase. "I tell you, if I really was a reporter looking to dig up some dirt on the store or the family, I have a good idea that O'Malley and this Norman woman would be able to provide it. What caught my attention, however, was O'Malley's mention of the photographs that the woman had apparently taken at various Bertrand functions over the years."

"You don't think the ones you got from the store will help us?"

Matt reached into his jacket's breast pocket and removed a letter-size envelope, then handed the thin packet to Jane. She flipped open the flap.

"This is it?"

"Carmichael assured me those are the only official photos of store functions. Apparently, most of them—the earlier ones, in particular—were kept at the Bertrand home, in special albums that Louise had put together. It seems that the old woman truly looked at the employees as her family. Anyway, all those were lost in that fire Aimee mentioned."

"So, I guess we should talk to this Vivian person."

Matt nodded slowly. Of course, if his current theory panned out, meeting this woman might not be necessary. At least, for the purposes of looking at photo albums.

"Well, Carmichael did say he thought a few of the older shots might be in there." He glanced at the driving rain before he went on. "I need to run into the office to get a few things. No need for you to get drenched. Why don't you look through those photos? I should be right back."

He didn't give Jane time to do more than nod before he

let himself out of the car. Shoving the door shut behind him, he hurried through the rain and up the stairs toward the large front door.

Jane watched him disappear into the building, then took a deep breath, closed her eyes and let her head fall back against the high-backed seat.

Matt's sudden mention of O'Malley and the pictures hadn't fooled her for one moment, since she had plenty of experience in changing subjects or redirecting conversations when questions about her past arose. It was clear that he didn't want to discuss his family. What wasn't clear was why he was willing to take her to meet them, if this was such an issue.

He'd mentioned an aunt and uncle and six cousins. If they all had spouses and children, this gathering could be quite large. After her reaction to the crowds in Bertrand's perfume aisle, she wondered if being crammed into a house with another bunch of strangers, making Christmas decorations and no doubt listening to Christmas music, was such a good idea. It could be quite uncomfortable for her, or for them, if some minor irritation should bring out that bossy, dark side of her personality.

Still, how could she pass up a chance to learn more about Matt? If he wasn't going to talk about himself, she was just going to have to learn about him from someone else. And who better than the people he'd grown up with?

That decision made, Jane took the stack of photographs out of the envelope. She stared at each of the twenty prints in turn, searching every face and item closely. Nothing looked familiar, other than the Bertrand star hanging atop the columns in several shots.

Sighing, she returned the pictures to their envelope, then crossed her arms against the growing chill. Trying to relax, she stared out the passenger window at the curtain of rain, which only served to remind her just how long it had been since she'd taken a bathroom break. She pulled her umbrella out of her purse and opened the door.

Several minutes later, when she stepped off the elevator on the brick building's third floor, she spied the light in the right-hand office area and called out, "Matt?"

As she moved in that direction, he appeared in the doorway. "What's up?"

"This—" Jane held out the envelope with the pictures. "They didn't spark one memory, but I thought you might want to put them somewhere safe so you can return them."

Matt seemed to be staring at the middle of her forehead. Suddenly, he smiled and took the envelope from her. When he turned back toward his office, Jane cleared her throat.

"Um…" She felt her face heat up. "Now that I'm here, could you direct me to the bathroom?"

Matt turned. "Oh, sure. Go through that archway. It's the first door on your right."

The all-white room was cold and small, consisting of a sink and a narrow shower stall, along with the fixture Jane was most pressingly interested in right now. Several minutes later, as she finished drying her hands, she glanced in the mirror and saw that the wind had blown her bangs back. Her forehead was naked for all the world to see, along with the jagged scar that rose from the innermost point of her left eyebrow and angled up to disappear into her hairline two inches to the left of her widow's peak.

Which explained what Matt had been staring at.

Using her fingers as a comb, Jane fluffed her bangs back into place. Noting that she was looking a bit faded around the edges, she regretted having locked her purse in Matt's car. As she gently ran an index finger beneath her lower lashes to remove some of the smudged liner, she told herself that sometime during the drive to Jack's house, she would have to make more extensive repairs.

When she stepped back into the main loft area, the light was off in Matt's office and he was nowhere to be seen. A second later she heard footsteps coming down the metal stairs to her left. She looked over as Matt reached the bottom step, now dressed in a dark green pullover and faded jeans.

"I decided it would be a good idea to change," he said. "It occurred to me that my cousins would have way too much fun teasing me about my 'Enry 'Iggins getup."

Jane chuckled, then looked worried. "I take it that this is a rather informal affair?"

Matt nodded.

"Well, aren't I just a little overdressed then?"

"Well, yes. But that's easily fixed." Matt glanced at his watch. "It's a little after two. I gave Libby a call, to tell her to expect us and see if I could bring anything. She put in a request for more microwave popcorn and, of all things, a sack of potatoes. I thought you and I should get something to eat before we leave, since we've completely missed lunch. Even allowing for traffic, we still have plenty of time to get across the bridge to Jack and Libby's before five, when everyone is gathering. And since Zoe's house is on the way, we'll just stop off and let you get into something more comfortable."

They managed lunch by grabbing a couple of turkey wraps and two bottles of juice from the café on the first floor of Matt's building. The trip to Zoe's house was more or less silent as Matt and Jane devoured both food and beverages. Jane left Matt relaxing on the settee in the foyer while she ran up to her room and changed into white Keds, jeans, and a red sweater with a cowl neckline. Even with taking the time to fix her makeup and wrapping one of the figures she'd finished the day before in tissue paper, then placing it in her backpack along with her wallet and keys, she was back downstairs in fifteen minutes. This earned her a surprised but generous smile from Matt.

"That was quick. I was figuring on being here a half hour, minimum."

Finding herself the target of such praise, not to mention the admiring glance Matt had swept her with as he spoke, Jane found herself suddenly shy. She managed a smile in return. "Well, I know that the traffic going north over the Golden Gate Bridge backs up early, so I figured I'd better make it quick.

"What's in the backpack?" he asked as they got into the Jeep.

Jane glanced at the item she'd put on the floor in front of her. "Oh...things."

"You're not going to tell me—are you."

"Not unless you tell me what's in your briefcase."

Matt started the engine and backed out of the driveway. "I told you, you'll find out later."

"Exactly," Jane replied. "And that's when you'll find out what's in the backpack."

An hour later, they were on the other side of the Golden Gate Bridge, pulling out of a grocery store parking lot, the bag containing the popcorn and potatoes on the back seat. The rain had become lighter, but as Jane rested her head against the seat back, she could hear it pattering on the windshield, in between the wiper's *swish-swish*.

"We're only a couple of blocks away from Jack and Libby's," Matt said. "So brace yourself."

"Brace myself?"

Matt glanced at her. "You know, you aren't the only person on the planet who doesn't handle large groups of people well. I love the entire McDermott bunch, but sometimes I find being with all of them at once a tad overwhelming."

Jane studied Matt's features as he concentrated on the winding road that took them beneath the canopy of trees growing across the residential street. She saw a tightness around his eyes, similar to the expression she'd noticed the day he'd walked into Maxwell's security office, and back into her life.

"You were up late last night," she said abruptly.

Matt glanced at her. "Yeah, I was. So?"

"So, you're tired. You didn't have to do this for me, you know."

The car slowed as Matt pulled to the right and stopped next to the curb. He switched the engine off, then turned toward her. "I didn't have to do what?"

"Bring me to meet your family, just because of what I said when we got back from Sausalito last week." For the second time that day, Jane was furious at herself for her outburst on the wharf. "I was wrong to be angry with you. It's your job to poke into my life right now, but your life is really none of my business."

Matt studied Jane's earnest, remorseful expression, and felt a slight ache in his chest.

There she sat, only hours after what had obviously been a very distressful encounter with her past on Bertrand's sales floor, and she was concerned about him—worried that he was tired, that she'd pushed him into doing something he didn't want to do.

He wasn't accustomed to being the object of such single-minded care. On the force, he'd been part of a team, just like when he played football in high school. His aunt and uncle had done their best to make him feel welcome when he came to live with them. But he'd always known that he didn't truly belong. When he played ball, he'd had a tendency to make up his own plays. On the force he'd been the Lone Ranger, the officer who never complained about patrolling the streets alone. When he lived with the Mc-Dermotts, he'd always been aware that he was an extra mouth to feed, an extra body to clothe. And before that, it had been clear that his mother and father—

Matt pulled his thoughts up short.

God, he hadn't let himself think about that in years. That was what came, he supposed, of looking into smoky eyes soft with concern.

"Jane." He placed a hand on her cheek as he forced a grin. "Did it ever occur to you that I might have brought you along as protection?"

Her eyes grew wide. "Protection?"

"Yes. The McDermotts are a merciless bunch—heartless teases. But if I have company along, they just might behave. So, are you ready?"

Jane nodded, but Matt could see a hint of fear in her eyes, an emotion he wanted to wipe away. His attention drifted to her lips. He leaned toward her, then tensed and held his position as he forced a jocular tone.

"Okay. Things are bound to be confusing at first. You'll be meeting my aunt Lydia and my uncle Charles. Jack has an older brother, Mike, who's married to Amanda. They have three children, twins Mick and Jake and a daughter named Hannah. The oldest sister, Patty, lives in D.C., so you won't be meeting her. Jack has three younger siblings. Sharon and Shawn are twins. They are both married. Sharon's husband is Sam, and they have a daughter named Paige. Shawn's wife, Jodi, is expecting. Kate is the youngest of my cousins. She's single but will most likely bring a date. Any questions?"

"Why?" Jane lifted her eyebrows. "Will there be a quiz?"

This lighthearted question eased Matt's tension. He smiled. "No, but we're likely to get separated. Once we're inside and the introductions are made, you'll be on your own." He turned to her as he prepared to exit the car. "Don't worry. They're always nice to newcomers."

Jane insisted on carrying the bag containing the popcorn and the potatoes. Matt figured she wanted to use it as some sort of shield, so he grabbed his briefcase and escorted her to the three-story, white Victorian house, decked with swags of evergreen dotted with tiny twinkling lights.

Once inside, he watched Jane while no fewer than eight people crowded into the entryway to be introduced. Slowly her deer-caught-in-headlights expression softened as the children filtered in. Two-and-a-half-year-old Hannah, wearing a red velvet dress and matching bow in her dark hair, held up a book and asked if Jane would read her a story about "Rudolph Snows." Ignoring Mike's protest, Jane handed the groceries to Matt, but insisted on keeping her backpack as the little child led her to a brown wing chair near the bay window in the living room.

Matt glanced around the room, draped with red-and-green garlands. There was a fire in the fireplace, and a large, naked pine tree in the corner. Seeing that Jane seemed comfortably occupied, Matt escaped to the kitchen, where he found Libby counting the bowls of popcorn arranged on the center island. She lifted her head, tucked a tendril of dark hair into the ponytail atop her head and smiled.

"Oh, good. You remembered the popcorn," she said. "I thought it would be easier if everyone had their own bowl to work from. I was afraid I didn't have enough, and sure enough, I'm three bowls short. You know where the microwave is. Give me those potatoes, and start popping."

Matt did as requested with a snappy, "Yessir, ma'am."

Libby rested the bag of potatoes on her very pregnant stomach and grinned. "Don't get smart with me, cousin."

Her gaze moved to the briefcase he'd place on the one free space on the counter. "And what is that doing here? You know the rules at these things. No business talk allowed."

"It's not business," Matt said. "At least, not completely. I need your photographic and computer skills. But it can wait until all the popcorn is strung and everyone else is gone."

With that, he placed the packet of popcorn in the microwave and pushed the proper buttons. When Sharon came in the room and offered to help. Matt turned popcorn duty over to her.

Stepping into the living room. he saw that two-year-old Paige had joined Jane and Hannah in the wing chair. Just as he considered rescuing her from his young second cousins, he saw Jane laugh at something one of the girls had said, then open another book, smile and begin to read.

This was just as well, because any rescue attempt would

have been foiled by Mick and Jake. Mike's twin boys way-laid Matt and dragged him into a wrestling match. When it ended in a draw several minutes later, Matt looked over to discover that his aunt Lydia had replaced Jane in the chair with the two girls. He had just enough time to see Jane walk through the French doors, carrying her backpack, before his uncle Charles stepped up to ask how business was going.

Jane crossed the foyer's shiny oak floor, through another set of glass-and-wood doors into a pale green kitchen. On her right, a table and six chairs formed an eating nook in front of a large bay window. Three women sat there—Jack's sisters Kate and Sharon, and the twins' mother, Amanda.

They all looked up from the large needles they were threading, to give Jane a welcoming smile. Jane nodded and smiled in reply, then turned to her right, where Jack's wife stood at the kitchen's center island, measuring popped kernels of corn into three bowls.

Libby looked up as Jane approached. "Hi, Jane. Come in here to escape the pandemonium?"

Jane glanced toward the other room, from which they heard whoops and taunts, followed by a stern, "Keep it to a dull roar, boys."

"Well, not exactly," she said. "I brought you something…sort of a hostess gift."

She opened her backpack as she finished speaking and drew out a winged figure with dark hair, wearing a dress of silver netting. When she held it out, Libby gasped.

"Oh, what a beautiful angel," she said as she wiped her hand on the apron that rode high on her bulging middle. "Or is it a fairy?" she asked as she came around the island.

Jane laughed. "Well, I started out making woodland elves and flower fairies. For the holidays I adapted these to create Christmas elves, Santas and angels." Jane handed the figure to Libby. "So this can be an angel or a fairy—it's up to you."

Libby looked amazed as she touched the gossamer wings. "Well, this one is destined to be a Christmas angel. And it arrived just in time." She shook her head. "When Jack was getting the ornaments organized this afternoon, he dropped the silver star we bought last year for the top of the tree. It shattered into a million pieces."

The image of a crystal star falling toward the store flashed through Jane's mind as Libby went on. "So, this little angel will take its place."

"Oh, what an honor," Jane said.

For some reason, the suggestion that something she had created would play such a special part in this family's Christmas made Jane's heart swell and her throat constrict.

Looking around quickly to keep threatening tears at bay, she asked, "Is there anything I can help you with?"

"Um...yes," Libby replied. She turned and spoke over her shoulder as she placed the angel on top of the refrigerator. "I was just about to wash the potatoes Matt brought. You can dry them for me."

Jane stepped toward the sack of potatoes on the ivory tile counter, next to the sink. "Are you going to bake these?"

"No," Libby replied. "I'm going to tell you what I've told everyone else. You'll find out what the potatoes are for when the time is right."

Jane shook her head. "You and Matt."

"What do you mean?"

Jane pointed to the briefcase on the island counter. "He refused to tell me what he had in there. Said I'd find out later."

Libby laughed. "He said something similar to me." She looked at the case again, then shook her head. "I'm tempted to take a peek, but that wouldn't be a good idea. If you haven't noticed, Matt's a very private person."

"He told me he didn't care much for crowds."

"Or family gatherings," Libby said as she turned the water on. "It's strange. He really seems to like everyone, and he and Jack are close. But since I've gotten to know him better, I've learned that some of Matt's joking is… something of a show."

She turned to Jane suddenly, a dripping potato in her hand. "Don't get me wrong. Matt is a *good* guy. He just doesn't let people get really close to him. I used to think this was because of his fiancée."

"Fiancée?" Jane repeated.

Libby placed the potato in the towel Jane was holding. "I guess I should say ex-fiancée. She left him shortly after he was shot. She claimed he was no longer the man she'd fallen in love with. Can you imagine?"

Jane shook her head as it struck her Matt must have been engaged when he was originally investigating her case. But then, she'd known nothing about his private life at the time, only that he made her laugh, made her feel safe. She couldn't imagine what sort of woman would have Matt's love and walk away from him—under any circumstance.

"I can't say I was surprised," Libby said as she scrubbed another potato. "I didn't know Amber long, but she was one of those showy, perfectly dressed Barbie doll types. In my opinion, not at all the sort Matt should be with."

The image of Aimee Bertrand flashed into Jane's mind.

Libby went on. "I thought maybe her leaving had caused Matt to withdraw. But Jack says his cousin was always something of a lone wolf."

Jane smiled. "Matt tells me his nickname is Lone Ranger."

Just then, Jane heard a loud whinny come from the doorway. She and Libby turned as Matt came in, on all fours, carrying Mick and Jake on his back.

Libby turned to Jane with a grin. "Maybe we should change that nickname to Silver."

Chapter Fourteen

Jane leaned against the living room wall. On her right, the half-open French door leading from the foyer shielded her from the bustle of goodbyes taking place beyond. On her left stood Jack and Libby's Christmas tree, festooned with multiple rows of popcorn strings. More of the strands, strung with lots of McDermott love and laughter, were going home in paper bags to grace other trees, while the crushed remains littered the green-and-red area rug, along with a few shriveled pieces of potato.

A weary smile lifted one side of her mouth. The mystery of the spuds had been solved when Libby gave every family member two potato halves, then instructed them on how to carve the cut ends into organic versions of rubber stamps. With the adults helping the kids, they soon had a collection of shapes: Christmas trees, stars, bells and even an elaborate snowflake.

Then they had all traipsed out the back door to Jack's newly constructed garage, where the spotless concrete floor was carpeted with lengths of plain white paper. A half hour of dipping potatoes into paint then pressing them onto the paper had resulted in long rows of homemade wrapping paper, which were now dry, rolled up and going home with the popcorn garlands.

Jane couldn't remember a more eventful day. She still hadn't had time to process what had happened to her at Bertrand's perfume counter. And, until she was alone in her attic apartment where she felt safe to give vent to her emotions and fears, that experience would just have to stay unexamined.

This evening, however, was a different matter. From the minute she was introduced to Matt's family, she'd been swept up in a swirl of teasing voices, popcorn fights and laughter, all accompanied by Christmas CDs playing softly in the background. There had been great food, too—a table full of salads and casseroles provided by the various family members, with a delicious apple cake for dessert. And, of course, eggnog. Fortunately, no one had questioned her when she refused to partake.

And during all the madness, she had been constantly aware of Matt—watching him roar at a joke his uncle told, or whisper to Mike's twin boys when they became a tad too rambunctious.

For most of the evening, Matt's dimpled smile had been in evidence. Once or twice, however, Jane had caught a lost, almost anxious look in his eyes. It was one she was quite familiar with, having seen it reflected in the hospital mirror so many times when she'd been preparing to meet the latest searcher who'd come to attempt to identify Jane Doe. It was a look that said she wondered if she would measure up to whatever expectations this person, or persons, might have. But why Matt should have such concerns, when it was clear that everyone in this family was crazy about him, was a complete mystery to her. As were his current whereabouts.

"Oh lord."

Jane started, straightening away from the wall as she turned toward the man standing in the doorway. Jack McDermott ran his fingers though his brown hair as he surveyed the disaster area that was his living room. When his gaze reached her, his lips twisted into a rueful smile.

"Looks like it snowed popcorn in here. Guess it's as close as we get to the real thing, here in *sunny* California. It's raining again. Pouring, actually."

"Oh." Jane couldn't think of anything more intelligent to say. She hadn't had any trouble talking earlier because so many conversations and jokes had been crossing one another in the packed room that she had just been caught up in the melee. Now, speaking one-on-one, she felt suddenly shy. She searched for something to lighten the mood. She didn't have far to look.

"Why don't I help you pick up a little?"

"You're a guest," Jack replied. "And as such, relieved of the responsibility for cleaning this mess up."

"Don't be silly. I helped make it, after all."

She smiled suddenly, recalling the teasing, flirtatious way Matt had tossed popcorn at her, and how she'd returned the volley.

"Well, if you insist," Matt said. "Libby's down in the basement with Matt. When she gets back up here, I'd like the worst of this cleared away. Otherwise, she'll be up half the night trying to restore order, instead of getting to bed early."

He turned, speaking over his shoulder as he walked from the room. "I'll be right back with a broom and dustpan."

He returned with those items, as well as a large plastic garbage bag. He handed this to Jane. "Why don't you take care of the bigger items," he said. "I'll round up the stray kernels. And while we're at it, you can tell me what sort of magic you've worked on my cousin."

Jane paused in the act of bending over to retrieve several almonds still in their shells that the twins had been attempting to skewer with their needles.

"Magic?"

"Yeah. I can't remember the last time I saw Matt so relaxed. Well, as relaxed as he ever truly gets, anyway."

Jane picked up an almond and dropped it in the plastic bag. So, her assessment of Matt's smile-as-a-shield had been correct.

"Of course," Jack continued as he wielded his broom, "he's had a rough year or so, and some of that is my fault."

Jane glanced at the man, to find him staring down at a nicely formed pile of ivory niblets. She told herself that what went on between Jack and Matt was family business, none of hers, but she couldn't help ask, "How do you figure that? My understanding is that you pulled him out of a deep depression when you suggested the two of you start your own detective agency."

Jack looked up. "He told you that? Well, it's partially true. What he probably didn't tell you was how hard it's been for him. Matt only stopped physical therapy for his knee recently. It's also been difficult for him to switch from actively going after the bad guys, to spending the majority of his time tracking them down on the computer and the phone."

He fell silent and began brushing another line of popcorn toward the larger clump. Jane plopped two more nuts into her bag, then crossed the room toward a tangle of white thread someone had thoughtfully piled on a side table.

"It couldn't have been all that easy a transition for you, either," she said.

"Well, I've always been more attracted to the mystery elements of a case, following the clues leading to who-dunit."

"Like Sherlock Holmes?"

Jack glanced up with a grin. "My cousin filled you in on that, too, did he? Well—" his smile faded "—Matt's always been more interested in the chase, doing the actual catching and bringing someone to justice. That's why this new way of working is so hard for him. And then, there was losing Manny.''

For the next few moments the room was silent, save for the whisper of the broom along the rug and the occasional *plop* as Jane dropped a nut into the trash bag or disposed of some other unidentifiable bit of food one of the children had dropped onto the rug.

''I think that's why solving the mystery surrounding you has Matt so…energized,'' Jack said. ''Losing a partner is hard enough for a cop. But when there are no clues to follow, and there's no way of bringing anyone to justice…well, it's just a helpless feeling that any cop would hate. And given Matt's background…''

Jack paused and his gaze slid toward Jane. They stared at each other across the room as the air filled with unspoken words. Jane considered asking Jack to go on, but remembered what Libby had said about Matt valuing his privacy.

And yet, he had brought her with him tonight. He must have known that his family would talk about him. Perhaps this was his way of revealing things that still hurt him too much to discuss—like the fiancée that had left him so coldly when he was injured.

It was on the tip of her tongue to ask Jack about this, when the man drew a deep breath and gave her a tight smile. ''I think it's been good for Matt to get caught up in trying to unlock the mystery of your identity. I was afraid he was getting bored with what we do, but now he seems totally revitalized. Take tonight, for example. It's been years since he's been to one of these things. Of course, I know he had an ulterior motive, but playing with Mike's boys brought out the kid I remember messing about with. It's been a long time since I saw even a hint of his old, devil-may-care self.''

The idea that investigating the mystery of her past was having a beneficial effect on Matt gave Jane a great deal of pleasure. However, her attention had been caught by something else Jack had just said.

"What ulterior motive are you referring to?"

Jack had just knelt down to begin brushing his popcorn pile into the dustpan. He looked up. "Well, I'm not sure. I think it has something to do with my wife's photographic expertise. I was busy getting my family out of the house, when Lib told me that she was going to help Matt with something in her workshop. And speaking of help, would you bring that garbage bag over here and hold it open for me?"

To cover her disappointment that Matt's "ulterior motive" was not a romantic one, Jane did as Jack requested. Jack scooped several loads of popcorn leavings into the plastic sack. When he finally finished, he stood with a relieved sigh and surveyed the room.

"Well, it could use a vacuuming, but that can wait until—hey, how did that get in here?"

Jane followed his line of sight, and spotted one of the potato halves she'd noticed earlier but had somehow missed in her cleanup efforts. She became aware of footsteps crossing the entryway as Jack moved toward the misshapen item. He picked it up just as Matt and Libby entered the room.

"Here you go, cousin," Jack said, tossing the potato to Matt. "This spud's for you."

Matt caught the item, looked at it, grinned and shook his head. "Thanks, Jack. You shouldn't have."

He then tossed the item into the open garbage bag and turned to Jane. There was an excited gleam in his eyes and an intense air of expectation about him, which inexplicably filled her with trepidation. That feeling only increased as he said, "I have something I want you to see in the kitchen. You too, Jack."

Matt took Jane's hand and led her across the foyer into the kitchen. As they approached the island in the center of the green-and-white checked floor, she saw Matt's briefcase lying open, surrounded by several manila folders.

She couldn't imagine why the scene seemed so ominous,

unless perhaps it was the faint scent of the detested eggnog that filled the air. But as Matt drew her to the waist-high counter, her knees began to tremble.

Jack and Libby stood arm in arm on the other side of the island. "Okay, Matt," Jack said. "What have you and my wife been up to now?"

Jane wondered the same thing, but an inexplicable sense of dread outweighed her curiosity. In a desperate attempt at delay, she looked from the open briefcase to Libby's dark blue eyes. "Oh," she said. "That reminds me, I was supposed to ask you about the night that Matt...*killed* you?"

Libby smiled and opened her mouth, but Matt spoke first. "That explanation will have to wait." He turned to Jane and squeezed her hand slightly as he said, "This is more important. Are you ready?"

His green eyes held hers, no longer gleaming with excitement or laughter, but offering silent encouragement. Slowly Jane nodded.

"All right." Matt released Jane's hand and opened the folder directly in front of them. He took out two sheets of paper and laid them side by side. "I want you to look at these. You, too, Jack."

Jane stared at two black-and-white photographs. The subject in each was a woman's face, of approximately the same size and shape. As she looked from one to the other, Jack came around to stand at her side.

"I recognize that," she said as she pointed to the picture on the left. "It's the photo of me that the *Chronicle* ran, a year ago July."

In the photo, the scar that raised one side of her mouth was much more noticeable than it was now, and the one marking her forehead darker. Her hair, barely an inch long, stood almost straight up from the widow's peak that shaped her face into a heart.

"Now," Matt said, "compare your face to the one in the photograph on the right."

Jane couldn't help but notice that this woman's hairline

also dipped in the center. But she had a much fuller face, with a wider nose. Her hair was drawn tightly back, with the ends curling forward from behind her ears, lending a bit of softness to the severe lines of her square jaw.

"That woman is Noelle Bertrand," Matt said.

Jane turned to him. "I don't understand. Why would you want me to look at—"

"Ah," Matt said, "never question a magician in the middle of a trick. *Voilà.*"

With that, Matt flipped open another folder and drew out a sheet of transparent film. Jane had just enough time to notice the irregularly shaped gray oval in the center, before Matt placed the sheet over the photograph of the woman he'd just identified as Noelle Bertrand. She watched him match up the outlines of the gray image on the film with those of Noelle's face.

"Now watch this," Matt said.

Jane felt her stomach knot as Matt shifted the transparency created from the photograph of Noelle onto the picture of herself, lining up Noelle's widow's peak with her own. He made a few adjustments before lifting his hands and saying, "Look closely, now."

The lower portions of the two faces didn't match up at all. The pale gray outline of Noelle's jaw was much wider and more angular than the jaw in the picture beneath. The nose area was a confusing blur, but as Jane looked closer, it became clear that the top one was wider and shorter.

However, the upper portions of both faces lined up perfectly—not only the widow's peaks, but the width of each forehead, the shape of both women's eyes and eyebrows, along with the position and size of their ears.

Jane felt weak as she stared at the eyes gazing blankly up at her. She crossed her arms to keep from shaking as she looked at Matt. "If you're suggesting that I am Noelle Bertrand, then you may have had a little too much spiked eggnog."

Matt placed his hands on her shoulders. "I'm afraid the

proof is incontrovertible. Libby worked this up for me. In her business, she creates photo collages composed of several negatives and, more recently, computer images. This was a simple matter of taking two photos, blowing them up to the same size, then making a transparency to match up the important features.''

Jane shook her head.

Matt leaned toward her. ''Jane, remember, I told you that the area around the eyes rarely changes. That's how they get those computer-aged pictures of missing children. Libby didn't need to do any computer aging, however. Here, look at the photo she used to get that image of Noelle.''

He swiveled her toward the counter again, then opened yet another folder to reveal what appeared to be a photocopy taken from a newspaper article. At the top, a woman stood in front of a man, both facing the camera. The woman's features matched the larger image she'd just looked at. Not only that, but Jane could see a marked resemblance to Aimee Bertrand, in spite of the difference in hairstyles and the fact that Noelle appeared some twenty pounds heavier.

Jane looked at the caption beneath the picture. When she read the words ''Bertrand heir to marry,'' her heart sank and her stomach clenched. She glanced at Matt's large, strong hand gently covering hers and thought she might cry.

No, she told herself. She made herself look at the photo again. This couldn't be true. She could not be Noelle Bertrand, the woman whom half the employees at Bertrand's seemed to find cold and arrogant. And she most definitely could not be engaged, or worse, already married. Besides...

She turned to Matt. ''I can't be Noelle. She's dead.''

He gave her a slow smile. ''So we thought. I have one more article I want you to look at. You too, Jack.''

He turned over the engagement shot of Noelle, to reveal another piece of paper lying beneath. ''This was among the items I copied from the *Chronicle* Web site. It ran in the business section, a year ago November. It states, 'Aimee and Phillip Bertrand have announced that Bestco is still interested in purchasing Bertrand's Department Store. However, they cannot finalize any sale without the participation of their sister, Noelle, who retains controlling interest in the family business. On the third of June, Noelle was to have married Glen Helms, a partner in the firm that represents the store. Two weeks before, she called off the wedding and flew to Europe, leaving her brother and sister in charge. They say that Noelle has recently informed them that she intends to relocate permanently to France, so they feel she will agree to the sale.''

Jane had begun to relax when Matt read that Noelle had called off her wedding. She didn't know why, since none of what he'd said convinced her that she and this person were one and the same.

''Jane,'' Matt said as he placed his hand on her arm, ''do the math. Noelle flew to Europe two weeks before June third. That would make it May twenty-first—the date of your so-called accident.''

Matt watched Jane closely as she looked up at him, saw the exact moment she accepted the truth. Her eyes darkened a moment, grew wide, then narrowed.

''Oh,'' she said. ''Then, the reason my picture didn't match up with anyone in the missing persons file was that I...Noelle...was never reported as missing.''

Matt nodded. ''Between the weight you lost while you were in that coma and the plastic surgery, the shot taken of you doesn't look like Noelle at all. Your voice was altered, too, because of the infection. Besides, anyone who knew Noelle thought she was off in Europe.''

''Except,'' Jane continued for him, ''whoever tried to kill me.''

Matt grimaced, then asked, ''Does knowing who you are bring back any memories?''

Jane had turned to look at the picture of Noelle again. She continued to stare at the photo as she shook her head.

Matt tried not to show his disappointment. After all, it

was ridiculous of him to have hoped that learning her identify would somehow jolt all of Jane's lost memories into
place. He was about to tell her not to worry about this,
when Jack spoke up.

"So, if I follow you, you think that someone boarded the
plane the night of May twenty-first, using Noelle's ID and
some kind of disguise, then later somehow faked her death
somewhere in Europe?"

"In Paris," Matt replied. "According to another report
in the *Chronicle,* Noelle drowned in the Seine. However,
her body was never recovered. And, of course, there was a
witness to this."

"How convenient." Jack's dry tone made it clear that he
shared Matt's skepticism regarding this story.

"It gets better," Matt said. "Now that we know who
Jane is...or was, we have a motive, which would be—"

"Oh, let me guess," Jack broke in. "Ownership of the
department store?"

"Bingo. And, of course, this leads to suspects, which in
this case—"

"Would be Noelle's brother and sister," Jack finished.

"Oh, but wait. There's more," Matt added with a grin.
He shuffled through the papers on the counter until he came
to the printout of another article. "We can't forget Glen
Helms."

As the two cousins bantered, Jack had returned to his
wife's side. "That name sounds familiar," he said.

"The man was an assistant D.A. over in Oakland several
years back, before he went to work for the corporate law
firm that represents Bertrand's Department Store." Matt
turned Noelle's engagement picture toward Jack. "Helms
also happens to be the man that Noelle left at the altar last
year, so to speak, last year. And today, I noticed that he
seemed awfully friendly with Noelle's younger sister."

Jack's eyes widened as he stared across the kitchen island
at Matt. Then his glance shifted to Jane.

"Well, Noelle," he said to her, "it seems that you must

have been quite the discerning woman to ditch a lowlife like Helms.''

"Can…we—" she hesitated "—not call me that?" Jane appeared to be gazing at the picture of Noelle as she spoke. Slowly she looked up at Matt. "You…you're probably right, about me being her, or her being…well, you know. But I still feel like…Jane.''

There was no way Matt could miss the pleading look in her eyes, or the attempt to appear as if she was taking all this in stride.

God, he thought as he smiled at her, *I love this woman.*

He froze. It was the second time that day he'd had that ridiculous thought. Ridiculous not because Jane wasn't a woman worthy of love, but because *he* was incapable of giving himself in that way.

He took her hand. "Of course we'll call you *Jane,*" he said. "You chose to keep that first name because that's what you were called from the moment you regained consciousness. And, somehow, I think it fits you far better, anyway.''

Gazing up at him, Jane's lips trembled. "Thanks.''

Matt squeezed her hand, then turned to his cousin. "How's our caseload?''

"We've got a couple of minor investigations going. But I have time to help you with this, if that's what you were going to ask. Not tonight, however. I've got to get the mother of my soon-to-be-born child upstairs and into bed before she falls asleep standing up.''

Matt glanced over at Libby. Her eyelids were already at half-mast.

"Jeez,'' he said. "I'm sorry. Go on up. I'll finish the dishes and get—''

Jack cut him off with a shake of his head. "They'll wait till morning. Gather up your evidence and get that poor girl of yours back across the bridge. She looks almost as wiped out as Libby.''

* * *

Matt looked at Jane as he waited to pay the toll on the San Francisco side of the bridge. Her features were clearly visible in the glow of the overhead lights. She sat rigidly, staring ahead, her hands clasped tightly over the articles he'd printed out earlier that day regarding Noelle Bertrand. She'd spent the earlier part of the trip bent over the pages, reading by the illumination of a small flashlight. As they crossed the Golden Gate Bridge, she'd extinguished the narrow beam and stared forward, as if carefully tracking the path of the windshield wipers.

"You said you had more articles about Noelle back at the office?" Jane asked.

Matt nodded as the car in front of him stopped.

"I'd like to read them," Jane said. "Tonight."

Glancing over, Matt saw that she was still staring straight ahead. He could almost feel the tension that held her straight in her seat.

"It's late, Jane," he said softly. "You've had a very long and rather eventful day. I think you should get some sleep. And perhaps talk to Zoe about all this."

Jane shook her head. "Zoe's not home tonight. She stays with a friend in Berkeley once a month." She turned to him. "There isn't a whole lot about Noelle in these articles, and I have a lot of questions about her. I won't get any sleep until at least some of them are answered."

Matt pulled up to the tollbooth to pay. He was aware of his intense desire to protect this woman, to take care of her. He wanted to insist she get some sleep before she tackled anything more, but he respected her need to face her demons.

As he drove away from the tollbooth he said, "Okay. My office it is."

Traffic was light, so the silent drive to the building where Matt worked and lived was short. Other than the few moments Jane spent placing the articles back in the briefcase and snapping it shut, not a sound came from her side of the car. More than once he looked at her, trying to think of words that would ease the tension that held her so erect.

This was one of the toughest parts of any sort of police work, he reminded himself. Telling someone something they obviously didn't want to hear, then standing by as they worked through the emotions that came with assimilating the information.

The only problem tonight, he told himself as he parked next to his building, was that the person doing the struggling was not just some stranger. It was Jane, someone he'd watched work so hard to become her own person—a person he liked very much, he admitted as he turned the car off.

Liked? Who was he kidding? he asked himself as he turned toward her, resting his arm on the steering wheel. His feelings for this woman went far beyond like. If he only *liked* her, he wouldn't be battling the desire to take her into his arms, to lower his mouth to hers, to kiss her until she moaned, to make love to her until she didn't care who she was.

To lose himself completely in her.

Matt tightened his fingers into a fist, clenched his teeth and took a deep, steadying breath.

Jane needed information. He understood all too well how filling the mind could shut off the ache of a wounded soul. He'd been doing that for years, reading all he could about missing persons, about alcoholism, about suicide, until some of what had happened in his life began to make sense.

He released the wheel and touched Jane's shoulder. She started and turned to him.

"We're here," he said. "It's pouring buckets, so we'll need that umbrella of yours."

Jane shook her head. "I didn't transfer it to my back-pack."

"Well, I guess we'll have to run for it."

Matt grabbed the briefcase as he spoke. He heard Jane's door open at the same time as his. Then both of them were sprinting through the rain toward the building's entrance.

He beat her by only a few seconds, just long enough to get the door unlocked and let them both escape the downpour.

As it was, Jane's hair was plastered to her head. When they exited the elevator into the loft and started across to his office area, loud squishing sounds drew his attention to Jane's feet. His familiarity with the parking lot had enabled him to avoid the spots where rain collected into deep puddles. Jane had obviously stepped in at least one of these, for her tennis shoes were soaked, as was the lower three inches of her jeans.

"You might want to get out of those shoes before you start in on the articles."

Matt stepped into his office as he spoke, flipping the switch that lit the area over his worktable on the right and the computer on the left. He led Jane to the computer, and turned it on. "I have copies of the information regarding Noelle over on the desk. If I remember, there's some stuff from the society pages as well as the business section. However, it's not in any particular order. It'll be easier to locate what you want in the files I created on my hard drive."

He paused to type in his password. As he waited for the screen that would allow him to access the Bertrand folder, he turned to Jane, and found her staring blankly at the monitor.

Again he could feel her nervousness. Again he wanted to pull her into his arms. But he understood her need for facts. He could hold her later.

"Sit down," he said as he pulled out his desk chair. "And get out of those sopping shoes. Your socks are probably drenched, as well. I'll go get you some dry ones, then show you how to run a search."

Matt came down from his loft several minutes later, carrying a towel and a pair of heavy socks left from his snowboarding days. When he entered the room, a now barefoot Jane was staring at the computer screen, her hand moving the mouse around its pad. As he came up behind her, he saw that she'd opened the file and had initiated a search for Noelle's name.

"Where did you learn to do this?"

Jane replied without looking up. "Occupational therapy. One of the reasons I worked so hard to make my business work was the fear that if I failed, I might have to spend most of my working life doing this sort of thing."

"I know the feeling."

For the first time since getting into the car after leaving Jack and Libby's, Jane turned and met his eyes. "Is that bad?" she asked gently.

Puzzled, Matt asked, "What?"

"Doing so much of your investigating on the Internet?"

"Oh." He gave a small smile. "You've been talking to Jack. Look, even when I was on the force I used the computer and the telephone for a lot of my investigations. They're damn good tools. Where I get frustrated is when Jack and I crack a case that the police failed at, and then have to let *them* get the guy."

"You don't think you play a part in bringing this person to justice?"

"Of course I do. But I miss the thrill of clipping those cuffs on a perp's wrists." He shrugged. "I guess I need to work on getting over my adrenaline addiction. I'm sure there's a twelve-step program for it somewhere. Anyway, here's some dry socks and a towel to dry your hair. Let me know if you run into any problems. I'll be over there, working out a plan of attack."

Jane noted the oversize gray armchair in the corner next to the worktable, then nodded and turned back to the computer screen, placing the towel and dry socks in her lap, forgotten. Matt shook his head, grabbed a pen from the cup on the desk and moved across the room.

After unearthing a notepad from the papers strewn all over the large table, Matt made himself comfortable in the chair, then began listing all the avenues of investigation that had suddenly opened up with the discovery of Jane's true identity. Starting with background checks on Aimee and Phillip Bertrand, along with Noelle's former fiancé, Glen Helms, Matt moved on to the question of Noelle's "death" in Paris.

A half hour later, he had three full pages of notes, listing people who needed to be interviewed in person, others he could call, along with bits of information he required but wasn't quite certain how to go about digging up. Just yet, anyway.

A strong gust of wind blew rain against the overhead window. Matt looked at his watch and got to his feet. As he crossed to the corner television, used primarily to study surveillance tapes, he noticed that Jane was engrossed in a document on the screen in front of her.

"Do you mind if I turn on the news?" he asked. "I'd like an idea just how long Mother Nature is going to treat us this way."

Jane turned toward him just long enough to give him an overly bright smile and shake her head before she went back to the monitor. Matt frowned as he switched on the set. There was something about Jane's smile that sent chills down his back, reminded him of something that he just couldn't quite put his finger on, something—

Matt's thoughts were broken by the news anchor's assurance that "We'll have more about the havoc all this rain is creating in the Bay Area in our weather segment. Now, however, Tasha Nichols has an update on a story we haven't heard much about in over a year. Tasha, what's new with Jane Doe Number Thirteen?"

Chapter Fifteen

Matt immediately turned from the television to Jane. She was still staring at the computer screen, but her rigid posture told him she was listening to Tasha cite a recent unconfirmed report originating from a local department store. Jane Doe Number Thirteen, the reporter said, was apparently still living in San Francisco, and may have begun to remember something of her past.

Jane turned toward the television as Tasha concluded with ''I would like to help Jane in her search for her memory. So if she, or anyone who might know of her whereabouts, is watching, please contact me.''

The moment the camera switched back to the anchorwoman, Matt glanced at Jane again. Her hands were clasped tightly in her lap. He could see that they were shaking. Her body appeared to be one taut muscle. When he softly said her name, she jerked toward him as if he'd shouted. Her eyes were bright, her lips curved in a smile, despite the fact that she had begun to shiver.

Matt realized suddenly why that smile of her seemed familiar. It was the expression he so often adopted—a grin that said everything was all right, that no one had to worry about him.

He also recognized the first signs of shock setting in.

And why not? Matt asked himself as he moved toward Jane. Her encounter at Bertrand's perfume counter had been upsetting, and the holiday crush with his family must have been draining for her. Finally, she had come face-to-face with the woman she used to be—only to hear him and Jack hypothesize that own brother and sister were the ones responsible for her attempted murder.

Matt reached her side in two long strides. Without saying a word, he bent forward, slid one arm around her back and the other beneath her legs. Bending his knees slightly, he lifted her, and after adjusting her weight against his chest, carried her out of the office and up the stairs leading to his loft.

Beneath the high-pitched roof, his living space ran twenty-five feet from the top of the stairs to the brick wall at the front of the building. He'd installed a tall divider wall to block the view from the floor below and make the forty-foot-wide space feel a bit more cozy. Matt carried Jane down the hallway formed by the wall and the metal railing at the edge of the loft. He passed through the open doorway at the far end, then turned right.

A king-size bed with an iron-and-wood headboard sat against the wall, facing the huge multipane window in the center of the brick wall on the opposite side of the room. He could turn on the electric blanket, Matt thought as he neared the bed, but he stopped as he realized just how violently Jane had begun to shake.

Turning, he made for an area that had been walled off to form a generous-size bathroom. He stood in the center of the dark-blue-tiled floor, looked at the bathtub, then the shower. Jane hadn't spoken a word, perhaps because she had gone further into shock, or because her teeth were chattering so violently. Warm water was the quickest way he knew to heat someone up. But would it be better to place her in a tub full, or make her stand beneath a steady stream?

Jane suddenly stopped quaking. Matt looked down to see that she was staring listlessly at the tan wall, and realized he didn't have time to fill the tub. Or, he told himself as he carried her toward the toilet, for worrying about her modesty. Balancing on one foot, he flipped the toilet lid down with the other. After depositing Jane there, he opened the shower's glass door, reached in and turned on the faucets. He checked to make sure the water wasn't too hot, then let it run at full blast while he went back to kneel next to Jane.

"Hey," he said.

She blinked twice, then slowly turned her head to look at him. Her eyes were darker than he'd ever seen them, the pupils large and only half-focused. Matt placed his arms around her, to offer both warmth and encouragement.

"I want you to take a shower. I'm not sure if you're in shock or just reacting to being wet and cold, but this is the quickest way to get you warm. Can you get undressed by yourself, or should I help?"

Jane stared at him for a moment before she blinked and drew in a sharp breath. "I can do it," she said. "You can leave now."

Not sure if he was relieved or disappointed, Matt released her. When he saw that she was standing on her own, he left the room, pulling the door shut behind him. He walked over to his bed, turned the electric blanket to its highest setting, then glanced across the room where a black wood-burning stove sat in the corner, flanked by a wooden chair and leather sofa.

He moved in that direction, then looked back at the bathroom door and headed there. When his knock wasn't answered, he opened the door an inch. No protest followed, so he peeked in to see that the floor was littered with Jane's red sweater, jeans and...other things.

Steam had rendered the shower door nearly opaque, revealing only the shadow of the slender body within. Matt stepped into the room and quickly picked up the damp sweater and jeans. Leaving the underthings where they lay, he grabbed the large brown terry-cloth bathrobe from the hook on the back of the door, draped it over the closed toilet seat, then left the room and shut the door again. He took the clothes with him to the far corner and draped them over the back of the chair, before squatting in front of the iron stove.

Opening the metal-and-glass door, he placed some crumpled pieces of newspaper on the stove's floor, added a few sticks of kindling, then unwrapped a manufactured log, threw in several rounds and lit a match from the metal holder he kept on the hearth. After shutting the hatch, he watched the fire through the door's glass window to make sure it caught, then returned to the bathroom door.

The sound of running water had stopped, and this time, when he knocked on the door, it was pulled open. Jane stood on the other side. Her hair was plastered to her head and dripped onto the collar of his robe, which hung to her ankles and looked like it had tried to swallow her.

She blinked as she finished tightening the belt at her waist, then said, "My clothes. Where did they—"

"I took them," Matt answered.

Her confused frown told him that the shower may have cured her shivers, but had done little for the numbed mental state she'd fallen into as she listened to the reporter promise to revive the story of Jane Doe Number Thirteen. He reached out and took her hand, drawing her forward as he spoke.

"They're over there. See?" He pointed across the room. "I have them drying and warming by the fire. And for you, I have a nice toasty bed."

He grabbed a towel, draped it around her shoulders and led her to the head of the bed. She stopped, stared at the triangle of white on the dark blue bedspread where he'd pulled the bedding back, then gazed up at him.

"I...I think I should go home."

Matt gave a wry smile. Hardly the most flattering response to the idea of getting into his bed. "Later," he assured her.

Jane shook her head. Her lips formed a thin line. "No. Now. I need to be alone, where I—"

She stopped speaking, lowered her eyes, swallowed and blinked. But even with all that, a film of tears shimmered in her eyes when she turned back to him, and her voice was raspy as she went on.

"I need to make sense of what's happened—to figure out who I am, how I fit into all this."

Matt cupped her face with his free hand, leaned down to look deep into her eyes. All he could manage to say was "I know."

Jane's eyes suddenly narrowed. Tears spilled onto her cheeks. "You can't know. And it's just too hard, being around people who have no idea what it's like to feel so...blank, so lost—people who know where they belong in the world. It's easier to deal with this by myself."

She turned toward the end of the bed, no doubt planning to make for her clothes. Matt moved around to block her path, placed his hands on her shoulders.

"You're wrong," he said. A hollow spot opened in his chest. "I do know. Believe me, I've spent more than my share of nights trying to figure that out myself. They were long and lonely and empty, despite the fact that they were spent in a house where love was in abundance. Only I couldn't figure out how to be a part of that."

Jane stared at him for several heartbeats. "The McDermotts?"

Matt nodded silently as he battled with warring needs. It had always been important to keep the pain of his childhood locked carefully inside. That was where he derived his strength, the drive to do the job he loved. But before him stood a woman fighting her own war, where the shadow-self of her past threatened the person she'd become.

He didn't think his own story had anything particularly encouraging to offer, other than the assurance that someone understood at least some of what she was going through. Yet, looking into the agony of her smoky eyes, he decided it would be worth whatever pain it cost him if there was any chance it would help Jane.

"I'll tell you what," he said quietly. "If you climb into that bed and stay warm while your clothes dry, I'll tell you all about it."

Jane glanced at the bed, then back to Matt. "All right."

As Jane got into the bed, Matt slipped out of his loafers. If he was going to tell bedtime stories, he might as well be comfortable.

"Scoot over," he ordered.

When Jane complied, he got into the bed next to her, pulled the covers over their laps and leaned back against the pillows piled up against the headboard. Jane sat next to him, her hands resting atop the navy-blue bedspread. Matt crossed his arms over his chest and stared out the window at the black night. Without looking at Jane, he started speaking.

"I don't know if you remember, but when we were looking at Bertrand's window, I mentioned that one of my few good memories of Christmas was of standing in front of it. That would have been the year I was six. My mother and father had taken me downtown. My brother, Jeremy, came too. He'd just turned ten. The four of us went to dinner, took in the lights, and Jeremy and I both sat on Santa's lap. By the time I was seven years old, that evening was like a distant dream."

Matt paused, momentarily holding on to images of that long-ago Christmas. "The next July, Jeremy took me to the park. I played on the swing, while he went down the slide behind me. After maybe five minutes, I jumped off and turned to join him. But he wasn't there. I thought he was hiding from me, teasing like he did sometimes. I pretended not to care and went down the slide a couple of times, went back to the swing for a while, then swung across the monkey bars for good measure. I lost my grip just before I reached the last rung and fell to the ground. When Jeremy didn't come out of his hiding place to laugh at me, I got worried. I called his name. I looked up into and behind every tree in the park. Then I ran home.''

Matt paused, clenched his jaw as he drew in a few deep breaths, but the ache in his chest grew. Fear gripped him, just as it had that long-ago day.

"The police came. They questioned me. They left and returned. More questions—from the police, my mother, my father. My mother cried, my father shouted. And drank. Nothing new. Anyway, a week later an officer came to tell us that my brother had been found. Dead.''

Matt's mouth was dry. He swallowed with difficulty before going on. "My mother started drinking that day. She sobered up occasionally, but not my father. Jeremy had always been his favorite son. Half the time Dad didn't even acknowledge my presence. The other half he screamed at me, said it was my fault that Jeremy had been taken.''

"Oh, Matt.'' Tears clogged Jane's voice.

He shook his head. "I knew that wasn't true. One of the detectives had sat me down when the investigation first started. He told me that I had done everything I could by coming home as soon as I knew Jeremy wasn't in the park. He made me promise not to blame myself. I kept my promise—even if he couldn't keep his.''

"What do you mean?''

"He promised to find whoever took Jeremy and make sure he paid for what he'd done. But that never happened. I know the policeman tried, but there just wasn't anything to go on.''

Jane's hand covered his. "You know that now,'' she said. "But you couldn't have known that back then.''

Matt considered her words. Slowly he nodded. "Yeah.

You're right. Now that I think about it, I was furious for a very long time. Not that I could do anything about it. Not unless I wanted to get hit.''

Matt tightened his crossed arms. He hadn't meant to say that. It had been a long time since he'd allowed himself to think of those days. He hadn't dared to let anything like that slip out back then, when even the most innocent remark might send his mother into a fit of tears, his father into a rage.

"No one knew about this, of course," Matt said. "Both my parents put on a good show whenever we got together with my mother's relatives."

"The McDermotts?"

"Yeah. Those were the only times I felt I could breathe, could feel safe. The two families always spent a lot of time together at the holidays. When December came around, I hoped things would get better. They didn't. Dad drank more. Mom cried more, anytime she looked at Jeremy's picture."

Matt paused again to collect himself. He felt Jane's hand on his.

"You must have missed him, too."

Matt nodded. He swallowed several times before he went on. "One night, my mother pulled herself together and told my father they were going Christmas shopping. He was in one of his mellower moods, just sullen. They left me at my aunt and uncle's and headed downtown. Five blocks away, their car was hit in the middle of an intersection, and they both died. Oddly enough, my father was not at fault. Some other drunk had run a red light. Anyway, that's how my aunt and uncle got stuck with me."

Matt stared out the dark window as the room echoed with silence, broken only by the soft popping noises coming from the stove in the corner.

"I was wrong," Jane said. "You *have* experienced the sort of thing I've been going through the past year and a half. I can only imagine how helpless you must have felt—

just a kid and having your world turned upside down by some faceless person who was never found, never made to pay for Jeremy's death and everything that came after.''

Matt frowned and turned to her. ''You're doing that thing, aren't you.''

Jane blinked. Matt watched a single tear slowly trickle down the side of her face as she asked, ''What thing?''

''That trick where you put yourself into another person's skin. You once told me you did that when you watched movies or read books, so you could learn how people felt, how they became who they were.''

''So I could become—me.'' Jane nodded. ''Yeah. I guess I was doing that. I'm sorry.''

''Sorry? Why?''

Jane glanced away. ''I…well, it's a sort of invasion of privacy, isn't it?'' She looked into his eyes. ''And rather presumptuous of me to think I really know what you are feeling.''

''No, it isn't.'' Matt reached over and gently ran a thumb down the moist trail left by her tear, a tear he knew had been shed for him. ''You hit the nail on the head. All these years I believed that I became a cop because of the games Jack and I played as kids. This might be hard to believe, but until this very moment I'd completely forgotten that policeman's promise, had never once connected what happened to Jeremy with my desire to work in law enforcement.''

She shook her head and gave a short laugh. ''Right,'' she said. ''I can't imagine that anyone could actually *forget* some part of their life.''

She laughed again, as tears slid down her face. Her head fell back onto the pillow and, as she laughed harder, her eyes shimmered up at Matt, inviting him to join her in the joke. He found his own lips curving, felt laughter well up from his chest, and fought the sudden tears that threatened as he collapsed against his own pillow.

He won the battle to keep his eyes dry, but only just. His

chest ached—from laughing, from all the years of emptiness stored there, and from the sudden, unlooked-for joy that came with knowing that someone else had seen into that emptiness and understood. Someone who recognized that this was what had made him into the person he was, and who wasn't going to try to "make it better," or run from the pain.

Someone warm and soft. Lying next to him. In his bed. Someone whose dark eyes were now looking into his with a mixture of warmth, understanding and...desire?

That could be wishful thinking. He could continue to doubt that anyone would really desire him as much as he desired them. Or he could test that assumption.

With another kiss.

Still looking into Jane's eyes, Matt slid his hand along her jaw, then slipped his fingers into the silky hair at the back of her head. Her eyes widened and the smile faded from her lips as they parted. Slowly he bent toward her, closing his eyes as his mouth moved over hers. Gently, firmly, he savored the warmth, the softness of her lips, the flood of heat that rushed instantly through his body. He shifted his weight onto one hip, angling toward her as he prepared to intensify the kiss.

Then he halted. With his blood humming in his veins, body tight with need, he forced himself to lift his lips from hers, then pull away two...three inches. He opened his eyes and studied her face.

Jane's eyes were still closed, her lips slightly open. A soft breath whispered past them, only to be drawn in with a tiny gasp as she opened her eyes and stared up at him. Her eyes were darker, the expression of longing deep. Suddenly her palm was resting on his cheek, then sliding toward the back of his head. Slender fingers curled into his hair and a gentle tug drew his face toward hers.

Again Matt attempted to be gentle. But as his lips met hers, he felt her fingers thread more urgently into his hair. Rolling toward her, he kissed her more deeply, moving his mouth over hers, feeling her lips part farther, then answer his kiss with a fervor that seemed to burn through his brain, to flame in his chest, then blaze into a need deeper and more powerful than any he'd experienced.

Kissing her was not enough. He needed every inch of her. His fingers slid from her hair to rest upon the cool flesh of her neck. His thumb tested the slender grace of her collarbones, the pulse beating in the soft dip in the center. His lips recorded the vibration of her soft moan, and he kissed her more thoroughly.

His fingertips barely acknowledged the barrier of terry cloth as they moved downward, slipped between rough fabric and silky skin. When his palm came to rest over her small, incredibly soft breast, the pleasure was almost too much to bear. A moan escaped his lips. As he lifted his head to draw a breath, he heard her groan softly in response.

More than pleasure colored that sound. Matt heard a hint of fear. In an instant his head was clear, his body prepared to do battle.

He opened his eyes. Jane was staring up at him. Her eyes were shadowed, unreadable. But the tension in the slender form lying half beneath his and the palm pressing against his chest said she was afraid.

Of him? Or was she reacting to the only other time, in her current memory, that a man had kissed her? A man who had been planning on using her in the worse way, with no regard at all for her innocence.

Matt gently rolled away from Jane. What had he been thinking? Here he was, halfway to seducing a woman he was supposedly trying to protect, a young woman who was, for all intents and purposes, a virgin. Noelle Bertrand may have shared physical intimacy with a man, but Jane Ashbury had no memory of that.

He had no business moving so quickly, taking advantage of the emotional state that had brought her to his bed, naked beneath that robe, after a day full of shocks. It had all left her too emotionally fragile to maintain that cheery facade

of hers, let alone make a conscious choice about love-
making.

As space opened up between Matt's body and Jane's, he
whispered, "I'm sorry. This isn't... This is too soon."

Jane stared at him. Her body felt as if it were on fire.

"Too soon for what?"

"For this," he said. "For us."

Jane stared at him, saw the lines of worry around his
eyes, could feel the conflicting responses in the body so
close to hers. He wanted her. The way he had kissed her,
held her, caressed her had made that abundantly clear. But
now he intended to stop. Because he thought it was too
soon.

For her, or for him?

He had faced rejection for most of his life, so had held
himself apart from others. Did he feel she would reject him,
too? Or was he concerned that she was still too immature
to deal with an adult relationship?

"It is not too soon," she said. "I've been waiting for
this moment, wanting it, for over a year."

She saw the surprise in Matt's eyes, and felt herself hesitate. She heard the whisper, *too soon,* in her head.

But life was short—too short. Hers was little more than
a year long, and she had too few truly wonderful memories.
She wasn't going to pass up the chance to make one now.

"You couldn't have known about that, of course," Jane
said. Rolling onto her side, she rose on one shoulder until
she was looking directly into his eyes. "And back then, this
would have been too soon. Emotionally and mentally I was
barely an adolescent. But there isn't anything adolescent
about how I feel now. About what I want now. I want you."

With that she placed her hand on his cheek and lifted her
lips to his. Matt instantly joined the kiss. His hand tugged
at the tie of the bathrobe, then slid inside to caress her naked
skin. Jane murmured against his mouth, then began tugging
at the hem of his sweater.

They worked in concert to finish removing her bathrobe

and get Matt out of his clothes. Then they came together, flesh against flesh, kissing, gasping for breath, then kissing again while their exploring hands raised desire to a fever pitch.

Jane gave herself to the moment, smiling against Matt's lips each time a deep moan escaped them. All the love scenes she'd ever read told her where all this was leading, but when she finally held Matt inside her, she realized that none of them adequately described either the pleasure that pulsed through her body or the emotion that filled her heart.

Chapter Sixteen

Jane opened her eyes. High above her, large windows set in a slanting ceiling let in bright morning light.

She squinted at the unfamiliar sight, wondered idly where she might be, then sat straight up. Her heart raced as she glanced frantically around the large room. Nothing looked familiar. Not the brick wall opposite her or the large window set in the center, or the wood-burning stove in the corner next to—

Jane stared at the chair next to the large black cylinder. Those were her jeans and sweater draped over the arms. Releasing a deep sigh, Jane fell back against the pillow. Her heart continued to pound. She was in Matthew Sullivan's bed, where the night before he had held her, kissed her, caressed her. Where she had given herself to him.

Her heart rate slowed.

What self? she found herself wondering. Just who had Matt made love to? Jane Ashbury, who wasn't much more than a figment of her own imagination that might fade into the ethers if and when her memory returned? Or had it been the grumpy Noelle Bertrand, a person so disliked that it seemed her own siblings had wanted her dead?

I want you. Those words, the ones she'd said to Matt last night—how very selfish they sounded this morning. How could she have offered her love, how could she have encouraged him to love her, when there were so many questions left unanswered?

Slowly Jane sat up. Matt had been right last night when he tried to keep things from going so far. It *had* been too soon. And perhaps that explained why he wasn't here with her now.

Turning, she noticed the clock on the side table. Ten o'clock. Could that be right? Sliding out of bed, Jane hurried across the room, gathered up her clothes and headed for the bathroom.

Twenty minutes later she emerged, fully dressed, running her tongue over her teeth to make sure she'd done a thorough job with toothpaste and finger. She looked around for her shoes and socks, then remembered Matt had made her remove them down in his office. Vaguely recalling how Matt had carried her up to the room, she found her way onto the open hallway that ran along the iron railing to the stairs. As she crossed the expanse, she heard Matt speaking below.

''Here's the thing. Wilcox is convinced that Jane's accident was a suicide attempt. We're going to have to do all the legwork and hand him the entire case on a silver platter if we hope to get any police cooperation, and an arrest. I was up half the night, going over the articles I'd downloaded from the *Chronicle* Web site. I found a small item hinting that Bertrand's Department Store was having financial difficulties. I'd like you or Paula to find out if this was true, or if it was just a rumor started by Bestco to get a better price when they bought the place.''

''All right.'' Jane recognized Jack's voice as she reached

the top of the stairs. "Did you learn anything more about Noelle Bertrand?"

"Well, she got an MBA from Stanford, and was active in several service organizations—mostly charities that worked with children, and, of course, she belonged to the normal business organizations. Nothing that would suggest—"

"Matt," his cousin said. "You're doing it again."

"Doing what?"

"Burying yourself in facts. Distancing yourself. That's what you always do, when anyone gets too close."

As Jane started down the stairs, she heard Matt say, "Jack, I'm just staying focused. Now, as I was saying, nothing in the business section or society pages offered the kind of information that would suggest a motive for murder. My money is still on the brother and sister, but that's why I set up that meeting with the woman the security guard told me about. I got the impression that if there are bodies buried anywhere, so to speak, Vivian Norman would know where."

"Well, if you and Jane are supposed to be at the woman's house at eleven, don't you think you should get Jane out of—"

"I'm not taking Jane with me."

Jane stopped at the bottom of the stairs. At first she'd been feeling awkward, wondering how Jack knew that she'd spent the night. Then, when Jack had accused Matt of burying himself in his work to keep someone from getting "too close," she'd begun to worry that Matt was also regretting what had happened in his bed.

Suddenly none of that mattered. With growing apprehension, she stared at the two men standing in the middle of Matt's office. Jack had a clipboard and pen. Matt was flipping through a small notebook.

"Learning her identity was pretty…upsetting," Matt went on. "I think she needs to spend some time with Zoe."

"I don't know," Jack said. "Something tells me Jane

might want to hear what this Norman woman has to say about her.''

Matt looked up from his notes. ''I don't care what she wants, dammit. Without her memory, Jane's a sitting duck. She's like Manny, intelligent but impulsive. I wasn't around to save him when he went into that alley without backup, but I'll be damned if I'll let Jane walk into the line of fire. She's the victim, I'm the professional, and I'll call the shots.''

Jane felt as if she'd been turned to ice. Is that what last night had been about for Matt? Had he started out to coddle her, the poor confused victim, only to have her encourage him to take things further than he'd planned?

Jane went down the last few stairs, then crossed the space to the office in three quick steps. Matt and Jack turned as she reached the doorway.

''So I'm a victim, am I?'' she said. Spying her shoes and socks next to the desk, she made for them. As she passed Matt, she continued speaking. ''I suppose you see me as some helpless little girl, waiting for Santa to wrap her case up and put a pretty bow on top. Well—'' she picked up her footwear, turned and walked toward the door ''—go ahead. Wrap it up. But don't bother putting it beneath my tree. It isn't what I want.''

She got halfway to the elevator before Matt yelled, ''Wait!''

She took one more step, halted and turned to him. ''Why should I?''

Matt walked forward, stopped two feet in front of her. ''So I can apologize. You're right. You deserve to be part of this. I…just thought that after last night…''

A frown formed as he looked down at her. Jane wondered if he was remembering, as she was, everything they'd shared in that big bed of his. Her breath slowed, became more shallow, her lips grew suddenly warm.

''I was wrong,'' Matt said at last. ''This is your past

we're talking about, and you have a right to learn everything you can.''

For one moment she thought he was going to say more.
Instead he flipped open his notebook and turned to his
cousin.

''I need you to get started on some of this while we're
gone. First off, verify that Noelle took that flight to Paris
on May twenty-first. I suspect that someone dressed as
Noelle did just that. Whoever pulled this off was smart
enough to use a stolen car, and either knew how to set it
to explode when it crashed, or hired someone who had that
expertise.''

As Jack moved to Matt's side, Jane realized that the man
was right. Matt *was* using work to avoid his emotions—
and her. Her heart ached as Matt continued speaking.

''Aimee Bertrand is the clothing buyer for the store. I'm
assuming she travels to Europe. In an interview following
the report of Noelle's death, last December, Phillip Bertrand
is quoted as saying that Noelle sent several postcards from
Europe. Again, I'm guessing he would still have them, to
use if he ever needed to prove that Noelle was in Europe
at the time in question. We'll eventually want to look at
them, but in the meantime, see if you can find out what
dates Aimee was in Europe during the period that Jane—I
mean, Noelle was supposedly there.''

''Let me do that.'' Paula spoke up. Jane turned to the
secretary, who was sitting at her desk, grinning. ''I can find
out which designers the store buys from, then call with
some made-up story about missing invoices that I need
dates on. I do a mean French accent.''

''Okay,'' Matt replied. ''That's yours. Jack, you're going
to have to call the Paris police. See what they can tell you
about this drowning incident. The paper said Noelle was
the victim of a mugging, hit over the head and thrown off
a bridge. Get whatever details you can. And one more
thing—see what you can get on the personal finances of
Aimee and Phillip Bertrand, along with anything you can

learn about Glen Helms. With any luck, we'll have more details to go over after we speak with Vivian Norman. Jane, get your shoes on and let's go.''

Forty-five minutes later, Jane and Matt sat in the Jeep, finishing up the meal they'd purchased from a fast-food drive-thru on the way to San Francisco's Sunset District. Several blocks up from the Great Highway, which ran along the ocean, they were parked in front of a white Tudor-style house. Other than the conversation required to order the food, neither had said a word.

Now Matt glanced at his watch. ''We'd better wait another fifteen minutes. Miss Norman quite clearly said she would see me at eleven o'clock *sharp*. I took it to mean she didn't want me to show up one minute earlier or later.''

He turned to Jane. She sat tense and stiff in the passenger seat, her eyes looking at him from behind the black-rimmed glasses he'd suggested she wear. It was clear that something was bothering her as she slowly lifted her foam coffee cup to her lips, took a sip, then returned it to the cup holder, before staring blindly out the front window.

Matt drew a slow, uneven breath. Of course something was bothering her. She had woken up alone, in the bed in which the two of them had made love, and he hadn't had the decency to say one thing about what had happened between them.

This morning hadn't gone at all as he'd anticipated. He'd planned on making breakfast for her, but he'd woken late, drugged and satiated, to the sound of Jack calling his name. Then, when the two of them were putting together a plan of attack for proving that Jane was indeed Noelle Bertrand, the doubts had crept in.

He had been about to do the right thing last night—pull away from Jane, give her more time to get her emotions straight. Then she had looked into his eyes and told him she wanted him. Wanted—not loved.

That thought, and the ache in his chest that came along

with it, ate at him. Dammit. He knew better than to get involved with a client—even if the attraction he felt was only physical. And with Jane, his feelings went so much deeper. How deep he hadn't had time to figure out.

But what about Jane? Had her desire for him been only that—physical? Or worse, had she been acting on the sympathy for him that he'd seen in her eyes after he told her his story?

"I'm sorry about last night."

Jane's words startled Matt. She was looking at him, eyes dark, lips set.

"I put you in an awkward position," she said before he could speak. "I feel like I've tricked you, somehow."

"Tricked me?" Matt shook his head. "Believe me, you didn't get me to do anything I didn't want to do. Very much."

Jane's lips twitched slightly before she said, "Last night you were with Jane Ashbury. We have no idea if you would even want to be in the same room with Noelle Bertrand, let alone make...have sex with her."

"Make love, Jane," he corrected. "That's what we did last night."

"Really?" Jane looked into his eyes. "Do either of us have any idea what love is? My understanding is that love is about sharing oneself with another. What or who my *self* is, is questionable at best. And you? You bury your emotions in work, let other people tell me about your pain."

Matt opened his mouth to protest, but Jane looked at her watch and said, "It's a few seconds before eleven. We'd better go," then turned and opened her door.

Matt followed her up the path. He didn't like the note things had ended on. After this visit, he was going to insist they have a long talk.

Matt knocked on the arched door. A second later it opened. The woman standing in the doorway was on the tall side, wearing an oversize blue chambray shirt over jeans and white tennis shoes. She had short gray hair, a square face and bright blue eyes. Her wide mouth smiled as she greeted them.

"You must be Mr. Simmons and Miss Martin. Harold called me about you, which is the only reason I agreed to this visit. Well, I'm Vivian Norman—call me Vivian—and I'm packing for another trip, so you'll have to excuse the disarray. Please come in."

The woman led them to a small living room. The walls were cream, and a dark green sofa and matching love seat were arranged in an L-shape in the far corner. A square oak coffee table in front was cluttered with notepads, several photo albums and a large cardboard box.

Matt and Jane had barely taken their places on the couch, when the woman spoke again.

"I understand you're interested in the Thanksgiving Eve decorating party that Bertrand's held for the employees, until this year."

Matt nodded as the woman took her seat on the love seat, placing Jane between the two of them.

"I see," Vivian said. "Harold felt you hadn't been given nearly enough family history when you were at the store yesterday. If you don't understand the family, you can't properly write about the Christmas traditions."

"Well, I do know that the store was established by Jean-Philippe Bertrand in 1906, that he started the tradition of the automated Christmas window and the Bertrand star."

"That's not entirely correct," Vivian said. "Jean-Philippe I did put the Christmas window in, and he did use a star to decorated the store, but it was just a simple five-point ornament. The one now known as the Bertrand star has eight arms—four large ones in the shape of a cross, and four more smaller ones filling the angles between. It didn't come into being until the year 1911. Jean-Philippe commissioned the crystal ornament for his new wife's birthday, December twenty-fifth."

Matt lifted an eyebrow. So that older woman, Wanda Hassock, had been right about all this, and Philippe Bertrand wrong. Interesting that the man should be so oblivious to his family's history.

"I put a pot of coffee on. I'll be right back," Vivian said after relating more of the history of the family.

After she disappeared into the other room, Matt turned to Jane. Her expression was troubled.

"There is something vaguely familiar about this place." She frowned. "The moment I walked in, I somehow felt like I was…home."

"Well, you probably knew this woman. She worked for—"

"Here we are," Vivian said.

The woman carried a tray that held three cups, along with a sugar bowl and creamer.

"Could you make room for this?" she asked. As Matt moved albums and books to one side, she said, "Harold told me you were interested in pictures of Bertrand's and the employees."

She put the tray down. "Help yourself to cream and sugar, while I find…" She paused as she opened one of the albums, flipped through several pages. "Here's a picture of the first Thanksgiving Eve function I attended. It was 1964, and I was all of eighteen. The girl next to me is Barbara Lawford, my best friend. She worked part-time for the store while she attended art school."

The woman sat down, cup in hand, a soft smile on her lips. "Barbara was the most flowery of flower children. And who does she end up marrying? The boss's son, the very serious and businesslike John Phillip Bertrand."

Vivian stopped speaking. Her smile faded as she stared at the photo for a moment.

"Barbara and John had three children. For a while, though, it looked like there would only be one. It was almost four years between Noelle's birth and that of her brother, John Phillip, Junior. Then Aimee came just thirteen months after Phillip. Shortly after that, Barbara was diagnosed with a brain tumor—inoperable. She died just a little over a year later.''

Silence filled the room. Matt sipped his coffee as he glanced at Jane. She showed no reaction to the story of her own mother's death, unless it was concern for the woman telling the tale.

"It must have been hard," Jane said quietly. "For you to lose your best friend."

Vivian looked up. She took a sip of coffee, nodded, then cleared her throat. "You are probably wondering what all this has to do with Christmas at Bertrand's. Well, as I mentioned earlier, Louise's birthday was December twenty-fifth. She loved everything about Christmas, and wanted all the employees to enjoy the season as much as she did. From the beginning, she and her husband treated Bertrand employees as part of their family. It was Louise's idea to close early on the evening before Thanksgiving and have the store workers help decorate the place. Because the season was so busy, they had an early Christmas celebration for the employees, their spouses and children, complete with a buffet dinner and gifts for everyone. And, of course, the children were treated to the first visit from the store Santa."

Vivian took another drink of coffee. "Yes, for many years, Christmas was a truly magical time at Bertrand's. Barbara loved Christmas, too, and got along famously with her grandmother-in-law, especially after she gave Louise her first great-grandchild on Christmas Eve.''

Matt heard Jane gasp. He realized this was the first time she'd learned the date of her own birth. Before he could do more than glance her way, Vivian continued speaking.

"Anyway, the two women started preparing for the Thanksgiving Eve festivities sometime in July. After Barbara died, Louise kept the tradition going on her own for another six years, until she died at the age of ninety-one."

The woman gave a deep sigh. "John had kept the tradition going after his grandmother's death as a way of honoring Louise and his wife, since they'd both loved Christ-

ELANE OSBORN 207

mas so. But his heart wasn't in it. Something had died when
Barbara did. It was worse after his grandmother passed on.
John wasn't so much devoted to Bertrand's as obsessed
with keeping it a success. Unfortunately, he passed this obsession on to Noelle.''

Matt managed to keep from looking at Jane as he said,
''Noelle? The one born on Christmas Eve?''

Vivian nodded. ''She went to work for her father directly
out of college. Noelle inherited her great-grandmother's
concern for the welfare of others, so she managed personnel
very well, at least at first. She didn't inherit her father's
business acumen, so she forced herself to learn it.''

''What do you mean, forced?''

''Well, Noelle was her mother's daughter.'' Vivian
shrugged. ''I mentioned that Barbara was an artist. When
Noelle was little, Barb used to draw pictures of elves and
fairies, then make up stories to go with them. She put some
into a little book. I encouraged Barb to try to get it published, but she put all that away when the next two babies
came along. Then, of course, she died. A couple of years
after, though, Louise taught Noelle to sew, and she made
herself little elf and fairy dolls from memory.''

This time Matt didn't even try to keep from looking at
Jane. She was sitting quietly, her face as white as snow,
staring across the coffee table at Vivian.

''I was at the house helping out,'' the woman said, ''after
a heart attack had taken Louise. Noelle was twelve. Her
father ordered her to put her dolls away, saying she had a
younger brother and sister to take care of now. Fortunately
she was saved from the job of surrogate mother when John
was remarried later that year, to a woman who doted on the
two younger children and also encouraged Noelle's artistic
abilities. Noelle was halfway to a degree in art, when the
woman died in a fire at the house. Noelle switched her
major to business when her father, who had paid little attention to her thus far, expressed a desire to have her work
for him at Bertrand's.''

Again Vivian paused. Her eyes grew sharper as they met Matt's. "All this must seem rather off the subject of the Christmas traditions you are researching. But it's because Noelle wanted to please her father in his obsession with honoring her mother and great-grandmother's love of the holiday that she took over planning the Thanksgiving Eve party during her last year of college, and continued doing so for the next seven years."

Matt managed to hide his excitement behind a neutral nod. When he had made the appointment to see this woman, he'd hoped to learn a little more about Noelle. Now it seemed Vivian might be a true gold mine, if he could get her to expand on the current subject.

"Noelle would have been twenty or so when she took this on," Matt commented. "That must have been a big job."

"The amount of work involved was only half the story." Vivian frowned as if mulling something over. "Not everyone knows this, but I want you to understand Noelle. The year her mother died, the six-year-old child climbed up in the store Santa's lap on Thanksgiving Eve and whispered that the only thing she wanted for Christmas was a healthy mommy. The poor man told me later that he was too stunned to say anything before Noelle jumped down and ran off with her candy cane. Her mother died just a month later, the day after Christmas."

Vivian blinked, glanced at the picture in the album, then looked back at Matt. "Anyway, over the years Noelle's birthday was all but forgotten as her father battled competition from chain stores. He gave his children expensive Christmas gifts, but they were rarely anything on their wish lists—rather, they were things he thought they *should* have. That wouldn't have been too bad if he'd taken the time to get to know any of the children."

She shook her head. "Somehow, though, in spite of what must have been very disappointing holidays for herself, Noelle made sure that the employees enjoyed the season."

"I guess she wouldn't be at all happy to learn that the decorating party has been done away with," said Matt.

Vivian's eyes shimmered. She blinked again, then sniffed and said, "Sorry," she said. "I know better. Regrets never help anything."

"Regrets?" Matt prompted.

"Yes. I'm afraid I had harsh words with Noelle at our last meeting, not long before she died."

Matt arranged his features into a puzzled expression. "I understand that Noelle died in Paris, just about a year ago. Are you telling me you saw her there?"

Vivian shook her head. "No. The conversation I'm referring to took place here, the previous May."

Chapter Seventeen

Jane took another sip of Vivian Norman's strong coffee. She had purposely refrained from adding cream, feeling the bitter taste would have a bracing effect. So far, it had helped her stay focused, despite the vague but persistent sense that a memory hovered on the edge of her consciousness.

"A year ago May," Matt was saying. "I seem to remember reading that Noelle left for Europe about that time, just a couple of weeks before she was going to get married."

Vivian nodded. "That's what we argued about. Noelle was quite put out with me when she arrived here. She had just returned from a business trip to New York, and learned not only that I had retired, but that my going away party had taken place in her absence."

"Was retiring a sudden decision on your part?"

"Yes, actually. In the previous several months many of the longtime employees had been offered quite generous retirement packages. It was clear to me what was happening, of course. These were all people who, along with me, had banded together the year before in an attempt to strike a deal with Noelle, Phillip and Aimee to sell the store to the employees.''

"So, when your attempt fell through, you think, Noelle and her siblings wanted to get rid of all of you?"

Vivian shrugged. "Some of us. But I don't think Noelle was truly aware of what was going on, although I did believe so at the time. After all, the lawyer who offered the retirement packages was her fiancé, Glen Helms.''

"I see. What changed your mind about Noelle?"

"Noelle herself. She seemed totally surprised when I told her about all the retirements. Several of these people had been in their early sixties, so she had just assumed it was—time for them to go.''

"You aren't near that age, though," Matt said.

Jane almost smiled at the way this subtle bit of flattery brought a faint blush to Vivian's cheeks.

"I was fifty-five at the time," the woman said. "I wouldn't have been able to consider leaving my job if not for a nice little inheritance from an aunt in England. And, of course, the package Glen offered me was…quite generous. The chance to get out and do some traveling while I'm still hale and hearty had been too good to pass up. Noelle seemed to understand this. But when I told her I would be leaving in three days, therefore wouldn't be attending her wedding, the proverbial can of worms was opened.''

"How's that?"

"Well, as I mentioned, Noelle's mother was my best friend. All three children called me Aunt V. I was particularly close to Noelle, so she had assumed I would be at her wedding. When I told her that wasn't going to happen, she demanded to know why. I lost my temper and said I not only didn't like the man she was marrying, but didn't trust him.''

Jane grew very still. She was aware that Matt had glanced

her way, but she didn't take her eyes off the woman sitting at the far edge of the love seat on her left. She willed Vivian to go on, to explain the creepy feeling she'd gotten yesterday when she'd seen Glen Helms, in spite of his boyish looks and his generous smile.

"I've met the man," Matt said. "He was quite friendly and very helpful."

"I have no doubt." Vivian's tone was icy. "He's the sort who slides through life on smiles and empty promises, dazzling as he goes. I told Noelle that she'd been so busy battling her brother and sister to keep the store afloat and out of the hands of Bestco, that she hadn't really looked at the man she was going to marry. I pointed out the persistent rumors that his first wife had divorced him because of multiple infidelities. Then I told her that, in my opinion, Glen Helms was taking advantage of the fact that she was in love with love, that she was desperate to please him, just as she'd tried to please her father. I said he was fulfilling all her fantasies of romance, but that he didn't truly love her at all. I also believed he was working with Bestco. If she wanted proof, I told her, she should have an outside accounting firm verify recent losses that Bertrand's had supposedly suffered."

"What was her response to that?"

"She walked out."

"You never heard from her again?"

"Well, yes. Two days later, I came back from a bon voyage party to find a message on my phone. It was Noelle. She said she'd done what I suggested regarding the accounts and I'd been right. She'd spent the day on the beach trying to decide what to do. The only conclusion she had reached was that she couldn't marry Glen. She was leaving for Paris the following night, she said, to figure out what to do about the store."

Vivian paused, then sighed. "I was hoping Noelle would contact me while she was in Europe. She knew I was staying with my cousin in Bath—even had Edwina's address. I did receive some postcards here, after I returned in September. One from Paris, another from Rome.''

The sofa seat beneath Jane shifted as Matt leaned forward. ''Do you still have those?''

Vivian nodded, but she appeared to be staring at the picture of Barbara Bertrand again. ''The messages were brief—the ruins were haunting, she wrote from Rome. Paris was rather wet, she said, and she wasn't ready to come home and face the mess she'd made at the store. But she'd be home before Christmas.''

Jane watched Vivian's eyes begin to shimmer, saw her features tighten. The tears fell, anyway. Vivian stood, reached into the pocket of her jeans, pulled out a white, lace-edged handkerchief and lifted it to her eyes. A scent wafted across the room to Jane. She drew a deep breath, inhaling the vaguely familiar combination of musk and flowers.

A second later, the woman sitting across from her was no longer a stranger.

She was Aunt V. Fragments of memories flicked through Jane's mind, images of a woman she recognized as her mother—laughing with Aunt V, then lying on her bed, pale as her pillowcase, smiling weakly at something Aunt V had said, then the tears in Aunt V's eyes as she told the girl Jane had been that her mother had gone to heaven.

Jane's heart burned, her eyes filled. She drew in two shuddering bursts of air. She felt Matt's warm, strong hand close over hers. She blinked, trying to stop the tears, but they continued to cloud her eyes.

''Janey, what's wrong?'' Matt's voice—low, concerned.

Through her tears Jane could see a blurry image moving toward her. Aunt V. She wanted more than anything to let the woman take her into her arms, to hold her the way she'd done all those years ago. But she couldn't. Not now. Not until she had a chance to make some sense of all the feelings that were flooding her, all the images flashing through her mind.

Shaking her head, she turned to Matt and managed to choke out, "The perfume."

"Perfume?"

Jane used the backs of her hands to brush the tears from her cheeks, then tried to keep any more from falling. She wanted to explain, but she couldn't speak. The pain in her chest was sharper now, the sense of loss deeper. All she could do was nod.

"Is she allergic?" Aunt V asked.

"Allergic?" Matt asked, then quickly followed that with "Oh, to the perfume. Oh…yeah. That must be it."

"I'm so sorry. I keep some on my handkerchief. It reminds me of Louise and Barbara. It was their favorite scent."

Jane didn't need to ask the name of the perfume. It was *Fleurs de Rochaille.*

"I'd better get her outside, to the fresh air," Matt said.

She felt his arm slide around her waist, then urge her to stand up. As she got to her feet, she drew in a shaky breath, dashed the tears from her eyes. By sheer will, she kept any more from falling as she crossed the room.

"Thank you for all your time and help," Matt said as they reached the front door. "I may have a few more questions. When will you be leaving on your trip?"

"I fly out Christmas afternoon. Feel free to call me anytime between now and then."

Jane let Matt guide her down the path to the Jeep. The moment he shut her door, a new wave of emotion washed over her. As the tears fell and sobs racked her chest, more fragments of her past danced on her closed eyelids. She was fumbling through her purse for a tissue, as Matt got in and switched on the engine, then turned to her.

"Can you tell me what happened?" he said.

Jane shook her head. She felt his hand fall gently on her arm.

"Take your time. I'm going to take you to Zoe's, okay?"

Jane nodded. He pulled the shoulder harness across her

body, clicked it into place, then touched her cheek softly. Jane tensed, fearing he was about to offer words of sympathy, which would surely destroy what little control she had over her raging emotions.

When he turned to take the wheel, she breathed a sigh of relief. A second later, as the vehicle began to move, her memory took her into its grip again, and all the people who had seemed like characters in a book to her just fifteen minutes ago came to life. She recalled holding one-year-old Aimee, lost without her mother, then saw Aimee again, an arrogant, angry teenager who resented any advice her older sister offered. Phillip showed up, too, the physical image of their father, but angry and sullen. Her mother, her father, her wonderful, warm Grandmere Louise, all moved in and out of her mind.

Most of the memories were fleeting, as if pushed on by the next one waiting to take its place. Some generated joy. Those were the earlier ones. The most recent images brought a tightness to her jaw, made her head ache. But eventually the kaleidoscope slowed down. Jane was able to breathe again, and when she dried her eyes this time, they stayed dry.

"We're here."

Matt switched the engine off and stepped out of the Jeep, while Jane glanced around. She recognized Zoe's gray house as Matt opened her door, and reached across her to unhook her shoulder harness. Then he placed his arms around her and gently drew her out of the car. He held her for several minutes, his cheek resting on the top of her head, his arms tight around her. Jane stood there, absorbing the silent solace he offered.

Then he straightened, placed his hand beneath her chin and lifted her face. Jane met his gaze. His eyes were a dark, dusky green beneath.

"How can I help you?"

"Kiss me." The words came out of their own accord. "Make all the pain go away."

Without a moment's hesitation, Matt lowered his head, placed his lips on hers and kissed her long and deep, his mouth soft on hers, his arms gentle around her.

When he lifted his head, he looked into her eyes and asked, "All better?"

Jane could feel her chest constrict. She shook her head.

"I didn't think so," he said. "That sort of thing only works in a fairy tale. I think we need to get you up to Zoe."

As Jane climbed the stairs, she prayed that Zoe was home, that the woman wasn't with one of her clients. Both prayers were answered. Once inside the door, Matt led her to Zoe's office, knocked on one of the french doors.

Zoe called out, "Jane, is that you?"

"Yes, it is," Jane managed to say, but when Zoe appeared at the door a moment later, she revised that statement. "I suppose I'm really not Jane anymore. I guess I'm Noelle again."

Zoe's expression of total confusion reminded Jane that the woman knew nothing about the incident at Bertrand's, or the composite picture that had proved her identity the night before. The mere idea of explaining all this drained her of what little energy she had left. Fortunately, Matt took on the job of giving Zoe a brief sketch of the events of the past day.

Twenty-four hours. It seemed like so much longer, Jane thought as she allowed Matt to lead her to the sofa beneath the window. Matt sat next to her. Zoe sat in her flowered chair.

"The perfume," Zoe said. "That triggered your memory. Am I right?"

Jane nodded.

"I wondered if that was it," Matt said. "Are your memories that bad?"

"Not all of them," Jane replied. "What started the tears was suddenly remembering that last visit to Aunt V. Before she took out that handkerchief, I hadn't felt a thing as she described the conversation we'd had that day. But then I smelled that perfume, and suddenly I found myself recalling everything we'd said to each other, along with the anger I'd felt, and how hurt I'd been by what she'd said about me and Glen. Then I remembered how good V had been to me over the years, almost like a second mother. I…''

Tears threatened again. Jane clenched her teeth, held her breath, then slowly released it. ''I was awful that day. I was awful a lot of days.''

''Perhaps,'' Zoe said gently. ''But from what little you have told me, I think perhaps you can see why you behaved that way. True?''

''A little. I'm not sure.''

''It is a lot to take in. We will work it through, a bit at a time.''

Jane nodded slowly.

Then Matt spoke. ''I hate to ask this, but do you remember anything about the night of your accident?''

The room suddenly felt like a freezer. Jane trembled. She cast her mind back, searching for an answer to his question. Finally she shook her head.

''The last thing I remember is that day at the beach.'' She looked into Matt's eyes. ''I was thinking about what the accountants had told me. They believed that someone had been messing with the store's financial records. I had ordered them to come up with proof, but I already knew what they would find. Aunt V had been right—Glen had made a complete fool of me. I was angry, then embarrassed, as I faced the truth. I had ''fallen in love with love,'' as Aunt V said. I had fooled myself. Then, I suddenly realized I didn't really care. Not about Glen, and not about what might happen to the store. Aunt V said I'd allowed it to eat me up—to make me into something I wasn't.''

Jane released a shuddering breath. ''The last thing I remember was deciding to call off the wedding and leave town—to go somewhere I could think, where I could find *me*. I had studied art in Paris my junior year of college, so

I decided to go there. I really don't remember anything after that.''

"Jane," Zoe said gently. "The experiences of that night were undoubtedly traumatic. I recall that drugs were found in your system when you were brought into the emergency room, so it is possible that you were unconscious when the car went over that cliff. Still, your brain was severely bruised. Often in such an injury, there is a period leading up to that moment that is lost forever. We will work with what you do recall, then see if hypnosis can bring anything else out.''

Jane turned to Matt. "I'm sorry. I know you were hoping—''

He cut her off with a shake of his head, then took her hands in both of his and looked into her eyes.

"You have absolutely nothing to be sorry for. Don't worry about remembering that night. Work with Zoe to put your life together. I'll worry about getting the proof we need to convict.''

Jane nodded. "I guess, then, that you should get back to your office.''

Matt seemed to hesitate a moment before he released her hands and stood up.

"You're right. Zoe is better equipped to help you than I am." He rested his hand on Jane's cheek. "I'll give you a call later, bring you up to date with the investigation and you can tell me how things are going.''

Then, with one of those quick, one-sided dimple smiles of his, he turned and walked out the room. A few moments later, Jane heard the door shut. The sound seemed to echo through the foyer, into the office, then vibrate in Jane's very soul.

"He is right, you know.''

Jane turned to Zoe. The old woman smiled gently. "I would imagine that you are feeling quite lost. And perhaps just a little schizophrenic. Like two people in one body?''

Jane nodded.

"Well. We have much work ahead of us. But first I want to say this to you. We all become what we focus on. I want you to believe, when we are through, that it is safe to be yourself, however that self should manifest itself." Zoe stood up. "I think, before we get started, that we both need a cup of tea. And perhaps a sweet or two."

Jane watched Zoe cross the room, then stop when she reached the door.

The woman turned and said, "Matthew paid you a very high compliment just now."

"What do you mean?"

"His leaving said he thinks you are capable of making this journey on your own, that he doesn't see you as a victim who needs a hand to hold."

Chapter Eighteen

Five days later, Matt finished arranging the pages of information that he, Jack and Paula had managed to gather together. As he stacked them in the middle of the otherwise clean desk in his office, he sighed.

"When are you going to call her?"

Jack stood in the doorway, leaning against the frame.

"I assume you're referring to Jane," Matt replied. "I have called. The first time was a couple of hours after I dropped her off at Zoe's. Jane said hypnosis hadn't brought out any memories, but she and Zoe would give it another try when she wasn't so tired. She asked me to call the next day. On Sunday she said she felt stronger, but that the time right before her accident was still a blank. I reassured her that the memories weren't all that vital. Because she suffered amnesia, any competent defense attorney would be able to cast reasonable doubt on anything she could recall."

"That's it?"

"No, Mother. I told her we were making progress in

several of our attempts to gather the sort of concrete evidence that would lead to a conviction. I asked if she wanted to get together so I could talk to her about what we'd learned up to that point. She said that she had work to catch up on, so I said I'd call and fill her in as soon as we had everything together.''

"Work to catch up on," Jack repeated. "And you bought that?"

"What do you mean?"

"She's not working, Matt. She's hiding."

"Hiding? From who?"

Jack shrugged. "Well, if I had to guess, I'd say you."

"Are you nuts?" Matt glared at his cousin. "What reason would she have to hide from me?"

"Oh, I don't know. Maybe, just maybe, she's having a little trouble coming to terms with being Noelle Bertrand, and worrying that you might have problems with that, too."

"What are you talking about?" Matt snapped. "She told us she still wanted to be called Jane. That's who she is."

"You think it's that simple, do you?" Jack laughed harshly. "Oh, I forgot. You know all about walling the past off, keeping old memories at bay, along with anyone who should be foolish enough to care about you."

"What are you talking about?"

"I'm talking about the way you never really let anyone in." Jack shoved himself away from the door frame. "Even as close as you and I are, there's always been this invisible line that can't be crossed, a part of you that you won't let anyone see."

Jack frowned as he went on. "Look, I know you took a beating, both emotionally and physically, from your father after Jeremy's death. Your neighbors told my dad all about that after your parents died. Dad told me to be there for you, but to give you space. We all tried to make you feel loved, but you wouldn't have it. Mom said it was because of what your father said."

Matt's chest felt tight. "My father said a lot of things. He was a drunk. I learned to ignore him."

"Even when he said you should have been the one to die? That's pretty hard for a six-year-old to brush off."

Matt shook his head but clamped his mouth shut, afraid of what might come out. After a few moments, Jack spoke again.

"Look, it hurt me when I realized that you would shut me out of your life if I tried to touch that pain, to help you with it. But I wanted to be your friend, so I let it go. However, it's one thing to accept a barrier between cousins, an entirely different matter when you ask this of a woman who's in love with you."

Matt thought about the moments he and Jane had shared in his loft—not just the pleasure they had shared, but the deep connection he had sensed flowing between them. Then he remembered the two of them in his Jeep, before they'd gone into Vivian Norman's house. She had referred to the night before as their having "had sex." When he'd corrected her, saying that what they had done was making love, her response had been that she couldn't know what love was because she didn't know who she was, Jane or Noelle.

That hadn't made any sense to him at the time. He remembered thinking as they walked up to Vivian's house that he would have to talk to Jane after the interview, to straighten all of this out. But the emotional storm that had swept Jane into its current once her memories returned had made him forget all that.

"Yeah, that's it," Jack was saying. "Give me that blank look. But believe me, Jane is in love with you. The signs are clear as rainwater, if you bothered to look. But then, you'd have to *let* her love you. I'm not sure you can do that. So maybe it would be better for both of you if you just left things as they are. Continue to play the detective, don't get close to her, and for heaven's sake, don't let her see into your heart."

Before Matt could speak, Jack pivoted and walked out

of the room, then shouted to Paula that he was meeting Libby for lunch. Matt turned to stare at the telephone, then crossed to his desk, lifted the receiver and punched in Jane's number.

For the sixth time in the past four days, Jane's machine took the call. Matt hung up, reached into his desk drawer for the phone book and impatiently plopped it on the desk. Several minutes later, he had Zoe Zeffarelli on the line. The woman explained that Jane had just left the house. She was on the way to the Embarcadero, to deliver some Santas and Christmas angels to a place called The Crystal Cave.

Matt rode the Jeep hard through traffic. He managed to find a parking space on Battery, several blocks from the Embarcadero Center, then practically sprinted to the second of the four buildings that made up the shopping area. The first directory he located told Matt that The Crystal Cave was in the first building, the one closest to the large outdoor plaza.

He was still a little out of breath when he stationed himself in an inconspicuous spot, where he could see Jane enter or leave the shop, without being seen first. He had no idea if he'd arrived before or after Jane. For all he knew, she had already come and—

No. There she was, in a bright red coat, leaving the store.

Matt suddenly realized he really didn't know what to say to her. He remembered her fears that she might become a different person once her memory returned. Was she the same young woman he'd dropped off at Zoe's, or had her personality undergone some radical change? Would he like the person she was now? More to the point, would that person like him?

Matt stepped back against the wall, but Jane walked in the other direction. Releasing a slow breath, Matt let her get several yards ahead, then followed. When he reached the doorway leading outside, he glanced to each side. Jane was nowhere to be seen. He started down the wide cement staircase that spiraled down to the bottom floor. When he didn't see her walking down the corridor leading to the first-floor shops, Matt stepped away from the stairs and examined the large cement area between the tables arranged in front of the ground-floor eating establishments and the two-story free-form fountain to his left.

The plaza wasn't empty, however. Matt looked at the huge outdoor ice-skating rink that had been set up here for the holiday season. It was an interesting contrast to the large palm trees that lined the street between the rink and the Ferry Building, but it was obvious that people were enjoying this taste of a New England winter in the center of California. A crowd had gathered around the four-foot-high fence surrounding the rink, watching those brave enough to chance the slippery surface on rented, narrow blades.

Jane would enjoy watching their antics, he knew. But would Noelle?

Apparently so, he decided a few moments later when he spotted the hem of Jane's red coat fluttering in the wind. She stood apart from the crowd, near the bottom of the oval, elbows leaning on the railing, her attention riveted on the couple skating in the center.

Matt drew a sharp breath. She looked so damn lonely. And why not? The second time he'd spoken to her, he'd warned her to stay out of the downtown area around Union Square, where Bertrand's was located, and to watch what she said to anyone. Like she knew so many people, he chided himself. She'd told him how few friends she'd made. She wasn't likely to call any of those people and announce that she wasn't Jane Ashbury, after all, but the supposedly dead Noelle Bertrand.

Damn, he thought as he crossed the walkway to the rink. He *was* a jerk. He should have insisted that she talk to him sooner, made it clear that he was crazy about her no matter what she called herself.

"Glad I caught up with you," he said as he stopped at her side.

Jane whirled toward him, eyes rounded and fear-filled.

As he reached out to touch her shoulder, recognition crossed her face and she released a sigh.

"Oh, hello, Matt," she said. "How did you know I was—of, course, you must have called Zoe."

Now, faced with the opportunity to clear matters up, Matt found he could only nod.

"Is something wrong?" she asked.

"Wrong? No. I just wanted to talk to you. Jack and I have been really busy, so…" Matt allowed his words to trail off. They were only going to be a polite lie. Jane deserved better.

"Look. I'm sorry," he said as he let his hand drop to his side. "I should have come to see you sooner. I'm sure that the past few days have been hell for you, struggling with all those new memories. I should have been there to help you—"

"You couldn't," Jane said. "Even Zoe couldn't help me, beyond giving me a few words of advice. Working through who I was, and who I am, is something I had to do by myself. That's why I didn't answer the telephone or return your messages."

She paused. A gust of wind caught her bangs, revealing the pink scar on her forehead. "And yes, it has been hell. I've spent the past several days walking around in a daze, feeling like two people in one body. Then I remembered something you told me."

"Me? What did I tell you?"

"You told me that I had chosen to create Jane Ashbury, that I could continue to choose who I wanted to be. Zoe said something similar—she said I had to believe it was okay to be myself, whether that was Jane or Noelle, or a combination of the two."

Matt nodded, then gave her a slow grin. "Well, have you decided which it's going to be?"

Jane shrugged. "I have no idea. I haven't had much chance to find out. With just myself and Zoe for company, I still feel like Jane. I doubt I'll start feeling or reacting like

Noelle until I come in contact with people from her life. And I guess I won't be doing that until I can prove that's who I am, right?''

Matt stared at her for several moments.

Jane frowned. "Is something wrong?"

He shook his head. He and Jack had been so busy attempting to prove that someone had tried to kill Noelle, that the fake death in Paris was just that—fake—that neither of them had given any thought to getting physical proof that Jane was actually Noelle Bertrand. This, however, was something she didn't need to worry about right now.

He glanced toward the rink, surrounded by crowds watching the skaters. The moment felt so awkward, so damn public. He wanted to say something warm, something encouraging, but the only thing that came to mind was "Do you skate?"

Jane said, "No," then surprised him with a big grin.

"What's so funny?"

"Nothing's *funny*," she said, but a laugh punctuated the end of her sentence. "It's just that this is the first time in a year and a half that I could just answer a question, without wondering if I had hated something in the past that I claimed to like now."

The conversation wasn't going where he wanted it to, but they had reestablished the teasing banter they'd always enjoyed.

"Things like eggnog?" he asked.

Jane made a face as the wind ruffled her bangs again. He felt himself relax. This was the person he remembered, the person he loved.

Matt waited for nervousness to set in. Nothing happened. He had admitted to himself that he loved Jane…or Noelle…the woman standing in front of him—and all he felt was joy.

And doubt. How did Jane-Noelle feel about him?

"Eggnog is something neither Jane nor Noelle like," she was saying. "But as to the skating, I've always loved watching it. Did you see that couple in the middle, ice-dancing?'' She turned to face the rink. ''Look how they glide along, in each other's arms, looking into one another's eyes,'' Jane finished with a sigh.

A smile stole over Matt's lips. ''I take it Noelle was a fan of romance, too?''

''Nope.'' Jane shook her head without taking her eyes off the skaters. ''She didn't have time to read such things, and her father would not have approved.''

''*Her* father?''

Jane's lips curved into a wry smile as she turned to Matt. As she suspected, his green eyes were twinkling, and he was grinning that one-dimpled grin of his.

''Okay,'' she said. ''I still feel a bit schizophrenic from time to time. Zoe says it's not a bad idea to look at my past with a certain amount of detachment. That way, I can decide which parts of my old life I want to keep and which I want to leave in…the past.''

Matt's smile faded slightly. ''It's that easy, is it?''

Jane sobered. ''I don't know. But I think it's worth a try.''

She stared at him, wondering if her reference to the bit of his past that he'd shared with her had been a little too pointed. She was preparing to apologize for this, when a ringing sound came from the pocket of Matt's brown jacket.

He reached in, flipped the phone open and said, ''What?''

Releasing a sigh, Jane wondered if the interruption was a blessing or a curse. The moment had felt awkward, and yet it might have opened up the silence that had existed between them for so many days—a silence she was responsible for.

But it was too late now. It was obvious by the way he frowned, then turned and walked several paces away to continue his conversation. She watched him briefly, then returned her gaze to the skaters again.

A few moments later, Matt touched her shoulder. His

features were set in grim lines. "That was Jack. He's at the Richmond police station. They've found the gun that killed Manny."

Jane heard no emotion in his voice. She reached out to touch his hand. His fingers closed over hers as he said, "He wants us to get there as soon as possible."

Matt's grip tightened, and Jane found herself being fairly pulled along as they hurried through the corridors of the first two buildings, then turned right and rushed down the street to the car.

As Matt drove, Jane wanted to reach over, touch the hand that gripped the shift knob, but restrained herself. Matt's tense posture and stony features told her all too clearly that any show of support wouldn't be welcomed right now. She knew from experience how important it could be to hold oneself together, how just the slightest act of kindness or even one word of understanding could break that sort of emotional control, knew how important it could be to hold on to that.

So she did nothing, said nothing, as Matt maneuvered through the streets, heading west. Finally, he spoke again.

"For some reason, Detective Wilcox is involved in this. Jack didn't give me any details, just said to meet him at the station." He paused. "On the way, I should probably fill you in on what we've learned in your case. First off, do you remember anything about the honeymoon you'd planned with Glen Helms?"

Jane considered the question, then nodded. "Yes. We were going to Switzerland."

"Right. We also learned that you'd taken some mountain climbing and ski lessons."

"Oh, yeah." Jane shuddered, then gave Matt a small smile. "What some people won't do for love, or for what they believe is love."

"I take it you weren't all that thrilled at the idea of skiing and mountain climbing?"

Jane sighed as they pulled to a stop at another red light.

"Glen convinced me I needed to try new things, that it would be exciting to be on top of the world and—oh."

She stiffened and turned to Matt. He looked into her eyes as she said, "Glen had planned on killing me on our honeymoon, hadn't he."

"That's what Jack and I think. We have no way of proving it, however. Glen cleverly set up your prenup so that he got nothing in the event of a divorce but would inherit if you died. However, your will left Bertrand's to your brother and sister. Now, here's where it gets interesting. Paula unearthed the information that Glen recently bought a diamond engagement ring. The rumor is that he's going to give it to Aimee on Christmas."

"They were after the store," Jane said. "Glen Helms was going to marry me, kill me in Switzerland so he could sell the place to Bestco. And when I refused to marry him, they grew desperate. Now he's going to marry my sister and share in her half of the profits."

"After a proper mourning period, of course," Matt said as traffic began to move again. "We think that when you called off the marriage, Glen and your siblings were forced to come up with a quick backup plan, which required that you die here, unrecognized, while Aimee took the flight you'd booked for Paris. When they faked your death several months later in Paris, no one would connect the two events. And if not for a faulty seat belt that let you fly out of that car, they might have gotten away with it."

Jane nodded.

The rest of the trip to the Richmond police station passed in silence. When Matt and Jane finally entered the building, Jack was waiting for them. He gave Jane a surprised glance, then turned to Matt.

"Wilcox is interviewing the suspect now," Jack said. "His name is George Dawson. He was picked up last night in the act of stealing a car up on Forty-Second near Cabrillo. The arresting officer found the gun when patting Mr. Dawson down, then brought him in here. While waiting to process the guy on the car theft charge, the police ran the gun and found no registration, so they ran a ballistics test, and hit the jackpot.''

"The gun that killed Manny," Matt said hoarsely.

"But wait," Jack said, face sober, "there's more."

Matt had been staring down the hallway to their right. Jane could practically feel the tension emanating from his body. He spun toward Jack with a jerk.

"More?"

"I happened to be here when all this came down. We've been so busy talking to the contacts we made in Paris and working the financial angle of Jane's case, that I hadn't gotten around to checking the car theft angle that you'd suggested."

Matt shrugged. "It was a long shot."

"One that paid off. I got Detective Jirovsky to look again, see if there were any other car thefts in the same vicinity last May, near the time of Jane's accident. He came up with an arrest the night before—a guy who was picked up attempting to steal a vehicle. It was his first offense, so his lawyer got him off the next day on bail."

Matt shook his head. "Impossible. Manny and I looked for that sort of thing."

"Timing, son," Jack said. "You were ahead of the ball. It seems the report didn't get entered for quite some time."

"Damn. Do you mean, if not for some paperwork snafu, Manny and I could have solved—"

"Matt," Jack broke in. "I don't think it was a simple screw-up. I have the feeling that if a mistake was made in this case, it was that the report got entered at all. You haven't heard, as they say, the rest of the story."

"Then, give it to me."

Jack glanced at Jane before he went on. "The gentleman who was arrested that night in May? He was none other than George Dawson."

Matt's features turned hard. "The guy Wilcox is questioning right now about Manny's death?"

"The very same. Jirovsky had no sooner come up with the name than one of the other detectives spotted me and told me about the ballistics test matching the bullet to the one that killed Manny. They knew you'd want to be informed."

Matt turned, started to walk down the corridor. Jack grabbed his arm.

"Hold your horses. You know you can't interfere with an interrogation. Besides, I've already had a conversation with Wilcox. I gave him a thumbnail sketch of all the evidence, circumstantial as it is, that we've collected on Glen Helms, Aimee Bertrand and brother Phillip. We're going to have to trust Bruce to connect the dots."

"Done."

Wilcox smiled at Jack, Matt and Jane as they turned to the man who had just stepped into the hallway.

"What do you mean—done?" Matt asked.

"Well, I've just had a very interesting conversation with George Dawson. He claims that he didn't shoot Manny. Says the gun we found on him used to belong to his brother, one Henry "Fats" Dawson. We've run the guy. Nasty fellow. Implicated in several murder-for-hire scenarios, always got off. You want to know where these killings took place?"

"Let me guess," Matt said. "Oakland. Oh, and that would undoubtedly be during the time Glen Helms was an assistant D.A."

Wilcox nodded. "Our friend George insists he's never shot anyone."

"Right," Jack said. "His brother gave him the gun for a birthday present."

"Not exactly. His brother gave him the gun for safe-keeping, after Fats shot a cop last year."

"Manny."

As the name echoed in the room, Jane bit the inside of her lip. She watched Matt's jaw work. Her stomach knotted.

Wilcox broke the silence. "According to George, his

brother brought him in on the contract to kill Noelle Bertrand—but only to steal the car, mind you. George got busted on the first attempt, but on the second night he scored.''

"Let me do the guessing this time," Jack said. "It was a 1999 Honda Accord, dark blue in color."

As Jane processed these words, she felt as if a blast of cold air had blown through the police station.

"Yep," Wilcox said. "The car that ended up at the bottom of the cliff off Camino Del Mar, just before midnight of May twenty-first of last year." He turned to Jane. "After throwing you out, and before bursting into flames."

Jane crossed her arms tightly to keep from shaking. She felt as if she was going to be sick, but refused to go looking for a rest room. She was determined to stay where she was and learn the entire story.

"Anyway," Wilcox continued, "George claims that Fats told him the guy who'd hired him to kill the young woman was ticked that she hadn't died, but didn't want another attempt unless it became necessary. The brothers thought everything was fine, until the middle of August, when a police detective showed up at George's house, asking questions about the arrest the night prior to the accident."

"Damn," Matt said under his breath.

"What is it?" Wilcox asked.

Matt shook his head. "Manny didn't have a large part to play in the undercover case we'd been assigned to. I bet he decided to use his free time to retrace every step we'd taken on Jane's accident, found the arrest report on George that hadn't been there the first time we checked, and decided to investigate on his own."

"I think you're probably right," Wilcox said.

The man's manner seemed to communicate sincere regret. Jane saw none of the pompous posturing she'd noticed in Wilcox that day in Maxwell's security office.

"From what George claims," Wilcox said, "his brother

contacted the man who had hired Fats to kill Jane—'' he turned to her ''—or should I say, Noelle?''

Jane shrugged, then managed to say, ''Either will do.''

''Well, the upshot is that Fats then got a contract to kill the cop. He somehow contacted Manny, set up a meeting with the promise of turning over the name of the man who had hired them. When Manny showed up, Fats shot him. The guy who hired Fats wanted the murder weapon, so he could destroy it, but Fats decided to keep it as insurance, in case he needed something to use against the guy. He gave the murder weapon to George for safekeeping, then took a different gun to meet with the client. Two days later, Fat's body was found on a dock, with three bullets in his chest.''

''I don't suppose George happened to witness all this?'' Jack said.

''We aren't that lucky. But he was able to give me the name of the guy that hired his brother to kill…Jane. Just like you two figured, it's Glen Helms. And he should be arriving here anytime now, courtesy of a police escort, along with Aimee and Phillip Bertrand.''

Jack looked surprised at this bit of news.

''Hey,'' Wilcox said, ''you two put together a hell of a case. I've ordered warrants for the Bertrands' home and the store. We'll get whatever financial items you weren't able to unearth, as well as verify the dates Aimee Bertrand was in Europe. I was particularly impressed with the way you worked with the police in Paris. I can hardly wait to hear Aimee explain why the suitcase found in her sister's hotel room in Paris contained all summery things, when Noelle was supposedly mugged on a very chilly December evening.''

''Well, I can explain that,'' Jane said. ''I do remember packing for the trip in May. If those things are available, I should be able to identify them.''

The double doors in the front of the building opened, and Jane turned to see Aimee, Phillip and Glen, their hands behind their back, ushered in by three uniformed officers.

Chapter Nineteen

It was the first time Jane had seen any of them since re-membering her past. She felt as if she were two distinct people staring out of one pair of eyes. As Jane, she saw three sullen-faced strangers. As Noelle, she felt a range of emotions from the concerned younger siblings she'd helped raise, to the pain of learning how they'd conspired against her. And Glen? She felt ill as watched the man who had made her believe he loved her while planning her death.

"What do you mean by bringing us down here?" Glen demanded. "I will not say a thing until I see my lawyer."

"Fine," Wilcox replied with a smile. To the arresting officers he said, "Place them in separate interrogation rooms. Get their lawyers for them. The D.A. should be here soon."

All three looked at Jane as they were led past in hand-cuffs. Her stomach churned. She swallowed, then glanced at Matt, saw him watching them move down the hallway.

"What's your plan, Wilcox?" Jack asked.

The detective shrugged. "Divide and conquer. You and Jack have made things pretty easy for us, uncovering Phillip's gambling debts and the astronomical amount Aimee owes to various credit card companies—giving them both ample motive."

This bit of information was news to Jane, but it dredged up an old memory. "They did that once before," she said. "About seven years ago, my father found out that they both owed large amounts of money. He bailed them out, just to keep the family name out of the papers."

"We know," Jack said. "A guy in Oakland accused Phillip of stealing from him to pay off some of this debt. Glen was an assistant to the district attorney there at the time. We figure that's when he became acquainted with Phillip. And, apparently, Aimee."

"Aimee?" Jane asked.

Jack nodded. "We found evidence that Aimee and Glen have been having an affair for years."

"You've got to be kidding. She was only nineteen when they met."

"And Glen was married. His ex-wife told me about Aimee, using only the vaguest of hints, you understand. I'm sure the exorbitant alimony Glen pays her is meant to guarantee her silence."

"Mr. Helms is quite the clever guy," Wilcox said. "Which is why the D.A. feels he'll probably need to make a deal with the Bertrand siblings in exchange for their testimony against Helms."

"No."

This was the first thing Matt had said since learning that Helms was responsible for Manny's murder. He glanced at Jane, then back to Wilcox.

"Phillip and Aimee conspired to kill Noelle. The police in Paris were able to find the woman Aimee bribed to say that she'd witnessed someone mug Noelle, then toss her over a bridge into the Seine. Her testimony will convict Aimee, at least, on accessory charges."

"Matt, the woman is a prostitute. You know that will taint her credibility. We need Aimee's and Phillip's testimony against Helms to lock in a conviction on the murder charge. Manny deserves that."

"Yeah, and Jane deserves to have her brother and sister punished, too. You have George Dawson. With his testimony and the gun you—"

"No," Wilcox said. "Given Dawson's criminal background, the jury is going to question anything he says, and you know it."

The detective turned to Jane. "I'm sorry. However, your brother and sister will definitely be brought up on fraud charges, and do time for it."

Jane felt too sick to do more than nod in reply. But her siblings, Phillip and Aimee, had made certain choices. They needed to face the consequences. She knew she wasn't responsible for their actions, nor for those of Glen Helms. Still, there was no escaping the fact that because of her connections to these three people, Manny Mendosa was dead.

The silence in the lobby was broken by a muffled ringing. Jack pulled out his cell phone and said, "Yes?" Then, "You're kidding… Are you sure?… Okay, I'll come get her."

He sounded more tense with each phrase. There was another pause before he said, "Yeah, that would be better. I'll meet you there, then."

He flipped the phone shut. "Libby's water broke. She's in labor."

"I thought she wasn't due until January first," Matt said.

"She wasn't." Jack reached into his pants pocket and pulled out his keys. "We were all set up to have the baby over in San Rafael. However, Sharon brought Libby into San Francisco today, for a surprise shower at Kate's. Looks like the baby decided to throw a surprise of its own. Anyway, Kate and Sharon are taking Libby over to the hospital Jane was at last year. I've got to go."

"Of course," Matt said. "I'll finish up here."

Jack turned and began striding toward the front of the building. Matt called out, "Good luck!" and Jack waved his reply as he stepped out the door.

"Miss Bertrand? Um...Ashbury?" Wilcox said. Jane turned to him. "I want to apologize for the way I handled your case. Or I guess I should say, didn't handle it. It's not that I didn't believe you, but from what I could see, Matt and Manny had done everything they could with the evidence that was available at the time. But I should have double-checked everything. I might have stumbled over Dawson's arrest on the night before your accident."

The man looked sincerely apologetic. Jane shook her head. "I don't know if that would have made any difference in the long run. Besides, as you explained, you had other cases to deal with, ones you felt you could solve. My father drummed into me the need to set priorities, to put your energy into areas that are most likely to be successful, so I understand."

"Thank you," Wilcox said, then turned to Matt. "Speaking of priorities, there isn't anything for you to do here. Don't you think you should be with your cousin when that baby arrives?"

Matt shrugged. "He won't need me. I'm sure his entire family will be there."

"Exactly."

Matt hesitated, then took Jane's hand and said, "Let's go."

As they walked through the door, Wilcox called out, "We'll keep you up to date on what's happening with these three."

Matt nodded as he pushed the glass door open and led Jane through. She followed him to the Jeep, feeling more reluctant with each step. She couldn't go with him, couldn't be there to see his face when it dawned on him that she was the reason Manny was killed.

As he started to unlock the passenger door, Jane touched his hand. "I'm not going with you," she said.

Matt turned to her. "Why not? I know it will be another crush of McDermotts, but you seemed to like them all. And I think Libby would want you to be there."

Jane gave him a wry look. "I think she'll be a bit too busy to care about who's there and who isn't, other than Jack. But I don't belong there. You do. I think Jack might need your support."

Matt frowned. There were so many things he wanted to say to Jane, but he couldn't forget the words Jack had thrown at him that morning, or all the times he'd shut his cousin out of his life. Slowly he nodded.

"You're right," he said. "But I think he'd like you to be there, too."

Jane looked into his dark green eyes for a moment. She so wanted to go with him, to feel a part of his family, to belong somewhere. But she couldn't take on a life that didn't belong to her. It was difficult enough trying to walk the balance beam dividing Jane and Noelle.

She took a step back and managed a weak smile. "Actually, I would love to be there. But I have—things I have to do. It suddenly occurred to me that with Phillip and Aimee locked up, someone has to look after the store, so to speak."

"You?"

Jane shrugged. "The Noelle part of me."

"You're going to go to the department store and tell them that you are Noelle Bertrand, back from the dead?"

"That's right. But first, I'm going back into the station to see if Wilcox will send someone along to make people believe that I am actually Noelle. I'd better hurry." She backed away. "You, too." She smiled a little wider, then turned and strode back to the police station.

Four hours later, Matt sat on an uncomfortable chair that some thoughtful nurses aide had brought into the small waiting room that was overflowing with McDermotts. And one Sullivan, Matt reminded himself.

His shoulders were tight. With everything that was going on around him, his thoughts kept straying to Jane.

The day she remembered her past, Jane had asked him for space, to let her work out who she was. He should never have agreed. He should have let Jack take over the case and insisted on staying by her side. When she didn't return his calls, he should have gone to Zoe's and insisted on seeing her. Today, he should have insisted she come with him, carved out some privacy and made her see how important she was to him.

But he'd blown it. He was going to have to find a way to get back into her life.

Yet, he was glad he'd come to the hospital. For the first two hours of Jane's labor, only the McDermott women and Libby's mother were in attendance, having come directly from the baby shower. They took turns talking with Libby and coaching her through contractions, giving Jack a few moments to walk off the nervousness he didn't want to communicate to his wife. Matt had accompanied Jack on these little jaunts through the sterile hallways. He wasn't sure how much help he'd been. After all, he'd simply listened while Jack muttered about effacement percentages and breathing patterns, and once or twice said something that made Jack laugh.

For the past twenty minutes, the only two people who had been allowed in the birthing room were Jack and Libby. Matt was just about to get up and stretch his legs when he heard Jack say, "Here she is."

Matt looked up. His cousin stood in the doorway, holding a tiny bundle wrapped in a pink blanket. All around the room, family members stirred, then crowded around the new father. Matt stood and listened to soft exclamations: "Oh, she's beautiful..." "Look at all that hair..." "She's so tiny..." "She looks just like her mother..."

He watched his cousin, in the center of all these people,

gazing down at his child. The smile on his face was pure joy, mixed with equal measures of pride and wonderment. Then Jack looked up, right into Matt's eyes. He stepped forward. Sharon and Kate moved apart to let him pass. He crossed the small room, stopped in front of Matt, and asked, "Would you like to hold your new second cousin?"

Jane stared at the line of customers waiting to leave through the revolving door. Forcing her lips to hold the smile she'd pasted on, she glanced at the large clock on the opposite wall. Six-fifteen on Christmas Eve. It was almost over.

Above the strains of "Jingle Bells," she could hear the repetitive clatter of cash registers as salespeople ran a final total of the day's transactions. Soon all the money would be counted and turned in, then the employees could escape Bertrand's, go home to their families and to their holiday celebrations. And she would—

A commotion on the opposite side of the doorway broke into her thoughts. She heard Harold O'Malley say, "Sir, you can't come in now. The store is—" There was a pause before Harold went on, "Oh, Mr. Sullivan, of course. Noelle is over there."

Jane drew a quick breath. Fighting the urge to turn and run, she watched Matt slip between two of the people in line. He wore his brown tweed jacket over the green crew-neck sweater that heightened the color of the eyes that held hers as he approached.

Her heart hammered in her chest. Hope warred with dread, joy with shame.

"I've tried calling," he said as he stopped in front of her. "Repeatedly."

"I know."

Jane was surprised he wanted to talk to her at all. She could barely look him in the eye. She wanted to glance away, to hide the guilt that had been eating at her for five days now. But he deserved better. He deserved an apology.

"I'm sorry," she said. "I got really caught up with everything here. Between reestablishing my identity, dealing with reporters and Bestco, I haven't had a lot of free time."

That was hardly the apology she'd had in mind. There were so many things she was sorry for, but standing in Bertrand's, surrounded by strangers, wasn't the place, and right now wasn't the time.

Matt stared at her, then said, "I have some evidence you need to look at."

Jane's heart sank. Of course, those calls had been about the case. That was what she'd been telling herself all along, wasn't it? After all, she'd seen the way Matt had drawn into himself at the police station, the way he'd stared at the wall just after Wilcox had explained how, and more important, why Manny had been killed.

"I talked to Wilcox yesterday," Jane replied. "He said the D.A. had everything he needed."

Matt shrugged. "This is some stuff I came across today. Wilcox had to catch a plane, and asked me to have you look it over. He said it might help move things along more quickly."

So, he was here on official business. "I don't understand," Jane said. "What could—?"

"It's financial in nature. We need you to verify that the figures are fraudulent."

Weariness felt like a weight upon her. She'd been hoping to leave once everyone else was gone, to go back to Zoe's for a long, hot soak in her claw-foot tub.

"Fine," she said. "We can go up to the office now."

Matt shook his head. "It's all on my computer at the agency. I can take you there, once you're all done here."

All done here? Jane almost smiled at that. "I'll let Graham know I'm leaving, and get my coat."

Fifteen minutes later, Harold was locking the revolving door behind them after wishing them a hearty "Merry Christmas." Jane walked silently next to Matt as they made their way to the Jeep in the underground parking area. Neither of them said a word until the car was in traffic.

Matt was the one who broke the silence. "So, how does it feel, being in charge of the store again?"

Jane stared straight ahead, into the lights of the oncoming cars. "It's been…interesting. Thank God for Graham Carmichael. Somehow, with all the publicity and the rumors circulating through the sales force after the media reported what had happened, he managed to hold everything together and keep the store operating. He'll make a good general manager."

Out of the corner of her eye, she saw Matt glance at her.

"You've promoted him from office manager?"

"Not exactly," Jane replied. "Graham won't be working for me anymore. He'll be working for Bestco."

"I don't understand. The papers said that the sale of Bertrand's would be declared null and void, since Aimee and Phillip didn't have the right to sell it, with you being alive and all."

His half-jesting tone brought a small smile to her lips. "Well, that is true. But, given that I have controlling interest, I was free to make a new deal with Bestco. In this one, all the management positions will be filled by longtime Bertrand's employees, not upstarts from the corporate offices. They didn't like it, but they've sunk too much capital into Bertrand's to turn down my proposal. And, as an outgoing gift to all the people who have worked for my family all these years, I negotiated a much better medical and dental benefits package for them."

Matt pulled into the agency parking lot, parked, turned to her and asked, "And what about the Thanksgiving Eve decorating party?"

"Reinstated permanently. With the provision that attendance is strictly voluntary."

He raised his eyebrows. "Congratulations. And what about you?"

"I'm out of it, completely." What was left of Jane's

smile faded as she unhooked her seat belt. "I'll make a lot of money in the deal, even after Phillip and Aimee get their shares. Their money will probably be eaten up by their defense lawyers. I hope to do some good with mine."

"I'm sure you will." Matt paused, then said, "Well, come on. Let's get this done, so I can get you back home."

Jane tried to maintain her composure as the elevator clanged shut and began its slow rise to the third floor. She had to approach the subject of Manny eventually. Maybe after she looked over this evidence of Matt's she would be able to find the words to tell him how sorry she was for her part in the loss of his friend.

When the elevator opened, she followed Matt. Just before they reached the door to his office area, he stopped and turned to her.

"I forgot. Libby wanted me to tell you how much she loved that outfit you sent the baby."

Matt was only about six inches away. His closeness and the musky scent of his aftershave filled her senses, made her feel dizzy.

"Well," she managed to say. "I wouldn't have known what to send, if not for your message on my machine. You said they had a girl, but you didn't tell me her name."

"I guess I didn't give many details. Well, the baby has her mother's black curly hair and dark blue eyes. Libby says she looks just like the Christmas angel you gave her at the popcorn-stringing party. So, they've named her Angel."

Jane blinked at the tears that instantly filled her eyes. "Oh." She cleared her throat. "How lovely."

"Angel is all that, and more. Would you like to see some pictures?"

"Of course."

Matt surprised Jane by taking her hand, then leading her up the iron stairway. She followed him into his loft area, then stopped when she saw the huge Christmas tree in front of the window. It glittered with tiny blinking white lights.

The only ornament was a crystal star, which hung on a branch near the very top.

She pointed at the ornament. "Is that—"

"The original Bertrand star?" he finished. "Yes, it is. Wilcox found it while searching the family safe deposit box for financial records. I promised to see that you got it."

Jane shivered. "I'm not sure I should be trusted with it. I almost destroyed it once."

"What do you mean?"

"I was on the ladder, getting ready to hang the star. The ladder suddenly wobbled, I fell backward and dropped the star. It caught on one of the lower boughs, but even though it didn't break, my father wouldn't speak to me for a month."

"And what happened to you?"

"The couch broke my fall, so I escaped with a broken arm."

Matt frowned. "I'd like to think," he said at last, "that when I have kids, I'll be more concerned about broken arms than broken ornaments."

Jane's lips trembled as she tried to smile. "I'm sure you will. Now, can I see those pictures of Angel?"

"I have something else to show you, first."

Matt took her hand and led her over to the tree, then pointed to a red box with a green bow beneath the lowermost limb.

"Santa Claus came early. That's for you," he said.

Jane stared at the package, then took a step backward. She shook her head. "I can't accept that," she said. "I can't believe you would even want to give something to me."

"What do you mean?"

Jane looked into Matt's eyes. Her stomach tightened. It was time. "Manny died because of me."

Matt slowly shook his head.

"Don't pretend that isn't true," Jane said. "He never would have been in that alley without backup if he hadn't been so anxious to find the person who had tried to kill me. And you wouldn't have lost a friend.''

"Is that why you haven't returned my calls? Because you've been feeling guilty?''

"Yes. And because I couldn't think of a way to make up for—''

"Don't!'' Matt stepped toward Jane. "You have nothing to make up for. Manny was a trained professional. He broke more than one rule going off on his own like that. He knew better. Fats Dawson may have shot him, but Glen Helms and Manny himself are responsible for his death. Not you.'' He took her hand. "Did you really think I blamed you?''

"No. Not blamed. But I was afraid that anytime you looked at me—''

"That I'd think of Manny, just like my father saw Jeremy each time he looked at me?''

Her eyes widened.

"I'm not like my father,'' Matt said. "Any more than you are like yours. I think being Jane for a while helped you see that.''

He was right, Jane realized. She'd been able to return to the store and claim the role of Noelle Bertrand without feeling that she had to perform her job the way her father would have approved of.

"Open your present, please.''

Matt was holding the red box. Slowly she lifted the lid, then peeked in.

Speechless, she reached in and drew out two soft figures. She found it almost impossible to breathe as she stared at the fairy and elf her mother had made for her all those years ago.

"There's more,'' Matt said.

Jane transferred the elf from her right hand to the crook of her left arm, then reached into the box again. She felt something small and flat, pulled it out and gasped.

"The book Vivian mentioned,'' she said. "The one my

mother wrote and illustrated. Where did you find these? I thought they were lost in the fire.''

''Again, you have Wilcox to thank. His men found them in a safe, at Bertrand's.''

Jane's eyes filled. ''Father...must have put them there for safe-keeping.'' She blinked, then looked up at Matt. ''Thank you. I don't know what to—''

''Hey,'' Matt said. ''I really can't take credit for those. You can thank Wilcox next time you see him. But I'm glad you like them. I do have something for you, though—to make up for the lump of coal I gave you.''

''Lump of coal?''

Matt nodded. All sign of amusement had left his face. His eyes were dark beneath a frown.

''Figuratively speaking. If you remember, I was determined to get justice for what had happened to you. I'd hoped, along with that, to give you an identity and a family. Considering that the family in question had been partially responsible for what happened to you, the value of that gift is questionable, to say the least.

''So—'' He bent over and reached under the tree, then stood and held out a small, flat oblong box covered in purple velvet and tied with a silver cord. ''I want to give you this. Happy birthday.''

Jane stared at the box. Her heart seemed to stop beating and to swell with excitement at the same time. She looked up at Matt.

''Nobody ever remembers my birthday. Except for Aunt V.''

''Well, I'm here to rectify that.''

Again he gave her one of those lopsided smiles. Jane smiled back. She felt all of six years old. She could barely contain her excitement.

''My hands are full,'' she said. ''Will you open it?''

Matt pulled on one end of the silver cord, then opened the hinged box to reveal a large oval of smoky topaz, attached to a thick gold chain.

"It was my mother's," Matt said. "I think it's the same color as your eyes."

Jane looked up at Matt. Her throat was tight, making her voice rougher-sounding than usual as she said, "It's beautiful. Thank you."

Then she caught her lower lip between her teeth. "This isn't right," she said at last. "I don't have anything for you."

Matt placed the purple box into the red one and popped the top on it. "You wouldn't have gotten me what I wanted, anyway," he said. "I didn't even know what was on my wish list until the day Angel was born."

"What is it?" Jane asked, as he took the large box from her hands and placed it on the floor.

Matt straightened, took her hands into his and gazed into her eyes. "I want what Jack and Libby have."

Jane's heart skipped a beat. "You want a baby?"

"Well, eventually," he said. His expression sobered. "I've spent most of my life feeling that I didn't deserve to be loved by anyone. When I looked into little Angel's eyes, I loved her. Then it hit me. Real love isn't conditional—it shouldn't need to be earned. That was when I realized that what I wanted most was to tell you that I loved you and have you believe it. I want you to say that you love me and be able to believe it."

He took a deep, shaky breath, then said, "I love you, Jane Noelle Bertrand Ashbury."

His eyes never left Jane's as he spoke. She had absolutely no desire to look away. She let her smile grow as wide as it wanted, then said, "I love you, Matthew Sullivan." She paused a beat. "Do you believe me?"

She saw the answer in his eyes even before he said "Yes."

"Well, you'd better."

With that, she grabbed the lapels of his jacket and pulled Matt toward her, at the same time as she rose to her toes to kiss him.

Jane's eyes fell shut as their lips met, then melded. She slid her hands up his chest to grasp his shoulders as Matt's arms encircled her, drawing her to him, his mouth making love to hers. Jane wanted to sigh, but she could barely breathe, so she continued to kiss Matt, to feel him grow hard against her.

Smiling against his lips, Jane's past fell away and the future shimmered before her. She could now give all her attention to the present.

This, finally, was what she'd read about, dreamed about. The moment when she could give her heart, herself, to the man she loved. They could explore each other fully, knowing where the wounds were, each trusting the other to touch gently. Having helped each other make peace with the past, on this oh-so-silent and special night, they could believe in tomorrow, believe in the gift of love.

* * * * *

Beginning in November from

V *Silhouette*®

SPECIAL EDITION™

by

PAMELA TOTH

From their Colorado spread meet Winchesters
Charlie, Adam and David: three sexy cowboys who
know how to lasso a lady's heart!

These rowdy ranchers are in for the ride of their lives
when a trio of big-city brides sets out to tame these
boys' wild ways. Cow…*men,* anyone?

Don't miss

CATTLEMAN'S HONOR (SE #1502)
available 11/02

THE MAN BEHIND THE BADGE (SE #1514)
available 1/03

And watch for David's story, coming in 2003!

Available at your favorite retail outlet.
Only from Silhouette books!

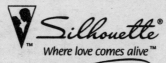

Where love comes alive™

Visit Silhouette at www.eHarlequin.com   SSEWB

#1 *New York Times*
bestselling author

NORA ROBERTS

presents the passionate
heart of the city that
never sleeps.

TRULY Madly
MANHATTAN

containing

LOCAL HERO
and
DUAL IMAGE

And coming in May

ENGAGING
THE ENEMY

containing

A WILL AND A WAY,
and
BOUNDARY LINES

*Available at your favorite
retail outlet.*

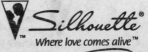

Silhouette®
Where love comes alive™

Visit Silhouette at www.eHarlequin.com

PSTMM

Coming from

SPECIAL EDITION™

THE SUMMER HOUSE
by
Susan Mallery
and
Teresa Southwick

Sun, sand and ocean. It was the perfect beach getaway,
and best friends Mandy Carter and Cassie Brightwell were
determined to enjoy it…alone. But summer could be
full of surprises. Especially when lovers, both old and new,
showed up unexpectedly!

**On Sale December 2002 (SSE #1510)
Two incredible stories in one fabulous novel!**

Available at your favorite retail outlet.

Where love comes alive™

Visit Silhouette at www.eHarlequin.com   SSETSH

If you enjoyed what you just read,
then we've got an offer you can't resist!

Take 2 bestselling
love stories FREE!
Plus get a FREE surprise gift!

Clip this page and mail it to Silhouette Reader Service™

IN U.S.A.	IN CANADA
3010 Walden Ave.	P.O. Box 609
P.O. Box 1867	Fort Erie, Ontario
Buffalo, N.Y. 14240-1867	L2A 5X3

YES! Please send me 2 free Silhouette Special Edition® novels and my free surprise gift. After receiving them, if I don't wish to receive anymore, I can return the shipping statement marked cancel. If I don't cancel, I will receive 6 brand-new novels every month, before they're available in stores! In the U.S.A., bill me at the bargain price of $3.99 plus 25¢ shipping and handling per book and applicable sales tax, if any*. In Canada, bill me at the bargain price of $4.74 plus 25¢ shipping and handling per book and applicable taxes**. That's the complete price and a savings of at least 10% off the cover prices—what a great deal! I understand that accepting the 2 free books and gift places me under no obligation ever to buy any books. I can always return a shipment and cancel at any time. Even if I never buy another book from Silhouette, the 2 free books and gift are mine to keep forever.

235 SDN DNUR
335 SDN DNUS

Name	(PLEASE PRINT)	
Address	Apt.#	
City	State/Prov.	Zip/Postal Code

* Terms and prices subject to change without notice. Sales tax applicable in N.Y.
** Canadian residents will be charged applicable provincial taxes and GST.
  All orders subject to approval. Offer limited to one per household and not valid to current Silhouette Special Edition® subscribers.
  ® are registered trademarks of Harlequin Books S.A., used under license.

SPED02   ©1998 Harlequin Enterprises Limited

eHARLEQUIN.com

community | membership

buy books | authors | online reads | magazine | learn to write

buy books

Your one-stop shop for great reads at great prices.
We have all your favorite Harlequin, Silhouette,
MIRA and Steeple Hill books, as well as a host of
other bestsellers in Other Romances. Discover a
wide array of new releases, bargains and hard-to-
find books today!

learn to write

Become the writer you always knew you could be:
get tips and tools on how to craft the perfect
romance novel and have your work critiqued by
professional experts in romance fiction. Follow
your dream now!

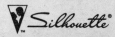

Silhouette®

Where love comes alive™—online...

Visit us at
www.eHarlequin.com

SINTLTW

New York Times bestselling author

DEBBIE MACOMBER

weaves emotional tales of love and longing.

Here is the first
of her celebrated
NAVY series!

NAVY *Wife*

Dare Lindy risk her heart
on a man whose duty
would keep taking
him away from her?

*Available this February
wherever Silhouette books
are sold.*

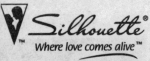

Silhouette®
Where love comes alive™

Visit Silhouette at www.eHarlequin.com   PSNW

SPECIAL EDITION™

From *USA TODAY* bestselling author

SHERRYL WOODS

comes the continuation of the heartwarming series

Coming in January 2003
MICHAEL'S DISCOVERY
Silhouette Special Edition #1513

An injury received in the line of duty left ex-navy SEAL
Michael Devaney bitter and withdrawn. But Michael hadn't
counted on beautiful physical therapist Kelly Andrews's healing
powers. Kelly's gentle touch mended his wounds, warmed
his heart and rekindled his belief in the power of love.

Look for more Devaneys coming in July and August 2003,
only from Silhouette Special Edition.

Available at your favorite retail outlet.

Where love comes alive™

Visit Silhouette at www.eHarlequin.com   SSEMD

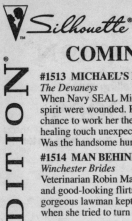

Silhouette®

COMING NEXT MONTH

#1513 MICHAEL'S DISCOVERY—Sherryl Woods
The Devaneys
When Navy SEAL Michael Devaney was shot, both his body and his spirit were wounded. Reluctantly, he gave lovely Kelly Andrews a chance to work her therapist's magic. But the beautiful therapist's healing touch unexpectedly stirred his senses and warmed his heart. Was the handsome hunk falling under her spell?

#1514 MAN BEHIND THE BADGE—Pamela Toth
Winchester Brides
Veterinarian Robin Marlowe moved to Colorado to escape her past—and good-looking flirts like Sheriff Charlie Winchester. But the gorgeous lawman kept showing up everywhere she turned—even when she tried to turn away....

#1515 MAYBE MY BABY—Victoria Pade
Baby Times Three
Emmy Harris knew better than to mix business with pleasure... except when it came to Dr. Aiden Tarlington and the mysterious baby who landed on his doorstep. Before long Emmy wasn't so eager to escape the small Alaskan town—or the handsome doctor's embrace!

#1516 THE ACCIDENTAL PRINCESS—Peggy Webb
Readers' Ring
No one realized how beautiful CJ Maxey was until she transformed herself for the dairy princess pageant. All she wanted was a scholarship, but soon she found hotshot reporter Clint Garrett gunning for her affection. When she gave up her newfound glamour, would Clint drop her like yesterday's news?

#1517 MIDNIGHT, MOONLIGHT & MIRACLES—Teresa Southwick
Wounded straight to his soul, Simon Reynolds needed the attention only nurse Megan Brightwell could provide. And though Megan knew better than to get involved with a patient, Simon's sacrifice had saved her daughter's sight. She was determined to show her gratitude by healing his body—and staying far away from his heart.

#1518 ANNIE AND THE CONFIRMED BACHELOR—Patricia Kay
Callahans & Kin
Self-made millionaire Kevin Callahan never thought he'd find love again—until he stumbled upon it in the form of the dazed woman weaving in front of his car. And though this woman he called Annie had no memory of who she was, would she still be able to remind Kevin how resilient his heart could be?